A Shark Out of Water

Other John Putnam Thatcher Mysteries
by Emma Lathen

A Shark
Out of Water

A JOHN THATCHER MYSTERY

EMMA LATHEN

ST. MARTIN'S PRESS
NEW YORK

THOMAS DUNNE BOOKS
An imprint of St. Martin's Press

Library of Congress Cataloging-in-Publication Data

Lathen, Emma, pseud.
    A shark out of water: a John Putnam Thatcher mystery / Emma Lathen.
      p.   cm.
    "A Thomas Dunne book."
    ISBN 0–312–17018–1
    I. Title.
PS3562.A755S53   1997
813' .54—dc21   97–23036

First edition: November 1997

10 9 8 7 6 5 4 3 2 1

Contents

A Shark Out of Water

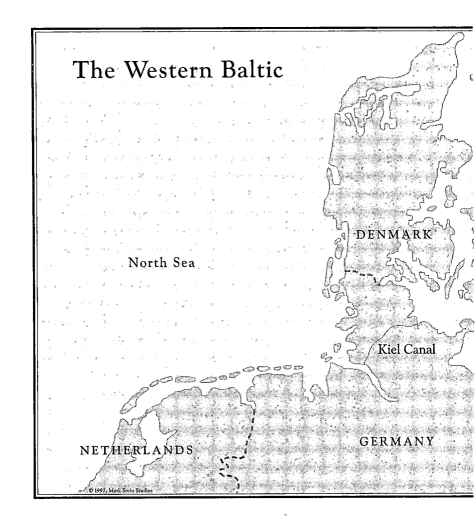

The Western Baltic

North Sea

DENMARK

Kiel Canal

NETHERLANDS

GERMANY

© 1997, Mark Stein Studios

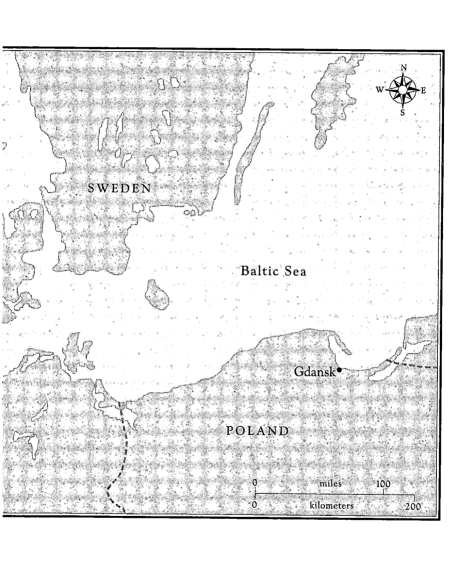

1. Setting Sail

WALL STREET IS haunted by ancient visions. Every investment banker is another conquistador lusting after fabled riches in distant lands. Let a sufficiently convincing prophet descend from the clouds and secular Wall Street becomes a community of faith until the victims far outnumber the predators. Then the outbreak subsides, leaving survivors older and sometimes wiser.

Among them was John Putnam Thatcher, who had learned enough lessons in his working life to reinforce the native shrewdness he had brought to his apprentice years at the Sloan Guaranty Trust. Now, many rungs higher up the ladder, he was CEO in all but name and the Sloan was flourishing despite booms, busts, and soft landings.

Wall Street had observed this phenomenon. More importantly the staff—having been spared mergers and downsizing—had also taken note.

Nonetheless, siren songs wafted into the Sloan every day, seductive melodies designed to lure innocents onto the rocks. Some of them, eluding an early warning system, reached Thatcher's desk. They were followed, on the double, by Miss Corsa and her dictation book. Since unbridled ferocity was not

1

one of Thatcher's management tools, his occasional thunderbolts were doubly effective.

But the real peril was not posed by sleeping watchdogs on the perimeter. Thatcher was surrounded by an elite corps of close aides, division chiefs, and assorted experts. Collectively and individually they were trustworthy beyond question, yet at the same time more insidious than any outsiders. They were, after all, closer to the action, exactly where the real mistakes happen.

So when Walter Bowman poked his head through the doorway of the spacious sixth-floor office to interrupt an informal conference with Charlie Trinkam, Thatcher's welcome was tinged with latent wariness.

Large, exuberant Bowman was the Sloan's highly regarded chief of research, a whiz at excavating shards of information from unlikely sources. His facts and figures were always impeccable but, like all his gifted kind, Bowman could fall in love with his own discoveries.

"Not interrupting, am I?"

"I was just about done anyway," said Trinkam, Thatcher's second-in-command, as he sketched willingness to leave his casual perch on the corner of the desk.

"Don't go, Charlie. You'll want to hear this too."

Bowman's transparent attempt at nonchalance redoubled Thatcher's suspicions.

"What have you got, Walter?" he asked.

Settling his bulk in a chair, Bowman beamed impartially at both of them.

"What do you know about the Kiel Canal?" he riposted.

Charlie and Thatcher exchanged long-suffering glances. Walter's standard procedure, when introducing a broad new subject, was to elicit a display of superficial knowledge before fleshing out that pitiful framework with his own exhaustive information.

"Suppose you tell us," suggested Thatcher, taking them directly to step two. "Or rather give us the basic outline."

It was still closer to a doctoral thesis.

". . . carries more traffic than any other canal in the world. It accommodates all shipments in and out of the Baltic and that's a helluva lot of timber and machine tools. Now, I don't have to tell you—"

"No, you don't," said Thatcher, cutting off the shipping minutia in favor of essentials. "Still, in view of its international importance, it's odd you don't hear more about it. I don't believe it's been mentioned in decades."

Charlie had the answer for that one. "No political problems," he suggested lazily.

Thatcher nodded. Of course that was it. When England wanted a shorter route to India it had to go to Egypt; when the United States wished to link its two coasts it had to go to Panama. But when Germany decided to dig its way from the Baltic to the North Sea it was able to stay on home territory.

"All right, Walter. So we have a canal that's entirely German—location, ownership, operation. What's in it for us?"

He settled back, prepared to pick holes in a gush of enthusiasm. Instead he found himself on the receiving end of an accusation.

"You shouldn't be here, John. You should be in Davos," Bowman charged.

Thatcher blinked. The Kiel Canal? Switzerland? Where was the connection?

"Shame on you, Walter," Trinkam said jovially. "Urging John off to the ski slopes so you can pull a fast one?"

His intervention had given Thatcher time to retrieve the missing fact.

"The World Economic Forum?" he hazarded.

"What else?" asked Walter.

Grand old Davos was keeping up with the times by offering Swiss hospitality and Alpine splendor to rich and famous groups as well as individuals. Every year statesmen and moguls gathered to pool their wisdom amidst conspicuous comforts. Thatcher was the first to admit that the Sloan Guaranty Trust had to be represented, while taking care that the assignment fell elsewhere.

"This year I passed the invitation on to the international division," he recalled.

"They were probably thrilled to pieces," grunted Walter, an inveterate critic of the information brought back by the Sloan's frequent fliers.

Thatcher was accustomed to this intramural rivalry. "Dissatisfied with the caliber of our delegation, are you? Well, go over yourself if you want. Or better yet, ask Everett to drop by. He's already in Europe."

Bowman took both suggestions at face value and shot them down. "I'm tied up with the comptroller and Ev, much as I admire him, would be a fish out of water."

Good gray Everett Gabler served the Sloan with great distinction, but he was a puritanical advocate of plain living.

"Oh, a short exposure to luxury won't kill him," said Thatcher lightly. "Then he can rush back to his poor Czechs and Hungarians."

These much oppressed peoples—and their need for seed money—constituted Everett's current mission.

"And I wish him lotsa luck," Bowman replied perfunctorily. "But he's not the man for the job even if he's willing to leave the huddled masses. You are. You see, your pal von Hennig is going to be at Davos. It's an ideal opportunity for you to pick his brains."

Peter von Hennig, recently named chairman of the board at Finanzbank in Frankfurt, was clout personified, both in his own person and as part of the German power structure.

4

"... and a good friend," Thatcher conceded. "But I fail to see why I should drop everything to meet him, Walter. He was over here last month and, while we had some very useful discussions—"

"What did you talk about?" Bowman interrupted.

"Nothing to put that gleam in your eye," replied Thatcher. "Look, you've given us the Kiel Canal and Peter von Hennig. Why don't you cut to the chase and tell us what you have in mind."

When it came to revealing secrets Bowman tended to ease himself into the subject. "I've been picking up rumors," he confided. "Nothing really solid, I admit. But if there's anything to it, the Sloan has a chance to get in on the ground floor."

"The ground floor of what?" said Thatcher, speeding the tempo.

"They're going to completely restructure the Kiel, maybe even double its capacity," Bowman announced on a swell of triumph.

Charlie whistled appreciatively. "You're talking a real megabucks project there."

"That's not all. It looks as if there's going to be international participation. That's because . . ."

Another flood of information washed over Bowman's audience. Pruning ruthlessly, Thatcher recapped the tutorial in his own mind.

Germany, reunited and back at the crossroads of Europe, was hell-bent on consolidating its position. Wielding deutsche marks instead of panzer divisions, Berlin was reclaiming markets and old spheres of interest. But this program, together with the overwhelming expenses of unification, strained even the vastest resources.

"Now the Federal Republic is under a lot of pressure to get going on the Kiel," Bowman continued. "Pressure from all sides, including its own ports. And God knows the plan fits in with their reintegration policies. So the potential returns are tremendous, but it's going to cost a bundle and the benefits will be shared by a large percentage of the world's shipping. That's why they're mulling over the notion of passing the hat some way."

"Germans do not pass the hat," Thatcher pointed out severely. "They solicit participation from the private sector. Of course it would all depend on the kind of syndicate that gets approval."

"Which is why you should talk to von Hennig before everyone else does. He's in the know if anybody is."

"Hmm," Thatcher mused. "It might be worthwhile."

Now that he heard a hint of concession, Walter was ready to reveal some reservations.

"I'm not sure whether von Hennig will be ready to talk dollars and cents—"

"He usually is."

"—because, as you can imagine, there's a tremendous amount of red tape to wade through."

Engineers and architects, unions and navies. And, as Thatcher added, "the far-famed German bureaucracy."

"Not just them," Bowman corrected. "You've got to include NATO, the European Union and, for all I know, the Court of International Justice. And now there's BADA too."

The brave new world was getting so overcrowded that Thatcher had to ask, "And what exactly is BADA?"

THAT QUESTION, IN the opinion of the chairman of the Baltic Area Development Association, was asked far too often. Annamarie Nordstrom had interrupted a promising political career in Sweden to become not only a delegate to BADA but its first executive chairman. Five years had been allotted for her to create an organization from nothing, to get it airborne and to work out the bugs. Now, at the end of two years and well ahead of schedule, she still had to deal with the total anonymity of her enterprise. Patiently she waited for her latest visitor to produce the customary opening remark.

"I'm afraid I know virtually nothing about BADA."

"I'll be delighted to tell you anything I can, Mr. Gabler," she replied cordially.

This sad state of affairs was, in part, a measure of her success. Ten member nations, five of them from the poverty-wracked east and five of them representing the wealth of Scandinavia and Germany, provided plenty of occasion for division and factionalism. Nonetheless, in spite of early threats to secede and endless grumbling from commercial interests hit by new regulations, damaging schisms had been largely avoided. No member state had stamped out, no lives had been lost under BADA's new safety regulations, no fishermen's protest had turned violent. And the net result was a complete news blackout. Nobody was interested in chronicling steady, prudent, undramatic growth.

As if to prove her point Mr. Gabler had dredged up a fugitive memory.

"I do believe that I did see an item in the German press about one of your operations."

This was the final irony. That story had featured BADA's only major gaffe in public. Fortunately interest had subsided when some fancy footwork on her part had retrieved the situation and ultimately soothed a foaming Estonian delegate and his supportive colleagues.

"That," she replied with a pleasant smile that gave no clue to her inner annoyance, "would have been in connection with our monitoring of toxic waste. Our mandate, I must tell you, is extremely broad, covering as it does the provision of marine services, environmental improvement, and economic development at both private and public levels."

As the familiar phrases fell from her lips she was covertly examining the spare man across the desk with the tight mouth and disciplined gray hair. She noted with amusement that he was not similarly engaged. Mr. Gabler's attention was split between listening to her remarks and checking them against the brochure he held. Probably he already knew about her training as an economist and her term as a junior minister of trade. He might even know that her husband was head of a firm making expensive crystal for the international market. Apparently that was sufficient.

At the end of her speech Gabler pursed his lips. "That sounds remarkably expensive," he commented.

"Of course it is," she agreed readily. "Our services, now almost all in place, have certainly not come cheap. But it's in the development area that we need all the financing we can get. Our program there began with loans to new entrepreneurs in eastern shipping. Now we are about to award our first grant for a major harbor revitalization."

"And where will that be?"

"The list of applicants has been narrowed down to two, with the final decision to be made by the council at its meeting next month. But I'm sure that I don't have to tell you that one harbor barely scratches the surface of the problem. You will have seen with your own eyes the state of the Baltic infrastructure."

That was one of the great advantages of having BADA's headquarters located in Gdansk, Poland, thought Madame Nordstrom. The Bay of Gdansk, situated halfway along the Baltic coast, boasted centuries of tradition as a great natural harbor with evidence of its glorious past still visible in the older part of the city. But visitors to BADA—whether delegates arriving for their regular sessions or bankers in search of investment possibilities—were forcibly reminded that today's reality was a port decaying beneath their feet. If she had her way, Gdansk would be the last spot on the Baltic to achieve a face-lift.

"In view of the extent of the undertakings you propose, I

would be most interested in seeing your financials," Gabler said sedately.

Having already labeled him in her mind as a numbers man, Annamarie was thankful that she had long since perfected her technique for dealing with that tribe. Congenitally suspicious of verbal communication, they tended to regard all general description as designed to obscure the painful numerical truth. It was her standard practice to provide them with a pleasant surprise. Without any warning they were allowed to discover for themselves that, while BADA might be financially modest, it was rock solid. Furthermore BADA was no longer entirely dependent on member contributions. Royalties from mineral development and subscriptions from the private sector were beginning to mount up. Indeed, the new computerized shipping service was generating a very healthy income and even the harbor grant would, in the richness of time, create a steady flow of dock fees. The sound psychology of Annamarie's understated approach had proved its worth in the past, and today it could almost be viewed as a humanitarian gesture. Mr Gabler did not look as if he had been receiving many pleasant surprises.

"Certainly," she said, a latent twinkle in her eye. "I know you merely dropped by today as a courtesy. Why don't I have the material prepared for you and we can meet tomorrow to review it? Just let me make sure that our chief of staff will be available. You'll want to tour our facility and Herr Zabriski is far more competent than I to discuss the technical aspects of our work."

"That would suit me admirably."

While these arrangements were being confirmed, Annamarie considered the form of tomorrow's tour. Stefan Zabriski, rightly proud of his equipment on the cutting edge of technology and personnel, would leave no corner of BADA unexplored. Enthusiastically he would expand on hydrology and meteorology as Mr. Gabler, his internal cash register ticking, confined himself to adding up assets. It was remarkable how long two single-minded men could be together without ever realizing that their interests were not congruous.

As soon as Gabler had made his courteous farewells Annamarie permitted herself an inward chuckle before turning to Zabriski's latest memorandum on inadequate container facilities in the eastern Baltic.

For six pages the report was a model. On the seventh page it strayed. As was happening all too frequently these days, the author had spied compelling proof for an immediate need to enlarge the capacity of the Kiel Canal.

Madame Nordstrom shook her head. She had already fielded several protests from the delegates about this recurring hobbyhorse. For eighteen months Stefan Zabriski had labored mightily by her side to structure a new institution. Now, with that herculean task behind, he was turning his attention to facets of BADA that he was far less fit to deal with. Zealous and dedicated, he not only believed that everything in the Baltic was BADA's business, he honestly thought this was a universally recognized truth.

"Poor Stefan," she murmured tolerantly. "As if we're going to be in any shape to consider the canal for another five years."

2. Crosscurrents

TWO FLOORS BELOW, Madame Nordstrom's chief of staff was also speeding a parting guest.

"Not at all, Herr Bach. It was my pleasure," Stefan Zabriski declared.

He sketched a formal bow and Leonhard Bach, a generation younger in years and style, responded with boyish enthusiasm: "And I sure learned a lot."

On this note of mutual satisfaction they separated. Zabriski was halfway back to his office before he discovered that he had been caught in the act.

As luck would have it his secretary chose this inopportune moment to return from errands elsewhere.

"Stefan," said Wanda Jesilko with mild reproach, "wasn't that Leonhard Bach I just passed in the hall?"

"Why, yes," said Zabriski vaguely. "Yes it was."

"The German shipper?" she continued. "The one who's here to lobby the Council into modernizing his home port?"

Wanda, a tall angular woman with enormous deep-set eyes, always dressed to emphasize her dramatic gypsy coloring. Today she was especially striking in a bold crimson blouse.

"You know quite well it was Bach," he said, falling back on quiet dignity. "Why these useless questions?"

Zabriski, a compact wiry man with close-cropped graying hair, was now striding around his office at a military clip. Wanda paused in the doorway to adjust a long, amber earring before planting herself in his path.

"I thought we decided that you would not intrude yourself," she reminded him. "At its next session the council will award the harbor grant to Estonia or Germany, to Tallinn or Rostock. Just wait for their decision, Stefan. No cozy talks with people who stand to benefit, like Herr Leonhard Bach from Rostock."

After an internal struggle he yielded slightly. "That is true enough. But believe me, Wanda, Rostock was barely mentioned. Nor was the council session, critical as that is. Bach and I were considering the larger aspects of Baltic development. In particular, a major renovation of the Kiel Canal, if you must know."

Shaking her head, she sighed deeply. After ten years as Zabriski's secretary she knew her man in and out. The five years they had spent as lovers scarcely counted.

"The topic of your conversation with him is of no importance," she began painstakingly.

Pulling away from her he assumed a new stance.

"Of no importance!" he thundered. "The Kiel Canal is of vital significance to every member of BADA!"

"Yes, yes," she said hastily. "But so are appearances, and look at how you're behaving. First you decline to see what's-his-name—that Estonian from Tallinn. Then you open the door to Bach. When, instead, you should be keeping all private fleet owners at arm's length."

"You're calling what Jaan Hroka runs a fleet?" he scoffed. "Those two rusted-out tubs of his? Hroka's nothing but a moneygrubbing little opportunist hoping for benefits he hasn't earned."

12

Before ascending to the giddy heights of BADA, Zabriski had served a long term in the limbo of the Marine Bureau of communist Poland. Wanda Jesilko had made the same transition but, unlike him, had shed old ways of thinking.

"You could say the same about Bach," she observed.

"Ridiculous," Zabriski blustered. "He is well informed and forward looking. Besides, unlike Hroka, he's a success."

"Because of a BADA loan."

"Exactly!" he cried, hearing only confirmation.

Many of the small BADA loans doled out to newly freed Europe had disappeared without a trace. Leonhard Bach's Valhalla Line was one of the happier exceptions. Zabriski persisted in regarding this achievement as a testament to his own acumen.

"Stefan," Wanda pleaded, "you're supposed to be impartial. And ever since that toxic dumping people are claiming that you're not."

"I was enforcing regulations that every member government has subscribed to," he said self-righteously.

"They think the whole incident was a setup." She lowered her voice meaningfully. "And I happen to know that it was."

"Now you're saying that I'm responsible for the crimes of others."

Ignoring the accusation, she continued: "You knew that stuff was being loaded on Hroka's ship. One phone call would have taken care of the situation. But no, you had to have his ship boarded at sea by BADA inspectors, escorted back to Tallinn and slapped with charges. You deliberately created a big public melodrama."

For a moment they stared at each other, narrowed light blue eyes challenging dark ones. As usual, it was Zabriski who blinked first.

But his shamefaced grin was not an apology. "It worked, didn't it? Nobody would have noticed if I'd simply aborted the loading. This way, the whole council knows exactly what tricks Estonia is up to."

"Not Estonia," she said gently. "One wretched little man with—as you said—two rusted-out tubs."

Brushing aside his own words he replied stiffly: "Hroka operates under license from the Estonian government."

"And you wonder why some members think you're pro-German!" she wailed. "You tell everybody you're pro-Rostock, you go out of your way to embarrass an Estonian national, then you have Herr Bach in for a clubby little chat!"

"You are making a mountain out of a molehill," he insisted, resuming his march around the office. "There's absolutely no doubt that Rostock will get the grant. After the delegates read my recommendations—by the way, you did get copies made, didn't you?"

"Yes, they're on my desk. That's exactly what I'm trying to make you understand. The more the council suspects you of bias, the less faith they're likely to place in your report."

He stopped dead, his face finally mirroring her anxiety.

"Nonsense," he declared. "That cannot be. My report embodies the technical findings of the staff. How can they possibly fail to give it full weight?"

"Because," she said, running out of patience, "when you start boarding ships on the high seas to make a point, people are not sure exactly what games you're playing."

Instead of being insulted he identified a flaw in her reasoning. "Aha, that shows you don't understand what I had in mind when I gave that order. I was not thinking about the harbor grant but about a display of BADA authority."

"One that nobody wanted!"

Sinking into a chair, he snatched a pencil and stared at it balefully. "Nobody?" he mocked. "You know as well as I do that it was madame chairman. If she had authorized a suspension or a heavy fine, every dockside worker in the Baltic would realize that BADA is a force to be reckoned with. But no, she is satisfied with a warning, the merest rap on the knuckles."

Stefan brooding over good work undone was Stefan seeking a villain. At the maritime bureau under communism it had been clumsy political apparatchiks. Here it was Annamarie Nordstrom and her insistence on diplomatic discretion. These dark moments of his soul required judicious handling.

"I know it was disappointing," said Wanda, beginning with sympathy before moving on to the unpalatable truth. "But Madame Nordstrom consulted the whole council and they agreed unanimously that your action was ill-judged and ill-timed. That's why she promised the Estonian delegate that there would be no sanctions."

"What do they know?" he muttered rebelliously.

She knew better than to answer him. Instead, passing behind his chair, she began to knead his tight shoulder muscles with slow, rhythmic pressure, reciting the current mantra as she did so.

"Now, you will not presume to tell a delegate or Madame Nordstrom how they should decide?"

"Really, Wanda," he protested in muted offense as the massage began to take effect. "After all this time I know how to deal with my so-called betters. These persons in fleeting authority are nothing new to me. I can deal with them very well, very well indeed."

Since there was no use puncturing this innocent vanity, she made another suggestion.

"And if there isn't anything urgent on your desk at the moment, why don't you check the computer room now?"

Every day Zabriski spent an hour before the monitors, tracking ship movements and simultaneously attaining psychic tranquillity.

"Good idea," he said, stretching his neck luxuriantly. Then with a touch of slyness, he added: "And while I'm at it, I'll just distribute some copies of my report."

Secure in the knowledge that most delegates were absent, Wanda remained calm.

WITHIN ITS FIVE-STORY structure BADA was a house divided. Zabriski ruled over the three lower floors, responsible for day-to-day operations. Policy was debated on the fourth floor in the council chamber, in the private offices of the delegates, and in their spacious lounge. At the top of the heap, Madame Nordstrom's suite shared the fifth floor with a small but elegant dining room.

Today, without a single delegate to be found, there was no need for exertion. Zabriski delivered his reports to several uninterested underlings, then fled downstairs to the basement where his cherished communication center was located.

The serried ranks of computers were stars in his personal crown. To the left was the BADA inspection service, enforcing uniform standards and safety measures on the flotilla of car and passenger ferries plying the Baltic. Nearby was the rescue command post, ready to answer emergency calls from St. Petersburg to Copenhagen.

Straight ahead was his favorite station where shipping traffic was continuously scanned. But what was this? A container ship scheduled to depart Malmö earlier that morning was still in dock, wasting untold dollars by delay.

"What's wrong with the SS *Leyden?*"

The response was immediate.

"Transformer blew in the facility at thirteen hours," said the nearest disembodied voice. "Power outage for three hours."

Zabriski swelled with pride. Who else had his finger on the pulse of all this activity? No admiral viewing his operations table experienced a greater sense of command than BADA's chief of staff in front of his screen. His compendious knowledge of Baltic ports transformed those green flickerings into a three-dimensional panorama.

Insensibly, his thoughts drifted further afield to construct a vision unsupported by his database. In that dream a magnificent modern waterway appeared, its broad expanse supporting an endless stream of traffic—and every inch of it was inspired and engineered by BADA under Stefan Zabriski's personal supervision.

Reality returned when he switched off and the screen went blank. He remained motionless for a moment before straightening.

"Something," he decided martially, "must be done."

3. The Burning Deck

I N NEW YORK and Gdansk it was easy to think in terms of the Kiel Canal's future. But that evening those actually operating and using it were just hoping to get through the night.

The man in charge of the office on a small bluff overlooking the locks knew that he was in for some long, hard hours.

"What kind of traffic is scheduled?" he asked.

"Busier than usual."

"Naturally!" he snarled.

With twilight had come the first fragile tendrils of fog. Writhing and coiling they had formed into balls. Then, with alarming speed, the balls became patches, the patches became drifts and, within the hour, a dense, suffocating blanket brought all traffic to a dead crawl.

Normally, when the Baltic itself was hazardous, entry into the Kieler Fiord spelled salvation. It was a long, narrow inlet, buffered against crashing waves and gale winds by gently rolling terrain. Its shores were dotted with suburban homes, industrial sites, marinas and, at the end, the city of Kiel. Embellishing the waters were commuter ferries zigzagging from side to side, low-slung commercial traffic plowing an arrow-straight course, and the white sails of recreational vessels circling at will.

But tonight the open sea was not the enemy. It was entry into the Fiord that was the beginning of a nightmare. Visibility, which that afternoon had been measured in kilometers, was now zero. Radar, with its multiplicity of blips, was proving useless. And the distorted echoes of foghorns, braying from every corner, added to the confusion. Pilots trying to negotiate the inlet in either direction were like blind men in a narrow corridor alive with moving obstacles.

Simply locating the entrance to the canal, on the right-hand side of the Fiord, was fraught with difficulty. The brilliant illumination of the Holtenau locks that usually made error impossible was tonight another distraction. The lighting, refracted by the fog, produced an eerie glow extending for half a mile.

Mishaps from those aiming at the canal soon began to bedevil the authorities. Immediately to the south of the locks two long moles thrust forward, sandwiching an inviting cul de sac into which a Greek freighter stumbled. Its plaintive call elicited scant sympathy.

"Tell them to stay there for the night. All we need is an idiot like that trying to back out."

As the hours wore on more and more vessels found themselves where they did not want to be. For some, this meant accepting the unwelcome hospitality of strange dry docks and piers. For others, with perils on every side, it meant dropping anchor in midstream.

At the canal, however, they had far too much to do with their own charges to worry about conditions in the harbor. Vessels exiting from the canal were relatively easy to handle, but coaxing new arrivals into their berths was a time-consuming and anxious business. Fortunately as navigation outside grew more difficult, the number seeking admission decreased.

"Good!" said the official. "The fewer the better."

He did not realize that the congestion outside was matched, on a smaller scale, by a growing clot within the canal. Ships traveling northward had slowed upon entering the fog: Those to the rear steadily closed the customary gaps.

"When are they going to let this lot through?" he asked.

Instinctively he looked towards the window only to see nothing but a wooly curtain banked against the weeping panes.

Down on the locks things were no better. The lockkeeper did not actually witness the arrival of new vessels. Instead there was a series of vibrating thumps, followed by the appearance of a ghostly visitor wreathed in white vapor. One and all, in a variety of accents, they made the same complaint.

"I had to feel my way around the building to find the door. I've never seen it as thick as this."

"Yes, it's a bad one all right. Here's your toll receipt."

After a large, Panamanian-registered freighter filled the last berth, the lockkeeper nodded to his minions and the time-honored procedure took place. The gates closed and water gushed powerfully through outlets for several minutes, then the inner gates opened and another contingent of vessels spilled into the canal. After the hell in the fiord outside, every helmsman breathed a sigh of relief. In the canal he would become part of a two-way stream, as ordered as anything on the autobahn.

Unfortunately the flotilla that had been inching its way upstream, growing with every kilometer, had lost its discipline. The abnormal crowding, the lack of visibility, and the diffused glow from Holtenau conspired to transform a defined string traveling northward into a loose wide-spread aggregate.

Simultaneously the lead vessel released from the locks chugged southward.

The results were foredoomed. For the crews swept up in the ensuing chain collision, the most horrifying aspect of their night of terror was that they never knew what was happening. The sounds echoed and reechoed from every point of the compass—metal crunching against metal, sirens hooting alarm signals, the anguished whine of desperately revving diesels, high-pitched voices yelling mindless obscenities. As every lookout hopelessly tried to penetrate the white cocoon in which he was immured, fancied perils became more dangerous than real hazards. A slight darkening of the surrounding murk assumed the shape of a menacing hull to be frantically avoided. Sometimes the misleading shadow would propel the unfortunate craft into an actual obstacle. Too often a genuine threat materialized without any warning at all.

The experience on board the *Lucinda*, an early victim, was typical. The man at the wheel was thrown off his feet by the force of an unexpected shuddering impact. Scrambling erect, he hurled himself at the wheel, only to discover that it no longer responded. With the *Lucinda* veering helplessly off course, he flew to the bows screaming a warning. Minutes later he was knocked down again by a collision astern.

But the ordeal had barely begun. The first flicker of fire appeared in the snarled tangle of two ships that had drifted into the center of the canal. Men who barely knew what they were doing downed crowbars to dive for extinguishers and hoses. Struggling along slippery decks and manhandling apparatus that felt covered with soapy scum, they were unaware of a greater threat spreading below. Ruptured fuel lines had long since deposited a flammable layer on the sea itself and now, beneath that opaque white blanket, the conflagration was burning viciously at water line.

The first explosion occurred shortly thereafter.

IN THE CANAL office the radio was jabbering nonstop. At first the brusque voices were controlled.

"*Lucinda* reports collision with unknown vessel . . . steering damaged . . ."

". . . reporting collision . . . still able to proceed . . ."

Then the tempo quickened.

". . . fire on board . . . need assistance . . ."

"*Lucinda* engaged in second collision . . ."

". . . chemical cargo spilling and on fire . . . request use of foam, not water . . . repeat, use foam . . ."

The explosion put an end to all pretense of calm. Erupting with sufficient force to be heard for miles along the canal, it was immediately followed by a logjam of pleas.

". . . hull breached . . . taking on water . . ."

"*Santa Christobel* must abandon ship . . ."

And finally there was near hysteria.

"Serious burn victims . . . request medical aid." The voice rose to a panic-stricken scream. "Jesus Christ, we need doctors and ambulances!"

Within seconds of the first SOS, the emergency services of the canal were deployed. Fire trucks sped forth to the nearest access point on land, the first aid station was manned and the water police in small maneuverable launches heroically began to thread their way into the heart of the disaster.

After the second explosion more calls went out, this time from the canal authority to surrounding communities. They were asking for additional manpower, additional equipment, additional medical personnel.

Before the night was over every agency within a fifty-mile radius was engaged. Hampered by fog, by unseen perils, by spills of burning oil, hundreds of men labored tirelessly to transport victims, evacuate sinking vessels, and extinguish fires.

And all through those endless hours, the office of the canal authority directed the overall effort without once having any conception of the general situation. All they could do was respond to points of alarm, scurry from emergency to emergency, and deal with each separate distress signal as it came. Only at dawn did the extent of the catastrophe become apparent.

* * *

23

"OH, MY GOD!"

It was sunrise and, the fog finally having dissipated, a clear day was breaking. From a fueling depot half a mile downstream the view was unobstructed.

"It wasn't this bad after the bombings," said an old-timer.

The carnage stretched as far as the eye could see. The two vessels where the fire had started still lay in their fatal embrace, half submerged. Burned-out hulks wallowed low in the water, blistered and peeling. Only the topmost superstructure of a capsized freighter was visible. Everywhere crippled ships canted at strange angles with red-eyed crews gloomily staring at the embankment. The smell of burnt rubber and freely flowing bilge hung like a pall over the water where unidentifiable wreckage mingled with shattered crates, barrels leaking ominous substances, and even a bright red bucket bobbing gaily in the muck.

And this was what was on the surface. God only knew what lay beneath, waiting to foul everything that passed.

The chief of operations of the Kiel Canal, roused from his bed at one o'clock, turned a fatigue-sodden face to his assistants. The daunting task of assessing the dimensions of the salvage operation and planning its implementation must now begin.

"Casualties?" he asked.

Of the burn victims, one had been dead on arrival and two were in critical condition. Twelve people, including three firefighters, required intensive care. Over forty comparatively minor injuries had received treatment.

"The locks?"

The senior lockkeeper, a white-haired veteran, shook his head sadly. At least two vessels had collided with the gates. There was considerable damage above water and an underwater examination would be necessary. He was not hopeful. At the very least significant repairs would be called for. Structural rebuilding was not inconceivable.

The next question came hesitantly and it was directed to a chemist.

"What about this mess?"

The CO was pointing to the seething scum visible between floating sheets of dirty foam.

When the chemist delayed his reply, the lockkeeper tried to be helpful.

"We do have cargo manifests from all the ships, so we can give you a list of the materials involved."

"It's not that simple."

Somehow the CO had suspected it would be complicated.

"Go on," he said tersely.

"There is the possibility of chemical combination between different spills. The testing procedures are elaborate and will take days. On the other hand I think I can tell you about one problem right away. I'm fairly sure that you have something corrosive down there."

The lockkeeper produced an anguished yelp that the CO ignored.

"And in the meantime? Can we start removing this filth?"

He was told that pumps of the size required were currently at work in eastern Germany. It would be days before they could be in place.

The CO gritted his teeth. Over and above this difficulty, there remained the vast physical blockage. Sunken hulls would have to be removed, other vessels must be repaired or towed, the floating debris had to be swept up, and underwater sweeps begun. With sudden prevision, he recalled those endless news items about projects in the east. Pumps, giant cranes, and experienced frogmen would all turn out to be somewhere near the Polish border.

"Well, we need all the help we can get. I'd better start calling. I'll contact the navy, the ministry in Bonn, the authorities in Holstein, and of course the city of Kiel."

But Town Hall in Kiel, which had responded magnificently to last night's calls for assistance, was now strangely uncooperative—in fact, almost hostile.

"No, you can't have any of our equipment. We need it ourselves," they snapped.

"But this is an emergency."

"My God, haven't you even looked at the harbor? They kept coming in to use the canal. When they couldn't, they entered the inner harbor. And of course nothing could leave, so now . . ."

There was a dramatic pause.

"So now we have gridlock."

The menace that loomed over all major urban centers had descended on the small city of Kiel in an odd fashion. Foremost among their embarrassments was a giant car ferry from Oslo, trapped in the middle of the mess.

"We will get those Norwegians ashore," vowed Town Hall, "if we have to take them off two at a time in canoes."

Then there was the final commuter ferry to set forth yesterday. It had made it as far as Kitzeberg before being sucked into the snarl and its passengers were in dire straits. The Norwegian ferry was basically a cruise ship; its occupants had showers, clean clothes, hot meals, and a bar at their disposal. The poor commuters not only lacked these amenities, but most of them were due at work within hours.

"City transportation is also affected," the steely voice continued. "With the ferries out of action, new bus routes must be established. We not only have to worry about the work force, but a large proportion of the school children as well."

An equivocal grunt simply stung Town Hall to further fury.

"My God, don't you understand yet? Those goddamned ships are still coming in."

Suddenly the CO realized that the performance of his own people was being criticized. Last night, after the first intimation of trouble, standard procedure had been followed and vessels rounding the Kiel Light had been warned that the Holtenau locks were out of commission. As the crisis developed, a message had flashed to the southern end of the canal advising that egress to the north was impossible. But no alerts had been issued to European shipping in general.

Grounding the phone, the CO began to remedy his omission. Grim-faced, he barked orders at his assistant.

". . . to the ministry of transport, to the admiralty, to IMCO in London, to the chamber of shipping. The same message . . ."

"And what about the BADA traffic service?" the assistant suggested. "Everybody listens to that."

"All right, BADA too. Tell them all that . . ."

The CO had to swallow visibly before he could bring himself to formulate the unthinkable.

"The Kiel Canal is closed indefinitely."

4. Trade Winds

SEVERAL HOURS EARLIER Wanda Jesilko's sleep-drugged mind had struggled to grasp the significance of the words just spoken.

"Inform Madame Nordstrom at once!"

Thanks to Stefan Zabriski's insistence on staying abreast of every fluctuation in Baltic activity, Wanda was accustomed to predawn telephone calls whenever he was spending the night. Long ago she had developed the ability to drift off as he was happily rapping out instructions. But this was different. Orders to rouse Madame Nordstrom at four o'clock in the morning meant that there was a real emergency or, alternatively, that Stefan had lost his mind.

"What's happened?"

He had already tossed back the covers and was padding over to the closet. "An accident in the Kiel Canal. And it sounds like a bad one."

"I'm coming," she declared, sounding more alert by the second. "Just give me a couple of minutes in the bathroom."

"I won't bother shaving," he called after her.

"Oh, yes you will."

As a result of this firmness they were both reasonably presentable when Annamarie, not a hair out of place, hurried into BADA headquarters a short while after their own arrival.

"How serious is it?" she asked.

"We can't tell yet," said Zabriski. "The information is coming in trickles."

The first details were not encouraging.

"Kiel is reporting casualties," announced someone scanning the wire. "The German news services are moving faster than official channels."

"That doesn't tell us what we need to know," Zabriski said impatiently. "They could all be the result of the same collision. If only one or two vessels are involved they can clear the canal quickly."

But succeeding hours brought more hulls disabled, more cargoes lost, more contaminants spilled. Fires, explosions, and sinkings were reported nonstop. As the list lengthened Zabriski became quieter and quieter.

"It sounds unbelievable," Madame Nordstrom commented after another grim printout.

Before Zabriski could reply communications rang through.

"The Kiel is closed to all traffic."

Drawing a deep breath Zabriski asked for the worst. "How long?"

"Indefinitely."

The stark announcement produced a moment of paralysis, then Annamarie rose. "That means you'll be very busy down here. I'll be in my office," she said to the room. At the door she paused and looked back. "Believe me, Stefan, I know how lucky BADA is to have you right now."

"Thank you," he said gruffly. "I'll do my best."

His promise initiated a spurt of activity that eclipsed previous BADA efforts. In a remarkably short time he had partial results to carry upstairs. Madame Nordstrom, as she reviewed the list of ships that had been scheduled to use the canal, was dismayed.

"And that," he pointed out, "is just for the next three days. A lengthy closure would involve much more."

Annamarie knew they were not talking just about shipping losses. Raw materials for manufacturing would not arrive. Finished products would not leave. Enterprises unaffected by either of these considerations could be shut down by a shortage of fuel.

"Good god!" she cried. "Everybody in the Baltic's been hit by a commercial earthquake!"

The ramifications reached further afield than that.

"The Japanese have two super freighters stuck," reported Zabriski. "And it will cost them three thousand dollars a day until Kiel reopens. Denmark's just imposed restrictions on passage through the islands. They've got more traffic than they can handle now. And if, god forbid, the weather worsens . . ."

Their immediate predicament was enough for Madame Nordstrom. "We can let the Japanese take care of themselves, Stefan," she replied with a pained grimace. "They, at least, have adequate insurance."

But Zabriski was already addressing the needs of BADA members. His list of emergency measures had been prepared a long time ago. ". . . and expanded regional traffic alerts," he added.

"Don't forget coordination with naval and civil defense people," she reminded him.

"Wanda's already activating our backup arrangements."

Zabriski's voice never varied in its gravity, but his whole body was vibrating with controlled excitement, his eyes gleaming with anticipation. Annamarie studied him sympathetically. His early insistence on acquiring all that expensive equipment, his lust for an ever-expanding database, his months of daily study were now all going to be justified. Who could blame the man if there was an element of satisfaction in his response to this emergency?

But he was looking beyond these considerations.

"You know, Madame Chairman," he said, bending low over the papers he was pushing together, "tragic as this occasion is, it might provide just the opening that BADA needs."

"Yes . . ." she murmured, "yes, that had occurred to me."

Raising his head to reveal what was now frank exultation, he sounded almost conspiratorial as he continued. "This might be the ideal time for you to speak seriously with the German government."

Then, without waiting for her reaction, he bustled back to his command post.

Annamarie shook her head sadly as she watched him leave. If only Stefan's perceptions about people matched his understanding of marine complexities. He had sensed correctly that they were sharing the recognition of an unexpected opportunity to further cherished plans. But she was willing to bet that he had not the slightest conception how far those plans might diverge.

EVERETT GABLER WAS not surprised to find messages at the hotel desk deferring his appointments with BADA's chairman and chief of staff. CNN—that beacon of light for English speakers in Eastern Europe—had already informed him of the Kiel disaster. Both notes were couched in the stately language of institutional apology, but Madame Nordstrom had enclosed, with her regrets, a thick packet of financials *in case Mr. Gabler wished to use the time for a preliminary review of BADA*. Very few potential borrowers from the Sloan had managed to elicit a nod of approval from Gabler and only his colleagues could have appreciated Annamarie's achievement.

Gabler, a lifelong adherent to the sane-mind-in-a-sound-body principle, took regular precautions when traveling. He had every confidence in the ability of his intellect to surmount any degree of disruption and deprivation. The weak reed in the structure was his cosseted digestive system. Accordingly, after four hours of intensive application, he sallied forth to combine wholesome exercise with a study of harbor conditions in Gdansk.

Having satisfied himself that reports of economic decline were accurate—that even the shipyard famous for the birth of Solidarity lay silent and moribund—he returned to his hotel with glowing cheeks and renewed dedication. Next on the agenda was a healthful meal to be followed by another bout with Madame Nordstrom's packet. He was drying his face in the bathroom when a knock on the hallway door brought him forth, towel in hand, and torpedoed his schedule.

"John! What in the world are you doing here?"

"I'm not entirely sure," Thatcher grumbled. "This is Peter von Hennig's doing."

"Von Hennig of Finanzbank?"

"That's right."

Briefly Everett considered the magnitude of the German's usual financial activities, the infinitesimal commercial opportunities in Gdansk, the fledgling status of BADA, then arrived at a conclusion.

"There is more to this than meets the eye," he said sternly.

"Absolutely," agreed Thatcher, plunging into an account of Bowman's hopes for the Kiel Canal.

Any project so worthy of the Sloan Guaranty Trust, as well as Finanzbank, was guaranteed to command Gabler's attention. Instinctively disposing of his towel and donning his jacket to signal the importance of their discussion, he perched his meager frame upright on the edge of his chair, looking like an alert sparrow on a tree branch.

33

"And what did von Hennig have to say?"

"Not much," Thatcher confessed. "I had barely been with him ten minutes when the canal disaster preempted his attention for the day. On top of that he's the German delegate to BADA, and there's an emergency meeting of their council tonight. He suggested I travel with him to Gdansk but I decided to come early so I could put you in the picture. According to Peter there's no doubt a canal project is inevitable. However, the best thinking puts the start of the venture about five years off. There's no consensus yet about the exact scope of the undertaking and there is going to be major jockeying between different factions."

Gabler had spotted a crumb. "But when did von Hennig say this?"

"Before we knew the extent of the disaster."

"Ah ha! So that could make a substantial difference."

Thatcher shrugged. "If current repairs are going to require massive costs, that certainly strengthens the position of those pushing for an early start to the project. They'll argue that while you're paying all those earthmovers and engineers, you may as well do the job thoroughly."

"A valid point."

Thatcher waved away this contribution. "True enough. But Everett, we have to be more concerned with the timing aspect. Finanzbank has obviously been hoping to put together an international consortium that would submit a proposal for financing the undertaking. Peter thought he had several years for all that involves. If they decide to jump-start the project, everybody's going to have to scramble."

"And no doubt reap the consequences of undue haste." Everett's reply was, by his standards, almost perfunctory. He was far too excited by the prospect to deliver his customary lecture about the need for meticulous preparation. "But what I do not understand, John, is BADA's role in all this."

"That's the mystery. And we'll have to wait for Peter to explain it."

IT WAS TEN-THIRTY before the long-awaited arrival. As always Peter von Hennig presented the appearance of an imperturbable aristocrat. Lean and vigorous, he moved with an air of effortless command. From his impeccable silver hair to his handmade shoes he was immediately recognizable in the West as one of the privileged few. In Poland he stood out like a visitor from another planet.

But, if hopscotching around Europe all day had failed to ruffle the facade, it had apparently taken its toll on the inner man. Thatcher had to step aside in the act of shaking hands as a waiter rolled a service cart into the room. Von Hennig had taken the precaution of bringing coffee and brandy with him. His first act was to pour himself a healthy tot as he waved Thatcher and Gabler towards the tray.

"I needed that," he announced after his first sip.

"Discord in Bonn?" Thatcher inquired delicately.

"The canal accident has been seized on as a platform by both the developers and the conservationists. We had to waste two hours listening to them. You would not believe the nonsense we heard—from making the industrial Baltic rival the Pacific Rim to prophecies of an ecological Armageddon if one more smokestack comes into the area."

"You're lucky some endangered species isn't nesting right by the canal locks."

"No doubt one will be found," von Hennig replied acerbicly. "Finally the powers of reason were permitted to address the problem actually at hand and some progress was made. You know, John, it is always a privilege to see intelligence in action. The older I get the more I seem to be surrounded by nincompoops. In politics, here at BADA, even in my own bank! To discover someone who knows what to do and how to do it is a genuine tonic."

Thatcher made a stab at extracting facts from this dithyramb.

"Are you referring to the current chancellor of the German Federal Republic?"

After a hearty guffaw, von Hennig said, "That twit? Not likely. No, I'm talking about Madame Nordstrom."

"You mean she was in Bonn too?"

But Madame Nordstrom had not left Gdansk. "She doesn't have to move around. She can play the telephone like a violin," said von Hennig.

"And exactly what miracle has Madame Nordstrom wrought?" Thatcher asked dubiously.

"She has convinced the German government to do everything she wants," von Hennig announced, "exactly as she wants to have it done."

Given Germany's notorious intransigence, this was impressive.

"Would you care to be a little more specific?"

"Germany is handing full responsibility for the investigation into the disaster at Kiel over to BADA. Not only that, BADA will act as clearinghouse for all insurance claims."

There was a stunned silence. While Thatcher inwardly grappled with the implications of this news, Gabler derived some satisfaction from restating the obvious.

"Good heavens, John, that means BADA will take charge of at least some aspects of a German problem within Germany."

"I had no idea BADA was such a force," Thatcher said at last.

Peter produced a schoolboy grin. "You're not the only one. You should have seen the faces of the other delegates when Annamarie and I broke it to them tonight."

That certainly told Thatcher who was orchestrating the loftier reaches of BADA policy. But it left quite a remarkable number of unanswered questions.

"I see of course that Germany will gain several advantages from this arrangement," he began probing cautiously. "An impartial outside arbiter will carry more weight than a national panel of investigators and that could be handy when the claims for negligence start pouring in—which they will any day now."

"Just what I told them myself," von Hennig admitted. Carefully he poured himself a cup of coffee before continuing. "And it goes without saying that Annamarie not only increases BADA's prestige immeasurably but also gains worldwide publicity for the organization."

Following his host's example Thatcher also engaged in delaying tactics with the coffeepot. Why was Peter so satisfied by Annamarie's success? It was clear that the two of them had been working in league today, but there was an element of detachment in Peter's account suggesting a pro tem alliance rather than a long established partnership. Thatcher began to look forward to meeting the redoubtable Annamarie. If she could maintain her independence with von Hennig, she was a major force.

"This seems to have been an overnight conversion in Bonn. Now I wonder what made them see the light," he mused, the glimmer of an idea forming.

With elaborate indifference von Hennig began: "You yourself just said—"

But as Thatcher swept over this interruption Gabler was nodding in comprehension.

"It's certainly something more important than a few negligence suits. Let's see . . . could it be that Germany is thinking of using BADA as bait to help attract international financing for your inevitable canal project?"

"The notion may have occurred."

Thatcher chuckled. If it had not, von Hennig would certainly have brought it to everybody's attention. This was jump-starting with a vengeance.

In the midst of all political complexity there often lurks a

37

beautiful simplicity—at least to a banker's way of thinking. Here the line was so paper-thin that Thatcher proceeded delicately.

"I'm sure your contribution to these decisions was invaluable, Peter."

Von Hennig was blandness itself. "Naturally, since the bank may be commercially involved, I felt it necessary to confine myself rigorously. I did recommend Madame Nordstrom's practical grasp of affairs and her chief of staff's technical expertise. Zabriski may be an idiot in geopolitics, but he is competent and he does employ some marine specialists who may be useful for more than the accident investigation."

"Useful in what way?" asked Gabler.

"Bonn has just okayed an engineering study for modernization of the Kiel."

"That's earlier than you anticipated, isn't it?" Gabler pressed.

"There was really no alternative."

The brisk note of finality indicated that von Hennig had come to the end of his disclosures, but Thatcher remained convinced that a major factor had been left unexplored. No doubt Peter would expand in his own good time.

"So that means everything is back on track, does it?"

"Not exactly." For some reason von Hennig was obscurely amused. "Annamarie is not wasting a golden photo opportunity. Tomorrow the BADA council is making a pilgrimage to Mecca. We're all leaving for Kiel in the morning."

"Under the circumstances that's a very reasonable decision," Thatcher said temperately.

"Yes, indeed," von Hennig replied with hearty cordiality. "But, John, now is the time for the Sloan to appear Baltic-minded. I strongly recommend that you join us."

"Oh, damn!"

5. First Class Passengers

T HE FACELESS MEN and women photographed at polished horseshoe tables cannot always delude themselves. They know they look dull as dishwater to the man in the street. All of them yearn for a theater of action where they can deplore extensive damage and console bloodied casualties. When the Kiel Canal offered BADA its first great opportunity, the delegates reached for overnight cases. Annamarie Nordstrom endorsed the enthusiasm, welcoming the showcase that Kiel offered. BADA would not only act, it would be seen acting.

To give the performance additional substance her office was instructed to pad the cast, filling extra space on the charter flight with available auxiliaries. As a result, when John Thatcher and Peter von Hennig arrived, they found all window seats occupied.

Their search for accommodation did not proceed far.

"Herr von Hennig! Good to see you again."

"Ah, good morning, Herr Bach," replied von Hennig with more courtesy than enthusiasm. Then he deftly inserted himself in the seat across the aisle.

Thatcher, left with no choice, sat down by the chunky, round-eyed unknown, whom he examined with interest. Could this be the Leonhard Bach recently puffed by *Der Spiegel*?

"... a bold newcomer from an ancient Hanseatic town," the magazine had gushed. "With gambler's nerves and a zest for trade, Bach reminds stodgy eastern Germans that the genius of capitalism is part of their birthright."

When the introductions confirmed this identification, Thatcher wondered why a buffer was so desirable between von Hennig and the wunderkind.

From the way he pumped hands to the way he plunged into conversation, Bach gave every evidence of adapting to the modern world. His English lacked von Hennig's aristocratic precision, but he knew the vernacular.

After the mandatory preliminaries, he plunged ahead. "... there's probably a silver lining to the whole screwup. At least this is real life, not a lot of theories. Now, no matter how much the foot-draggers keep yelling, people will finally understand we're running out of time to overhaul the Kiel Canal."

With von Hennig apparently absorbed by the instructions for exiting from the plane in case of emergency, Thatcher said mildly, "But disagreements about a starting date still exist, don't they?"

This evoked a snort. "I can see you've been getting fed the official line," said Bach, with cheerful disdain. "Believe me, though I'm sorry to say it, Germany's as bad as BADA. Hanging back, delaying decisions, ducking the inevitable. A new Kiel's got to be built, everybody knows that. So let's do it."

When this failed to detach von Hennig from flotation pillows, Bach grinned and carried on the debate alone.

"We need a canal that's ready for the twenty-first century. And that doesn't just mean handling increased traffic and cutting passage time. It means guaranteeing our outlet to the North Sea—no matter what happens. Look where we are now. One lousy accident and the whole Baltic's bottled up."

Von Hennig was almost forced to reply. "The decisions are not quite that simple," he said frostily. "We aren't talking about

40

right and wrong, but about how much to do and when. You speak about benefits, Herr Bach. Well there are costs too, and other factors as well. Take the matter of risk. This accident is truly unfortunate, I grant you. But it is only prudent to ask how often the canal has been closed in peacetime."

Leonhard Bach was not conceding an inch. "One closing is more than enough," he said flatly.

Unexpectedly he received support.

"You can say that again," said the man sitting beyond von Hennig. "The Kiel's too damned important for all these ifs, ands or buts. By the way, my name is Jaan Hroka."

"I've heard of you," said Bach. "You sail out of Tallinn, right?"

"Yeah," said Hroka, "and without the canal I'm out of business, like plenty of other people."

"God knows you're right about that. Estonia's showing more sense than Bonn."

Hroka's face tightened. "Who knows about Estonia?" he growled. "I talk for Hroka Shipping, and I've got a perishable cargo trapped in the canal."

"Christ, that's tough, Hroka," Bach replied. "Thank god Valhalla won't take any hits if they get things moving fast enough."

"That's luck for you," Hroka complained sourly. "I've got two stinking little freighters and one of them gets caught. And with your six or seven, you manage to squeak by. You probably cleared the canal at the last possible moment."

"As a matter of fact the *Fricka* made it by three hours," Bach said without apology.

"I don't need this right now." Hroka continued his lament. "Not with the harbor grant still up for grabs."

Bach remained tactlessly optimistic. "Looks as if I'm going to get a break there too. Rostock's chances are getting better and better. Isn't that right, Herr von Hennig?"

Peter opted for evasion in the grand manner.

"I never predict the outcome of elections."

The snub did not seem to surprise Bach. Shrugging it off, he confined his attention to Hroka until they landed in Kiel.

"Louts, both of them!" declared von Hennig as they strolled through the airport.

The shipping industry, Thatcher could have reminded him, is not a hotbed of perfect gentlemen. Instead he said, "According to *Der Spiegel* Bach is a countryman to be proud of."

"The man's a menace. Oh, I admit he was quick off the mark when East Germany fell. He was buying privatized freighters from their government even as the Berlin Wall was crumbling. By the time he asked BADA for an expansion loan he was head and shoulders above the competition. But he's still small potatoes. He cornered me yesterday for an hour with foolish suggestions while displaying utterly no conception of the larger issues."

"You've heard sales pitches before," Thatcher pointed out. "I'm sure you're able to cope."

"Naturally," said von Hennig with irritation. "But Bach's been running around Gdansk for two months now pestering every delegate he can find. He operates out of Rostock and he's convinced he has valuable counsel to offer."

"On what basis?"

Meddlesome individuals often tackle their own governments, but they rarely have the temerity to thrust themselves on others.

"Because he's been made into a celebrity by the press. He's been interviewed on television so often he now thinks he really is a role model for every would-be entrepreneur in the East. On top of that," said von Hennig acidly, "he's an expert on BADA. They tell me he drops by Gdansk regularly to discuss policy and, just because he meets his payments, he doesn't get kicked out."

Thatcher could not picture a cozy exchange between the brash Leonhard Bach and the Madame Nordstrom who could hold her own with Peter. When he said as much, von Hennig amplified.

"No, no, not Annamarie. It's Stefan Zabriski who's adopted him."

"The chief of staff?" said Thatcher, conning his memory.

"Yes," said von Hennig, "and he and Bach are two of a kind. They share a romantic vision of the Baltic's future. Bach of course has rosy dreams of commerce expanding, while Zabriski foresees BADA presiding over a Nordic renaissance."

"What in practical terms does that mean?" asked Thatcher prosaically.

"Among other things that they are both fervent, mindless advocates of a new Kiel Canal. They want some impossible megalithic project and they want it started today. You should see Annamarie's face when Zabriski lets loose on the subject. She—"

He broke off abruptly because they had emerged outdoors to find Madame Nordstrom directly before them, busy organizing the division of her party into vanloads.

Thanks to Gabler, Thatcher had been equipped with a brief resume of her professional career. It was typical of Everett that he had failed to mention—if indeed he had ever noticed—that she was still a very attractive woman looking a good ten years younger than her age. Very tall and long-legged, she could have been an advertisement for the Scandinavian way of life. The blond hair, blue eyes, and fair skin all glowed with a vitality that conjured up ski slopes and sailboats.

As soon as the first vehicle pulled away from the curb, with the second still waiting in the wings, von Hennig introduced his companion.

Responding warmly, Annamarie looked expectantly over Thatcher's shoulder. "Mr. Gabler is not with you? I was so sorry to be forced to defer our meeting."

"He quite understood the necessity and he appreciated the material you supplied. In fact, he's now proposing such an intensive study of BADA that he stayed behind to hire himself a bilingual secretary."

"Good luck to him!" snorted von Hennig, raising sardonic eyebrows.

Madame Nordstrom was sedateness itself. "Finding English-speaking help in Gdansk can be a problem," she admitted. "Nonetheless I'm delighted that he's taking time from his schedule."

Her eyes, however, were not shining because of Everett's employment plans. She had not so much as glanced at von Hennig while she was addressing Thatcher, but she was obviously alive to many implications in this conjunction of Finanzbank and the Sloan Guaranty Trust. In fact, thought Thatcher resentfully, more alive than he was himself. Peter would have to come clean very soon.

"And it goes without saying," she continued, "how pleased I am that you were able to join us on this inspection tour."

"I'm curious to see conditions for myself," Thatcher said truthfully.

What met his eyes was the same desolation that dawn had first revealed twenty-four hours earlier. Like the autobahn after a serious accident, the Kiel Canal was clotted with traffic going nowhere.

For those desiring a closer look, BADA was ferrying delegates and the press out to the wreckage. For those remaining ashore, the chairman of the council was providing a running commentary.

". . . yes, in cooperation with German authorities, BADA is assembling several special units from our member states," said Madame Nordstrom. "Of course, our own staff of marine engineers is already engaged."

Backgrounding is an art and one that Madame Nordstrom had mastered. The dignitaries hung on her every word; the journalists scribbled furiously.

". . . and bad as the situation is here," she continued, "you will see at our next stop the true dimensions of the challenge."

The next stop came after a short bus ride to Holtenau, the Baltic entrance to the canal. Disembarking, Thatcher beheld a sight he would never forget. The waters of Kiel harbor were hopelessly tangled by naval vessels, tankers, trawlers, and barges.

Madame Nordstrom raised her voice above the steady lament of horns and sirens.

"And the congestion at the southern end of the canal is, if anything, worse."

Had BADA been prepared for a disaster of this magnitude?

"Not this kind," said Madame Nordstrom. "As most of you know, we do have contingency plans. Data's already being fed into our central computer from everyone with dislocated schedules and stranded cargoes. But the situation here at Kiel is truly extraordinary, and we're still working out arrangements with the German government."

This steely determination to present BADA at its operational best led her to continue.

". . . rationalizing information from so many agencies would have been impossible if the experts on BADA's staff had not had procedures in place," she declared. "For everything we're able to accomplish, great credit is due to Stefan Zabriski, who's been working day and night. Stefan, would you like to add anything to what I've said?"

She was tall enough to look over surrounding heads to a satellite group where Stefan Zabriski was the center of a clamoring horde. He would engage in a brief exchange, then pivot to dictate instructions to his secretary before repeating the whole process. Madame Nordstrom's summons brought him forward, blinking at the ring of expectant faces. Only after prompting from Wanda did he brighten.

"We just received permission from Copenhagen," he said baldly. "We'll be assembling a team of pilots to convoy ships through Danish waters tomorrow morning."

Without further elaboration, he moved to return to his waiting suppliants but Madame Nordstrom detained him.

"Wonderful!" she exclaimed, hailing a triumph. "We all thought that would take much longer."

Zabriski ignored the cue.

"It's only going to help smaller craft," he said meticulously.

His perfunctory response cost Madame Nordstrom her audience. Separate discussions broke forth as the gathering dissolved into its parts. Madame Nordstrom bit her lip briefly, then startled John Thatcher by clasping his arm and stepping to Zabriski's side.

"Stefan," she said. "You should meet Mr. Thatcher. He is from the Sloan Guaranty Trust, in New York."

Zabriski was obviously itching to get back to work but he was a professional civil servant. He greeted Thatcher conventionally and produced some acceptable small talk.

"Then Mr. Gabler is your associate? I'm looking forward to my talks with him."

But his next remarks divulged his real order of priorities. Abandoning Everett Gabler, John Thatcher, and the money they represented, he turned to Annamarie.

"You know, Madame Chairman, now that everybody's attention is focused on the shortcomings of the present canal, this is our opportunity to initiate discussions with Bonn about a new system."

Ruefully she gestured toward the chaos engulfing Holtenau. "Stefan, let's all concentrate on getting this canal open," she suggested, "before we start building another one."

The reminder was more than enough. "You're right, there is

too much to do now," Zabriski agreed. "And I want to talk to Myers!"

With that, he hurried off.

"Just a minute, Wanda," said Madame Nordstrom swiftly. "Will you warn Stefan that the press will be out in force when those convoys leave for Denmark?"

"I'll tell him, all right," Wanda said cheerfully, "but he won't take it in. Maybe I'd better arrange the details."

Stepping aside, Thatcher was struck by the contrast between the two women. Annamarie, erect and composed, her tidy chignon glinting in the sunlight, was coolly efficient. Wanda, her thick cloud of dark hair whipping in the breeze, was agreeing to directions with eager nods and exuberant gestures.

Once she was at liberty, Madame Nordstrom sounded an apologetic note. "Stefan," she explained, "has his blind spots."

In other words, he had time for his grandiose hopes but was oblivious to the need for favorable publicity. Thatcher could have formulated a harsher verdict but he was primarily interested in the Kiel Canal.

"If you mean Zabriski's enthusiasm for a major new system, I understand that he's not alone. They were discussing it just this morning on the plane from Gdansk."

"But who was doing the talking?" she asked reasonably.

Thatcher's reply did not impress her.

"Oh, Leonhard Bach!" she sniffed. "I thought you meant BADA delegates. For example, I know that you're friendly with Peter von Hennig. Did he give you any intimation of the latest German thinking on the subject?"

Large blue eyes had been trained on John Thatcher before. Furthermore he had his own turf to protect.

"As a matter of fact," he said without a qualm, "the subject hasn't arisen."

* * *

AFTER HOURS OF salty breezes, bright sunshine, and healthy exercise on docks and embankments, Thatcher expected an evening of casual comfort. Instead he got a whiff of an older, statelier past. The Hotel Maritim, like the city of Kiel itself, was a postwar construction. Nevertheless, its atmosphere recalled a turn-of-the-century watering place. Garden paths were laid out for leisurely promenades, a series of lounges on the ground floor beckoned guests to elaborate tea and coffee rituals, and the dining room elevated dinner into a protracted, elaborate ceremony. At the Maritim, merriment was not the keynote.

Tonight Peter von Hennig was dining elsewhere with the directors of Germany's largest shipping line. He had, however, done his duty by Thatcher, first introducing him to Casimir Radan, the Polish delegate, and then providing a dinner companion in the shape of BADA's Danish representative.

Fortunately Eric Andersen, a rangy, weather-beaten Arctic expert who was the voice of environmentalism on the council, was not rabid on his subject. He started by comparing notes on what they had seen earlier that day.

"An incredible sight," he agreed. "Especially when you've sailed through the canal as often as I have. And the congestion in the Danish channels is breaking records too."

"What about the convoys BADA is starting tomorrow? Won't that make things worse?"

"Probably," said Andersen, "but you see . . ."

Deploying knives and forks he diagramed a course that relied heavily on superb seamanship.

"So Denmark is running some risk giving BADA permission to take more ships into the area?" Thatcher asked.

"It's our contribution to BADA," said Andersen with mock solemnity. "If Denmark can help sort things out, everybody will benefit."

Thatcher knew about selfless gestures. "A favor done is a favor earned, eh?" he suggested.

"I certainly hope so," Andersen replied. "I need all the goodwill I can promote."

Advocacy can be palatable when it comes leavened with good humor. But good sense is also desirable. A few cautious questions reassured Thatcher on that score.

"Despite what you may have heard, we're not all extremists," Andersen smiled. "Sure, some of the fringe types are against any commercial development. But for most of us, modest well-thought-out projects that improve what's already in place are totally acceptable. Take this harbor grant for example. Denmark voted for it because it will do a lot of good for Tallinn or Rostock—whichever way things go."

Like Peter von Hennig, he was not ready to commit himself.

"You sound quite sympathetic to your opponents," Thatcher observed.

"Let's just say I understand them. All they need is education."

At these dread words, Thatcher stiffened but Andersen remained low-keyed.

"It's up to us to explain why making a million marks is no good if it sticks you with two million marks worth of toxic waste."

His approach was more sensible than wholesale condemnation but there was a drawback, as Thatcher pointed out.

"Education takes time, especially when people are as desperately poor as they are in the East."

"It's uphill work with the rich too," said Andersen. "You Americans are worse than the poor bloody Poles with all your air-conditioning and automobiles."

Thatcher had long since learned that temperatures in Atlanta and distances in the Rockies were not regarded as sufficient justification.

"And are conditions in Denmark ideal?" he inquired.

"Touché," said Andersen. "But we are ahead of most nations."

49

After a short discourse about enlightened public policy Thatcher felt free to exact a return.

"Yes, I see the value of windmill farms," he said with some truth, "but sooner or later lines are going to be drawn over larger undertakings. For instance, these proposals to expand the Kiel Canal."

"Thank god that's not in the immediate future," said Andersen with sincerity. "The last thing the Baltic needs is more traffic before it's cleaned up. But you're right. When the time comes there'll be a pitched battle about the scope of the improvements. Some lunatics are actually talking about two separate, one-way canals. The construction alone would devastate the whole peninsula."

Thatcher suddenly saw the Sloan figuring as an enemy of planet Earth.

"Surely there are more responsible proposals," he protested.

"Hundreds!" snorted Andersen. "But every damned one of them will be big enough to require careful scrutiny from us."

Thatcher did not know whether to be relieved or not. But with the long-awaited arrival of the soup, Andersen turned to less contentious matters.

"My daughter is thinking of going to college in the States," he began.

Miss Andersen was only thirteen years old but Wellesley, Stanford, and Princeton lasted nicely through dinner.

6. . . . and a Bottle of Rum

ONVERSATIONS AT OTHER tables were just as desultory. Two hours of rich food and interminable delays had produced a pall of insidious lethargy. A small combo in the corner contributed to the prevailing somnolence. Its repertoire had been so carefully screened for genteel suitability that the musicians were bored to distraction. As the evening progressed they too collapsed into a remorseless diminuendo.

One guest was still alive and kicking.

Leonhard Bach raised his voice in genial complaint. "C'mon, we're all falling asleep here. Play something with a little punch."

The band nodded, grinned and began a selection marginally more animated than the "Dead March."

"Hell, no," said Bach, placing a meaty hand on the table to lever himself upright. With an encouraging smile, he urged: "Play 'Laughing Louise.'"

Mindful of management's admonitions, the band denied any knowledge of "Laughing Louise."

"But everybody knows it." Swinging around to appeal for support, Bach stumbled against a chair leg and would have pitched forward if his tablemate had not extended a steadying arm.

By now the attention of most diners had been attracted.

Some were indifferent, some amused, a few affronted. But the two German engineers Bach chose to address had missed what was going on.

"You've heard of 'Laughing Louise,' haven't you?" he challenged them.

Startled, they automatically agreed.

"See!" Bach bellowed triumphantly.

All hotels have experience with guests who over-imbibe but this maître d'hôtel was too inflexible to resolve the difficulty. Under his lowering glare, the band remained frozen until another guest took matters into his own hands.

"Now, Leonhard," said Stefan Zabriski, joining Bach and placing a calming hand on his shoulder, "if they don't know it, I'll play it for you. Didn't I see a piano accordion somewhere?"

There was one on a chair by the bandstand. Slipping into its straps, Zabriski beamed confidently and began a rousing rendition of the hoary favorite.

When Leonhard Bach responded by raising his voice in an off-key accompaniment, the issue trembled in the balance. As a soloist Bach would have been a social embarrassment, but the gods were with him. The two engineers, still baffled, obligingly joined in.

"Everybody sing!" Leonhard Bach commanded, waving his arms.

Amazingly, they did.

Stefan Zabriski had not only saved the day, he had become the indentured entertainer of the evening. Pelted with requests, he tossed off sea chanteys, sentimental ballads and then, at the urging of a young couple, a polka.

The twosome instantly took to the minute dance floor. Emboldened by their example other diners began pushing back tables and soon every one of the few women present had been swept up. Most of the hopping and skipping was more spirited than skillful. But one dazzling pair stole the show. When they swung past, Thatcher was astonished to recognize Stefan Zabriski's secretary. She and her partner—Casimir Radan, the stout white-haired dignitary Thatcher had met earlier—were proving to the world why the polka is named after Poland. Her olive cheeks flushed with color, her black eyes sparkling, Wanda magically conveyed the impression of voluminous petticoats flicking around her ankles.

"Amazing," Thatcher murmured.

But Eric Andersen was watching Wanda's partner.

"Casimir's still pretty spry for his age, isn't he?" he remarked indulgently.

At the end of the polka Zabriski, now accompanied by a band absolved of responsibility, moved on to even more robust selections. John Thatcher, who had been unable to identify any of the previous offerings, now knew he was listening to a student drinking song. While Zabriski belted out the melody, while the clarinet soared to new heights, the audience heartily stamped its feet and roared its lungs out until the concluding bars. Then: "*Hoch! Hoch! Hoch!*" they all shouted, raising their glasses high.

At ELEVEN-THIRTY A mutinous dining room staff finally forced the maître d'hôtel to take action.

"Ladies and gentlemen," he announced during a temporary lull, "we will now be serving brandy and liqueurs in the lounge."

On the principle that if the Pied Piper leaves town the children will follow, he descended on Stefan Zabriski. After warmly insisting that Zabriski regard himself as management's guest for the evening, the maître d'hôtel ushered him up the stairs. Instantly the waiters started clearing tables and the band began packing. But these prods were unnecessary. Zabriski had become such a magnet that his audience simply surged after him.

In the lounge it developed that Zabriski needed a rest. Mopping a glistening brow and breathing hard, he modestly disclaimed any personal merit.

"I enjoyed it. But, my, I haven't done that for a long time."

At his side Leonhard Bach, hoarse-voiced from his own exertions and now visibly reeling, shared in the triumph.

"I guess we showed them BADA knows how to celebrate," he declared to the world at large. "And why the hell shouldn't we? Everything's going our way."

"Yes, there won't be any doubt about our capability now," Zabriski agreed happily. After a revivifying sip, he produced a compliment of his own. "And it's good of you, Leonhard, to set aside your own losses to join in our victory."

Blinking owlishly, Bach tried to adjust to this portrait of himself. "Losses?"

"I remember the Valhalla's *Gudrun* was due to pass through the canal today. It must be costing you a pretty penny."

"Christ, after seeing those burnt-out hulls I'm just grateful she wasn't scheduled for two days ago." Unwilling to have the moment soured by insurance claims, he went on cheerfully: "But come on, Stefan, tell us where you learned to play the accordion that way."

Wanda Jesilko, now equipped with a double vodka, had made her way to their side.

"That isn't even half of it," she said, laughing. "Go on, tell them, Stefan."

When he did not immediately comply, she continued affectionately: "You should hear him on the violin. Or on the flute for that matter. And he can play anything from classical on down."

Basking in her tribute, Zabriski explained that it all came from his humble origins.

"You see, my father was a barge captain and we lived on board. So the family had to entertain itself. Whatever instrument anyone could beg, borrow or steal, we all learned to use."

"Despite all those forms and papers of yours, you're a regular, Stefan," Bach announced as he nearly flattened the slight Zabriski with a comradely pat on the back. "Off the barges, eh? That's a hard life."

"But a good one," said Zabriski after recovering his breath. "Oh, what stories we could tell, Leonhard."

Bach was momentarily taken aback. Before bursting on the world as a man of action he himself had been a paper pusher. A career in the Rostock harbormaster's office until the fall of East Germany had not furnished many anecdotes about life on the bounding main. Fortunately several old salts in the crowd were more than willing to contribute their own tall tales.

At least one spectator found nothing to admire in this feast of harmony. Jaan Hroka had sidled up to the improvised bar where John Thatcher and Eric Andersen were observing the scene.

"Would you look at that? It's enough to make you sick," he snarled. "Bach makes a fool of himself so Zabriski comes running to the rescue. And now it's Stefan and Leonhard all over the place even though Bach's as drunk as a skunk. Anything that damned German wants, anything Rostock wants, BADA just hands it over."

Andersen did not appreciate this outburst and, looking about for relief, was happy to point out that the Estonian delegate was beckoning Hroka.

"Vigotis, for Chrissake! Well, I've got a few things to say to him too," said Hroka, stomping off.

"Whew!" breathed Andersen, looking on with distaste. "Still, Zabriski should be more careful about Bach."

"What on earth are you talking about, Eric?" asked Madame Nordstrom, emerging from the crowd. "I for one was profoundly grateful to see Stefan exercising some tact."

While Thatcher procured a brandy for her, Andersen explained. "Yes, Annamarie, but you just missed Hroka complaining about favoritism. And you have to admit that, right now, friendly attention to a Rostock shipper invites misinterpretation."

"Good lord, I'd forgotten Hroka came along with us," she exclaimed. "It's a wonder the whole evening didn't turn into a debacle."

"A debacle?" asked a new voice. "That sounds good to me. I myself have just spent several hours of unutterable boredom."

Peter von Hennig showed no signs of wear.

"Were you expecting to have a rollicking time?" Thatcher inquired.

"Certainly not," said von Hennig. "The larger the shipping line, the greater the disruption caused by the Kiel catastrophe. I expected the directors to be worried, I expected them to be weighing alternatives. I did not expect them to be agonizing over their entire fleet. My god, we considered every individual vessel they own—its current location, its possible reroutings and, of course, every penny of additional expenditure . . . what is that noise?"

In a far corner of the lounge a scratch quartet had just burst into song. Their close harmony was almost drowned by the boozy chatter on every side.

"I'll be damned," accused the indignant von Hennig, "you've been having a party."

"You missed the sing-along," said Thatcher gravely, before going on to a fuller description of high times at the Maritim.

To Annamarie's dismay von Hennig donned his official mantle.

"Our Estonian delegate must have been pleased to see Zabriski emerging from his shell in the guise of a friend to Rostock," he declared sarcastically.

"Come now, Peter," she argued, "how else could Stefan have spared BADA real embarrassment?"

The response came from Eric Andersen, not von Hennig.

56

"But who elected Zabriski to do anything at all?" he asked at his blandest.

To John Thatcher, one thing seemed obvious. Stefan Zabriski was claiming more attention from BADA's council than any chief of staff should.

7. Full Steam Ahead

WHATEVER THE FAULTS of the BADA contingent, they had inherited enough Baltic hardiness to tumble out of bed early the next morning. Leonhard Bach was unwontedly subdued, Jaan Hroka's eyes were bloodshot and Casimir Radan winced at every movement, but they were all on time for Madame Nordstrom's media event.

Immediately after dawn, the small vessels planning to join the Danish convoy had begun to struggle free from the strangled mass clotting the inner roadstead. With busy hootings and tootings, one after the other edged its way through the available gaps. Crews lining the decks of stationary craft watched critically, helicopters hovering overhead barked instructions, and the canal authority maintained anxious radio contact with everything that moved.

In the outer harbor an air of fiesta prevailed. Pennants were flying from every mast, new arrivals were greeted with fanfare, and a small power launch darted about with men entering data on clipboards. At nine o'clock a blast from the horn of the pilot ship sounded the official start and the raggle-taggle fleet set forth to resounding cheers.

Glorious as the moment was, it represented the peak of Stefan Zabriski's popularity, destined now to sink steadily.

"My warmest congratulations," said Peter von Hennig. "It went exactly as planned."

"Yes, but it's only a stopgap. There is still so much for us to do," Zabriski replied soberly.

Von Hennig thought they were talking about the same thing.

"I assure you Germany understands the pressing need to repair all damage."

Zabriski barely allowed him to finish. "But even while that is proceeding we must be thinking about the greater damage—to the Baltic's reputation for reliable shipping."

"A never-to-be sufficiently respected ideal," said von Hennig evasively. "And one that will be receiving serious attention from all parties."

"Attention that will be swiftly translated into action, I hope," Zabriski said earnestly, "now that we all realize that a major canal project cannot wait much longer."

But von Hennig had no intention of being towed into a policy debate. Drawing himself up, he conveyed the formal appreciation of the city of Kiel, then skillfully directed the conversation back to the flotilla. Before Zabriski knew it, his quarry had slipped away.

Not everyone was as adroit as von Hennig. Jaan Hroka, finding himself next to Zabriski, followed up felicitations with an attempt to ingratiate himself.

"Everybody says they couldn't have done it without you."

"It's all due to my people," Zabriski demurred. "They've performed wonders. I now have no hesitation about returning to Gdansk."

"Yeah, but conducting operations from there will still mean a lot of work for you."

Zabriski shook his head. "Not so much. Of course I'll have

to review the computer readouts, but only to assure myself that the system is functioning properly."

"Boy, you stay on top of the smallest detail, don't you?" said Hroka, shoveling it on.

"The whole reason for a contingency plan is to handle an emergency while continuing ordinary routine. I do not anticipate any delays in council business."

Hroka knew that one item awaiting BADA was the vote on Rostock and Tallinn.

"Too bad," he muttered under his breath.

Still mentally revelling in the picture of a BADA working with two hands, Zabriski forgot that he was addressing an Estonian.

"BADA must not be deflected from its high purpose. This is the ideal moment to demonstrate that delinquency will not be rewarded."

Hopelessness silenced Jaan Hroka. It was painfully obvious that anything he said would be dismissed as naked self-interest.

Eric Andersen, however, represented the sovereign state of Denmark. Later in the morning, after he too had produced the mandatory compliments about the flotilla, he was not surprised to hear Zabriski sound the theme of canal construction. A noncommittal rejoinder received short shrift.

"Oh, I'm not talking about more discussion. Now that we're all agreed," Zabriski said serenely, "real planning can begin."

"But differences are bound to arise when ten countries are considering action. Only yesterday your own representative told me of his misgivings about costly undertakings."

References to Poland were not going to do Andersen any good.

"Some members had trouble understanding the urgency of the situation," Zabriski conceded. "But that's all changed. Casimir Radan will speak very differently on the flight back. I honestly do not see how any legitimate divergence can remain."

The other delegates had fled at the sound of that last preposterous statement. But a lifetime in the vanguard of environmentalism had made Andersen a teacher.

"As long as members have varying internal problems, there will be varying responses," he said slowly.

Zabriski's hand brushed aside this argument.

"Internal problems are not proper concerns of BADA."

"They are factors in every delegate's consideration of any BADA proposal."

"You're not saying you're against a canal proposal, are you?" Zabriski demanded, his eyes widening with incredulity.

"My decision will be based on a host of considerations. Furthermore, as no specific proposal is on the table, it's premature to talk about votes."

Zabriski had not listened to anything beyond the first sentence.

"But none of these internal problems affect Denmark. So there is absolutely no excuse for you to support further delay."

"I do not need any excuse for consulting my country's best interests."

If Andersen's refusal to pledge himself to the cause had been an unwelcome shock, his lofty tone was even worse. After hours of congratulations, flattery, and agreement, Zabriski was encountering his first intransigence. He did not like it.

Too quickly he shot back: "Denmark had no qualms about supporting the Aland project. But, of course, BADA employed a Danish firm for that cleanup."

The firm in question was not only Danish, it was owned by Eric Andersen's in-laws.

"And just what do you mean by that?" he demanded, stiffening.

Zabriski, intent on seizing the moral high ground, was oblivious.

"BADA's decisions cannot be made on the basis of immediate gain to individual members."

"Who the hell do you think you are?" Andersen roared. "Running around impugning my motives? It's high time somebody told you that the council runs things. The staff takes orders. If I can't make you understand that, maybe Madame Nordstrom can!"

THERE WAS NO rush to occupy the seat adjacent to Stefan Zabriski and Leonhard Bach sat exactly where he wanted on the flight back to Gdansk.

It was an unfortunate time for BADA's chief of staff to be cheek by jowl with an uncritical supporter. Here was proof positive that his views were endorsed by reasonable men. Leonhard Bach was not mired in the past; he was facing the future.

As the German's jovial tones rang through the cabin, everybody could follow the tenor of his remarks.

". . . there's bound to be consensus now . . . with two separate canals this can never happen again."

Those sitting to the rear could see both heads bobbing in accord and were not surprised, later in the trip, to hear that same booming voice say:

"It would almost be a pat on the back for Estonia . . . Fat chance of anybody paying attention to BADA regulations after that . . ."

WANDA JESILKO WAS delayed leaving Kiel in order to prepare lists of BADA personnel and equipment for transfer to the damage site. She was barely across the threshold of her office at eleven the next morning before she was on the receiving end of a spurt of complaints from Zabriski.

"Would you believe it? Even after seeing conditions at Kiel,

63

even after hearing of dislocation all over the Baltic, even after listening to people from the shipping companies, some of these idiots still do not admit the necessity for an immediate canal project."

Laying down her portfolio she examined him with tolerant amusement.

"Hello, dear. How are you? And did you have a good trip home?" she inquired in artificially dulcet tones.

Momentarily puzzled, he finally realized his duty. "Oh, sorry, Wanda. I'm glad you're back. Were there any problems?"

"No, everything's straightened out," she admitted as she sauntered forward in all the glory of a brilliantly patterned batik dress. "But it's nice to be asked."

He felt he had already done all that was required in that line.

"What does it take to make them face facts?" he demanded histrionically. "I was so sure this would do it."

"Now, Stefan," she murmured automatically. "You can't expect overnight results."

He shook his head. "It's not just that. There are some of them," he intoned darkly, "who are deliberately trying to stem the tide of progress, probably out of naked self-interest."

"Pooh!" she said, deliberately puncturing his high-flown rhetoric. One of the games Stefan regularly played was to despair at the monumental dimensions of any obstacle, however picayune. Probably, she suspected, so that his ultimate success was proportionately great. "You've always known there would be some resistance."

"Before yes, but not now. Nobody can have doubts any longer, nobody with an open mind."

"Like you?" she asked, her lips twisted by a half smile.

Zabriski saw no irony.

"Yes. Like me and like others. Just ask the people who are really involved, the ones who use the canal or depend on it. You should have heard Leonhard Bach on the plane."

"Oh, no!" she burst forth. "You didn't sit with him, Stefan, not after all I said."

"I didn't choose him. He sat down next to me," Zabriski replied. "What was I supposed to do? Tell him to go away?"

She sighed. However ill-judged Zabriski's rescue of Bach at the Maritim might have been, his subsequent entertainment of the crowd had more than recovered lost ground. In fact, Wanda had been pleased as punch at the rare opportunity for other people to see Stefan as she saw him. For once he had laid aside the mantle of official reserve and allowed some humanity to surface. But apparently there was a price to pay.

"I might have known Bach would exploit the situation," she grumbled.

"What is there to exploit?"

"He's not only creating intimacy, he's flaunting it. I'll bet it's all Leonhard and Stefan now."

"You're prejudiced," he accused. "At least he's open and aboveboard about his position. Not like some of those others."

Wanda grinned. Once Stefan had a bee in his bonnet he heard only what he wanted to hear.

"Come on," she said with a comforting pat on his shoulder. "You can't see sinister forces at work every time someone has different ideas."

"The hell I can't. And I told Andersen as much," he retorted with every sign of satisfaction.

Wanda's hand froze in midair but her voice was mild. "You shouldn't do that, Stefan," she chided.

"Somebody has to."

"Not necessarily," she groaned with a final pat. Abandoning him, she scooped some files from her portfolio preparatory to spreading joy among the chosen technical experts.

He ignored both her objection and the signs of departure. "And I certainly have given up expecting anything from

Madame Chairman. Why, she's so busy playing politics she's barely abreast of the situation."

Briefly Wanda wondered if Stefan had the slightest notion that it was those despised politics that had put him front and center at Kiel.

"That's her job."

"Well then, let her get on with it, while I take care of the important problems."

8. Pressure Falling

NDUSTRIOUSLY WORKING AN hour later, Zabriski was at a loss when Annamarie Nordstrom unexpectedly entered his office.

"I must speak to you, Stefan."

Immersed in a printout, he frowned. "Can't it wait?"

"I'm afraid not," she replied, composedly settling herself in a chair.

The departure from protocol finally registered. His thoughts flying to a new crisis at Kiel, Zabriski asked anxiously:

"What's happened?"

The chairman looked at him sorrowfully.

"You have really done it this time, Stefan," she began. "First I have had to pacify Anton Vigotis, who's alarmed by your loose talk with Jaan Hroka. Then, far more serious, Eric Andersen is in a fury and his complaint seems more than justified. I cannot have you trying to pressure the council."

Decompressing from the world of ship registries and cargo manifests, Zabriski was momentarily blank.

"Oh, Andersen!" he finally said, memory and irritation both returning. "That man is deaf to rational persuasion. Everybody else agrees on the urgency of a canal project."

In spite of an intimate acquaintance with Zabriski's myopia, Madame Nordstrom was astonished at the form his recollection took. Clinically she surveyed her chief of staff. Stefan was growing disturbingly fond of laying down the law.

"First let us deal with Vigotis," she announced, ignoring his remarks. "How can you possibly have given Jaan Hroka the impression that the harbor vote is an opportunity to penalize Estonia? That was settled last week."

"Only because you felt that the BADA union was still fragile. I thought at the time you were being unduly alarmist," he recalled pleasurably. "Anyway, what's all the fuss about? Rostock is going to get the grant in any event. Now it will simply be unanimous."

Annamarie bit down hard. But much as she longed to pierce Zabriski's complacence, she had no intention of departing from her script. Their head-on collision, when it came, would center on her second point.

"All that is irrelevant. As you well know, I gave my personal assurance to Tallinn that no further action would be taken, so the matter is closed," she said coldly. "Which brings me to Herr Andersen. In order to avoid further complaints of this nature it must be understood that you have no business airing your views, let alone attempting to force them on the members."

"But that is nonsense. My staff collects the data for an informed decision," he retorted. "It is necessary that I make known the conclusions derived from this material."

No matter what the fiction, senior civil servants always have ideas about policy. Their persuasive powers, however, are supposed to be confined to their ministers. Once they start electioneering, they cease to be civil servants. As Annamarie elaborated this thesis, Zabriski's jaw set tighter and tighter.

"I cannot agree," he protested. "The delegates have to be told on what basis to make their decision."

This was pure euphemism. What Zabriski meant was that they had to be told what to do.

"People are perfectly capable of reaching their own decisions," she snapped.

"How can you say that when there are men like Jaan Hroka and yes, like Eric Andersen, who are deflected by their own improper concerns?"

"Stop right there, Stefan," she directed crisply. "You cannot assume that opposition to a canal proposal implies corruption."

But Zabriski had laid back his ears.

"There are those who agree with me," he insisted.

"Like Leonhard Bach?" she asked with open irony.

"And what's wrong with Bach? He is worth listening to."

She shook her head impatiently. "He's simply Hroka in reverse. Understand I have nothing against Bach. I am trying to make you understand that everyone has interests."

"They should have only one goal—the success of BADA."

"And success comes from balancing different interests," she rejoined.

"Not at the price of failing to make the correct decision!"

Annamarie was fast recognizing another one of Zabriski's weaknesses. In his eyes there was a right way, ordained from on high; failure to conform to it was betrayal.

"I dislike saying this, Stefan, but it has become necessary," she said, showing steel for the first time. "Unless you make adjustments in your attitude, your very great value to BADA will be severely impaired. I shall say this only once. There are no right decisions or wrong decisions. There are only decisions made by the council after it has considered whatever it chooses. And the delegates from our member states are not going to be submitted to harassment by the staff."

Zabriski had never before been subjected to the iron maiden treatment. He goggled at her.

"What are you saying?"

She continued her shock tactics. "The staff, at whatever level, is charged with certain limited duties. Continually over-stepping the bounds of your jurisdiction cannot be tolerated."

"This is making a mountain out of a molehill," he said accusingly. "Simply because Andersen chose to take offense at some well-merited criticism."

"You are not in a position to criticize anybody, Stefan. I'm the one who's going to be doing that. I had hoped that we could work together as peers. You force me to remind you that I, acting for the council, hold supreme authority and I will not have it diminished."

"How can you speak for BADA? You'll be gone as soon as your term expires," Zabriski said, revealing his scorn for birds of passage.

She rose to her feet and began to leave.

"At which time I will be replaced by a different chairman with similar authority." At the door she paused for a parting shot. "You will have only yourself to blame if you are not here to witness that succession."

Zabriski, white with anger, followed her into the hallway. "You're simply looking for an excuse to get rid of me so that you can install some spineless yes-man," he charged.

With glacial precision she replied, "I will get rid of anyone who imperils the continued progress of BADA."

"The main reason for BADA's progress is me!" Zabriski ranted. "All you've done is pander to one group after another!"

"It's called compromise, Stefan, and without it we wouldn't have lasted a year," she said, rather pleased at his loss of control. At least she had gotten through to him.

"A meaningless word to cover what amounts to a bunch of payoffs. People don't know half of what's been going on here."

"They not only know, they understand. Which is more than I can say for you," she replied.

70

There was an ugly glitter in Zabriski's eyes.

"That's what you think. Do you really believe I've been blind to what you've been up to? Just remember this: I can blow BADA apart any time I want!"

EVEN DISAGREEMENTS CONDUCTED behind closed doors at BADA surfaced on the grapevine within hours. A blazing row in a public corridor made its way to the employee cafeteria in a matter of minutes.

". . . stalked out of his office yelling that he was fired . . ."

"You know he had a fight in Kiel with Mr. Andersen. I'll bet that's what got her going. . . ."

". . . Herr Zabriski was literally foaming at the mouth, they say."

". . . official complaint from the Estonian delegate."

"I heard Mr. Andersen had to be held back from punching him."

Arriving for lunch after two hours with the engineers, Wanda could scarcely believe her ears. Nothing else was being discussed on the line at the steam tables. And when Wanda carried her tray to a far corner the snatches from surrounding tables merely increased her confusion. Most of what she heard was obviously the colorful embroidery of people hungry for melodrama.

Unfortunately she could not dismiss the account of Andersen's secretary who joined her after a few minutes. Karen was totally absorbed in her forthcoming wedding. All her spare time was spent either writing long letters to her fiancé at some remote archeological site or discussing with her mother every detail of her future ménage from saucepans to curtains. Karen's work was at BADA, but the real drama in her life lay elsewhere.

"Oh, yes," she replied to a hesitant question from Wanda. "Something happened all right, but I don't know what. I do know I've never seen Mr. Andersen like that before. When he's angry he usually gets cold and distant. But not this time. He was really boiling when he stormed up to Madame Nordstrom's office."

Nor was there any doubt that the encounter with Annamarie, whatever its content, must have been extraordinarily heated. For Stefan to throw away the formality of a lifetime and allow their dispute to spill into public argued hostilities on an unprecedented level.

And everything had been going so well. For once Zabriski had been working in perfect harmony with the chairman, proving his worth every moment. And now just because she, Wanda, had been elsewhere he had destroyed all that budding goodwill.

But a moment's reflection persuaded her that the catalyst had not been her absence. Starting with that predawn phone call the last few days had been a triumphal march for Zabriski. Far better than Madame Nordstrom, Wanda realized that the canal disaster had been viewed by Stefan as a miracle from on high, expressly designed to allow him to fulfill his dreams and emerge as the savior of the Baltic. He had reigned supreme at his command post in Gdansk, then he had been the man of the hour beside the canal. Intoxicated by his victories, he must have lost his wits and started hectoring the wrong people.

Without knowing any of the details, Wanda, a veteran of office politics, feared he was in deep trouble. It was one thing to flick somebody on the raw occasionally; it was entirely different to raise a powerful anti-Zabriski party. And any combination of Annamarie, Vigotis, and Andersen spelled danger.

Abruptly she rose. Culling more tidbits in the cafeteria was a waste of time. She needed to learn exactly what had taken place, particularly with Annamarie, and only one person could tell her. Fortunately there was no doubt where Stefan would take his overflowing emotions.

She was right about his activity, but wrong about its location. He had left the computer room and was back in his office, glued to his own terminal. One look was enough to tell Wanda she was not dealing with an artificially contrived minidrama. This time things were so bad even Stefan realized that he had created a crisis.

His posture told the whole story. Normally he faced the screen with eager anticipation. Today he was slumped in his chair, defeated and inert.

"For heaven's sake, Stefan," she began urgently. "What happened with Annamarie?"

"What difference does it make?" he replied in a bleak monotone. "She's been waiting for an excuse to fire me."

Oh god, she thought, some of the gossip had not been exaggerated.

"She actually threatened that?"

He did not bother to look up. "She'll say I'm incompetent," he muttered.

"And Herr Andersen?"

"Him too. They'll gang up on me."

Wanda's frustration was mounting with every exchange. Long practice had made her adept at extracting facts from one of Stefan's biased tirades against his adversaries. But she could learn nothing from these fragmented doomsday responses.

"Listen to me, Stefan. I have to know what's going on. Was it about the canal?"

"None of this would have happened if it hadn't been for the canal."

She thought she could guess the rest. Inflated with his achievements, Stefan had stormed at opposition to his grand plans with shot and shell.

"It's not certain yet," he said, listlessly returning from some silent reverie. "I could be mistaken."

Relief flooded Wanda. Madame Nordstrom must have issued an ultimatum. Reform or go! That was a lot better than instant dismissal.

"Then it's simple," she announced. "You'll just have to back down."

Finally he raised his head and she was appalled. The only time she had ever seen that expression was in the pain-filled bewilderment of a stricken animal.

"Nothing can undo the past," he half-whispered.

Worst of all there was not one single word in his own defense. And this from Stefan, who never admitted the slightest flaw in his conduct. But at least that frozen inertia was beginning to thaw. Ever so slightly he was shifting his position.

"It will all have to come out, you know, and they'll blame me," he continued in dreary acceptance. "They'll probably claim I lack integrity, that I was going to benefit myself."

Wanda could imagine many possible charges being levied against him. Arrogance, egotism and pigheadedness were the ones that sprang to mind. But incompetence? Lack of integrity? Slowly she was being forced to a hideous conclusion. Stefan was not talking about something that had already happened. The quarrels had merely made him vulnerable to some future discovery. What, in god's name, had he done?

"But how was I to tell?" he suddenly exclaimed with a flicker of his old self-justification. "My only fault was believing what I was told."

Hailing this sign of recovery, Wanda leaned forward. "Look, Stefan, things can't be that bad. Tell me what's wrong and we'll come up with a plan."

"As if that were all it took," he said with a spasm of racked laughter that chilled her blood.

"That's not going to do any good," she rapped out sharply. "Stop feeling sorry for yourself and let me help you."

His lips set in a stubborn line. "There are other things I have to do first."

"Such as?"

To her surprise he produced a specific answer.

"I'm leaving tonight on an inspection tour of Baltic ports."

"Good!" she said, endorsing this program instantly. "That will give everybody time to cool off."

And, she thought to herself, it eliminated the possibility of Stefan antagonizing anybody else important. Let him vent his despair and frustration on hapless dock officials a long way from headquarters.

"In the meantime," she coaxed. "I could be shoring up your position. Just tell me what the difficulty is and I'll do my best. You know that."

"WILL YOU JUST LEAVE ME ALONE!" he suddenly exploded.

She backed a pace in alarm. A spasm of irritation would have signaled the old Stefan, but this sounded more like a scream for mercy.

"If that's the way you want it, Stefan," she said sadly, already in full retreat.

But back at her own desk she was at a loss. Throughout the ups and downs of official life for the last ten years he had unfailingly turned to her for assistance. He had not asked for her support—he had demanded it. Stefan had never before turned to stone, never shut her out, never acted as if he were carrying a burden of such shame and mortification that he was actually afraid to tell her.

9. Dead Reckoning

SERENELY UNAWARE OF the smoldering grapevine at BADA, of Madame Nordstrom's withdrawal into her own quarters, of Stefan Zabriski's blitzkrieg strikes from St. Petersburg to Stockholm, John Thatcher and Everett Gabler had at last succeeded in pinning down Peter von Hennig. For forty-eight hours they exploited this situation, immured in Peter's office on BADA's fourth floor. But even three men of steel can negotiate the complex details of a proposed bond issue only so long. At six o'clock they were more than ready to move across the hall to the delegates' lounge.

As their drinks were being served Gabler shifted aside for the waiter.

"Good heavens!" he exclaimed. "Who's that?"

Thatcher turned his head towards the entrance to see a Stefan Zabriski who was a far cry from the bustling, vindicated figure at Kiel. BADA's chief of staff, lines of fatigue etched deeply into his face, was sagging against the doorjamb as he scanned the crowded room.

"Excuse me," said Peter von Hennig, pushing back his chair. "I've been wanting a word with him."

Since six o'clock was a busy time in the lounge—with wait-

77

ers and busboys scurrying in all directions—progress across the floor was impeded.

"Just a minute, Zabriski!" Von Hennig called over various obstacles.

But the chief of staff had sighted his own objective. "Not now," he grunted, veering away.

Von Hennig was sputtering when he returned to the table. "What unbelievable effrontery!"

The incident had attracted the attention of Madame Nordstrom, who immediately hurried over.

"I saw that, Peter, and it was absolutely inexcusable," she said, sinking into the chair Thatcher had pulled out. "All I can do is apologize on BADA's behalf."

But von Hennig's gaze remained fixed on the culprit. "My god, he's going from bad to worse."

On the far side of the lounge Eric Andersen and Leonhard Bach had been deep in conversation. But Zabriski, ignoring the Dane's existence, fastened on the man he wanted. After some kind of protest, Bach shrugged helplessly and followed Zabriski to the bar. The party at Thatcher's table watched the two men collect drinks, then leave the room.

"Now Eric will feel insulted too," Madame Nordstrom predicted.

To Thatcher's ear, she did not sound entirely regretful. There was, however, no denying von Hennig's sincerity.

"Bach, of all people!" he choked.

His indignation echoed from the next table where Jaan Hroka spoke loud and clear.

"That's what I've been beefing about all along. When it's me asking Zabriski for an interview, he puts me off until next week. But he's got plenty of time for a drink with Bach."

The complaint had been delivered in English to the room at large but Annamarie, feigning deafness, replied to von Hennig's last outburst.

"There's nothing I can say, Peter, after Stefan's been openly offensive to one delegate after another."

"BADA," he replied, "can dispense with a chief of staff who is incapable of controlling himself in public."

Nodding solemnly she said, "I quite agree."

Von Hennig was now willing to dismiss the matter. Turning to topics worthier of the table, he said, "You'll be interested in what I was going to tell Thatcher about my call from Bonn."

"Yes, indeed," she admitted.

For a quarter of an hour von Hennig described the latest German response to the canal disaster. Despite minority cries for an accelerated pace, no further action had been taken beyond approval of the technical study.

"That should please you, Annamarie," he concluded. "The engineers will define the feasible options. When BADA is finally ready to start talking, the sillier suggestions will have been winnowed out."

"Yes," she agreed with a gleam in her eye, "and with all the preliminaries done at Germany's expense."

Restored to good humor, von Hennig was chaffing her on her parsimony when they were interrupted.

"I hope I'm not butting in."

"Of course not, Herr Bach," said Annamarie with automatic courtesy. "Do join us."

"Only for a few minutes," Bach promised. "You see, I'm worried about Stefan."

"If you mean his unfortunate conduct towards Herr Andersen, then I wouldn't . . ."

Her voice died away as Bach shook his head vigorously.

"No, no, this is far worse. Stefan is behaving oddly because he's half out of his mind with worry. In fact, I've never seen him spinning like this."

But Madame Nordstrom was through talking about her chief of staff.

"He's probably overtired."

"Then it's taking a weird form," Bach said bluntly. "He claims he's come across something fishy at BADA."

"It won't be the first time," she replied with a tight smile. "Stefan's an idealist. We all fall short of his standards."

Von Hennig snorted contemptuously.

"This isn't his usual line," Bach insisted. "Stefan's talking about fraud."

"Wonderful! Now he's trying to start another scandal," von Hennig jibed.

Like a frustrated bull Bach swung his head from one member of his audience to another.

"I'm not getting through to you. Maybe I shouldn't even be trying but I thought you and Herr Andersen would want to know."

"If Stefan was discussing something in confidence," she observed, "perhaps you should not be telling us."

Thatcher was not surprised to see this reproof brushed aside.

"No, that's not what worries me," Bach assured her. "The thing is, he may not realize how much he let out. Half the time he didn't remember I was there. The poor guy was so charged up he had to let off steam. But what it comes down to is this— Stefan thinks somebody is ripping off BADA in a big way, to the tune of millions."

Annamarie sounded almost indulgent. "You can't be serious."

"Like hell I can't!" he shot back. "Stefan's damn near frantic about it; says it's the last thing he expected his review of the Kiel dislocations to bring to light."

"And what exactly did he discover?" asked von Hennig skeptically.

Bach lifted his solid shoulders. "He refused to go into any detail. That's one of the reasons I thought this was important for you all to hear about." Half-apologetically he continued. "When it's a simple case of Stefan's being on his high horse, he doesn't hold things back."

Another thought occurred to Annamarie.

"Does that mean you've already discussed this with other people?" she asked in dismay.

"Only in broad terms." Defensively Bach went on. "I just tried to make Herr Andersen understand why Stefan acted the way he did. But I didn't say anything about the scam. Besides, Stefan is going home to write a report for the council. By tomorrow morning it will all be out in the open."

He was protesting too much. John Thatcher would have bet good money that, in the first flush of excitement, Bach had told Andersen the whole sorry story.

Peter von Hennig, however, felt that the blame for indiscretion lay elsewhere. "If Zabriski really has something serious to say, why this roundabout approach?" he asked Madame Nordstrom. "He should have come to you the moment he returned."

This at least she could explain.

"You've been out of touch, Peter. I had to dress him down just before he left. Stefan may be avoiding me right now."

Leonhard Bach addressed von Hennig's unspoken criticism. "And the only reason he grabbed me was that he wanted my input on trade usage. Of course by the time we got to his office he was on such a roll he never asked me anything. In the end he probably regretted approaching me because he said he had things to do. I've been racking my brains to figure out how he thought I could help him, but I haven't come up with a damn thing."

"As Stefan did not make himself clear, there's no point trying to guess what he meant. We'll just have to wait until morning," said Madame Nordstrom. Then, glancing at her watch, she reached for her purse. "I'm afraid you'll have to excuse me. My husband is arriving for a visit tonight and I'm already running late."

After her departure von Hennig continued the good work, snubbing attempts at speculation with enough vigor so that Bach also took his leave.

As soon as the coast was clear Thatcher lofted inquiring eyebrows. "So? Do you think Zabriski really has stumbled across something?"

"Possibly," von Hennig conceded with patrician distaste. "It is far more likely that he has come across some minor derelictions. Zabriski is not a person of balanced judgement."

Gabler found this inadequate as the last word on the contretemps they had just witnessed.

"Fraud," he began, rolling the word around his tongue like a connoisseur.

Hastily Thatcher intervened. "There isn't much to be gained from speculating on the forms that might take, Ev. Tomorrow morning Zabriski will present his report and we'll know all about it. Don't you agree, Peter?"

But von Hennig's thoughts were elsewhere. "I seem to have lost touch with BADA while the three of us have been closeted together," he murmured. "I'm beginning to wonder whether Zabriski himself may not be the major problem."

Thatcher considered and dismissed the possibility that Peter was still annoyed by Zabriski's rudeness. "Because Madame Nordstrom said she had to reprimand him?"

Von Hennig shook his head, not in disagreement but as an aid to ordering his thoughts. With a precision that Gabler, for one, approved, he began ticking off items. "There was more than that. First he seems to have had a row with Annamarie. Then he apparently had some kind of tiff with Andersen. Furthermore, whatever excuse there may have been for coming to Bach's aid at the Maritim, there is none for prominently singling him out here in the lounge. And finally there is gross discourtesy to two delegates right now."

Added up, these points came to an impressive total, as

Thatcher had to admit. "But you yourself recommended him in Bonn as a competent chief of staff."

"He is, or rather he has been. That's what alarms me. All of this is very uncharacteristic. Zabriski's manner has always been unexceptionable with the delegates. You know the kind of thing—a good deal of surface deference supported by the confidence that he's the real expert."

"And yet you've labeled him ignorant about vital concerns."

Von Hennig shrugged. "That didn't matter. We all know he has a vainglorious view of BADA's future under his direction, but it's as if he were some bore droning on about his stamp collection. He didn't try to force agreement—on the contrary, he rather enjoyed displaying more vision that the rest of us. I can only recall one instance when his fanaticism caused trouble and that was the toxic dumping."

"Ah!" exclaimed Gabler. "I saw the photograph."

"Too many people did," von Hennig said sourly. Then turning to Thatcher he continued. "Zabriski marched into the council with the most astonishing proposals for sanctions. We were not only supposed to put that wretched Hroka out of business but cripple Estonia with some kind of boycott."

"Surely that caused waves."

Peter smiled in grim recollection. "Vigotis was livid. Fortunately Annamarie took charge. She thanked Zabriski for his suggestions, dismissed him from the chamber, then went to work putting out the fire."

"So that's why Hroka is always accusing him of being anti-Estonian."

"Yes. But actually Zabriski's so anxious to have BADA's authority recognized he was simply grabbing at the excuse for a show of power. Silly, of course, but not dangerous with Annamarie riding herd on him. Unless it was the beginning of some kind of breakdown."

Thatcher wished that he had seen Zabriski in some other

context than his endeavors at the Kiel Canal. There he had certainly not looked like someone heading for a crack-up.

"It's hard to judge without knowing what's been going on," he said.

Gabler coughed delicately. "Surely the most egregious aspect of Zabriski's behavior was choosing Bach as his confidant rather than Madame Nordstrom?" he suggested. "Even if they are having difficulties."

"That's it! That's what's been nagging at me," von Hennig declared in a moment of self-discovery. "Mentioning those difficulties was a departure from Annamarie's usual style. Normally she would have corrected Zabriski in private and never referred to the incident even with a delegate, let alone outsiders."

"You don't think it just slipped out?" Thatcher ventured.

"Ha! Everything she does is deliberate. She was signaling a new plateau in her dealings with him."

Thatcher was remembering more. "And she was not all that bothered by Zabriski's brusqueness to Andersen."

"Lining up support," von Hennig said cogently. "I tell you one thing. This report we'll get tomorrow may be peanuts compared to what's going on between those two. I think I'll leave you now and see if I can catch Casimir Radan at the hotel. He's usually not averse to a little discreet gossip and he may know what's been happening around here."

As soon as von Hennig departed Thatcher addressed the unspoken thought behind Gabler's expression of disapproval. "Peter is not condoning fraud, Ev. He simply suspects that this famous report may be a gambit in some kind of power struggle between Madame Nordstrom and Zabriski."

"I would have thought the outcome of such a struggle self-evident."

"Probably, but Peter knows more about BADA than we do.

He may be concerned how much damage would be caused in the process."

Reluctantly Gabler agreed.

"And as we're not likely to learn anything more here we might leave ourselves," Thatcher continued. "I'd like to check in with Miss Corsa and Charlie."

"And I," said Gabler, rising briskly, "have to make arrangements for tomorrow with Mrs. Gomulka."

In the elevator Gabler explained that, after wading through a host of unworthy applicants, he had finally found a satisfactory candidate for employment. Thatcher hoped that the rate of pay would compensate this unknown woman for what she was getting into.

Gabler had been busy on other fronts as well, as Thatcher was reminded upon reaching the ground floor. He had automatically turned to the front entrance and its taxi rank when Everett plucked at his sleeve.

"Not that way, John. We're going to the parking lot at the back. I rented a car at lunchtime."

In Gabler's opinion the wait for a cab had often been unconscionable.

"Well, not any longer," said Thatcher, following Everett outdoors into the darkness of an early northern evening.

From what could be seen as they picked their way across the half-empty lot, the car of universal choice at BADA was the Fiat Polska.

"They all look the same to me, Ev. You lead—"

Breaking off, Thatcher peered at the isolated vehicle ahead. A large irregular shape lay in its shadow. With a frown he advanced several paces, then froze.

"It's Zabriski," he managed to say through a congested throat. Dropping to one knee, Thatcher forced himself to look at the battered head lying in an ominous dark pool. "And I'm almost sure he's dead."

Everett stared around the lot in bewilderment. "But how could . . . I mean nobody could be driving here that fast . . . and to just leave him . . ."

"It wasn't a car, Everett," said Thatcher, grimly pointing. "It was that."

A tire iron lay several feet away, ugly with Stefan Zabriski's blood.

10. Fishing Expedition

I N THE ETERNITY that followed Everett Gabler was first to recover.

"We have to summon help," he said shakily.

Although mesmerized by the horror lying at his feet, Thatcher did his best to adjust to the needs of the moment.

Then, like the answer to a prayer, approaching footsteps sounded.

"Thank god!" exclaimed Thatcher, hailing somebody—anybody—who could assist. "They can call—oh, no!"

"Don't come closer!" yelped Everett.

But it was too late. Wanda Jesilko, swathed in scarves, paused in a stray shaft of light and frowned an inquiry at the two men confronting her. Then she peered beyond them to the lifeless bundle tossed carelessly against the Polska.

"What's that?" she asked, sidestepping Gabler's outstretched arms. When she reached the body, she stared downward at the lolling mangled head. "It looks like . . . but it can't be . . . Stefan? Oh god, Stefan!"

Crumpling to her knees she began rocking back and forth like an old woman. "No . . . no . . . no . . ."

From whisper to denial to paroxysm her keening mounted steadily.

Even Everett was paralyzed. But this time, relief was at hand. Somewhere behind Thatcher, a door was flung open. Drawn like flies, BADA personnel swarmed outside, pushing forward until they formed a human shield around the stricken woman. Wanda's convulsive cries became the mechanical underbeat to their confused chorus. The questions and exclamations, all unintelligible to Thatcher, were nevertheless music to his ear. Already, excitement was dispelling the nightmare. Sooner or later, cold hard reality must follow.

IT WAS LATER rather than sooner.

"Over an hour, by my reckoning," said Everett, consulting his watch again.

"Just be grateful we're not out there with a corpse and a hysterical woman," said Thatcher callously.

Gabler shuddered retroactively, although their current situation did not have much to recommend it. The delegate's lounge, to which they had been herded with fifteen or twenty others, no longer glowed with warm, shaded lamplight. Instead, a harsh overhead fixture beat down uncompromisingly on an illassorted and unconvivial gathering. Frightened waiters were circulating with much-needed drinks like medics dispensing first aid, but apart from their muted bustle, only whispers broke the silence.

This left a clear field for the inveterate faultfinders.

"I repeat," said one of them, "notifying the local police was highly incorrect procedure."

Carping had begun with the arrival of the first uniform. Yes, there was a rapidly cooling body in the parking lot, but BADA was not a tawdry saloon. Crime on the privileged premises of an international organization required tact and diplomacy. Could these requisites be supplied by passing patrolmen?

The two stolid young giants currently guarding the door did not inspire confidence along those lines, but Thatcher was on their side. While they gave no indication of sensitivity, they had at least activated the system. Downstairs, homicide specialists were circling Stefan Zabriski with clinical detachment. Somebody had sped Wanda off to the infirmary. For this bonus, Thatcher counted confinement in the delegates' lounge a small price to pay.

Others differed.

"But why are they keeping us here? What are we waiting for?"

Thatcher's curiosity, as lively as the next man's, was still centered on the murder, not its immediate aftermath. Offhand, he would have guessed that they were waiting for more policemen.

Instead, they got Annamarie Nordstrom. Her entrance into the lounge was a work of art.

"I came as soon as they managed to contact me," she announced.

Every inch the chairman of the general council of the Baltic Area Development Association, she advanced into her realm with ironclad dignity.

Her lieges needed calming.

"Madame Chairman, do you realize that somebody prematurely called the local police?" said the fusser.

"So I understand," she said, grandly dismissing this quibble. "I don't care. Oh, I know BADA has extraterritorial rights— but we must remember that Stefan is . . . was . . . a Polish citizen, and a distinguished one. So instead of worrying about technicalities, will you please tell me exactly what happened?"

Thatcher was wondering how many others detected a slight crack in her veneer when he was catapulted into the spotlight.

"That's what we do not know," complained an eminent hydrologist. "But Mr. Thatcher here—and Mr. Gabler—they found Zabriski's body!"

When, several lifetimes ago, Thatcher had last shared a table with Madame Nordstrom, he had done the listening. As she sank into a chair beside him he decided that reciprocating with the discovery of a corpse did not constitute a significant improvement. His account was as bald and unvarnished as he could make it.

"How awful," she said at the end of his recital. "To have Wanda Jesilko come along just then."

Surely an odd, almost grotesque aspect of the tragedy to single out! An expression of profound gravity enabled Thatcher to conceal his surprise but Everett quivered slightly.

Without apparent self-consciousness, Annamarie explained herself.

". . . most of us will confine ourselves to simple facts, but after this shock, Wanda may . . . er . . . lose her sense of proportion."

Thatcher interpreted this as protectiveness toward BADA but Everett went further afield.

"A very unpleasant experience for anybody," he said gamely. "But do I gather that Mrs. Jesilko was particularly attached to Zabriski?"

"Lovers," she said briefly. "When Stefan's wife died—and Wanda's husband took off—well . . . they've been together for five years now."

A relationship that was as respectable as you could get, short of the altar, thought Thatcher. On the other hand, it did suggest that Wanda might know more than Madame Nordstrom wanted the police to hear.

As if reading his thoughts, she gave a small sigh, then indicated she could no longer ignore the call of duty. Tapping a spoon against her cup for attention, she rose and made her statement.

"This isn't the time for me to elaborate on the sorrow we feel at the loss of a valued colleague. I do want to allay doubts you may have about the investigation. Ordinarily, we prefer to keep some facets of BADA to ourselves—but this is an exception. We owe it to Stefan to be as helpful as possible, to transmit everything we have seen or heard. I'm sure anything irrelevant will be disregarded."

"Odder still," commented Thatcher.

While Gabler found much that was admirable in Madame Nordstrom's remarks, he recognized a contradiction. Following her misgivings about Wanda Jesilko, pleas for candor rang hollow.

Then a possible explanation presented itself. Unnoticed by Thatcher, the law enforcement arm of BADA's host country had joined the party. Together with an assistant, a heavily decorated policeman had slipped into the lounge. Large and unmistakably imposing, he had a thatch of prematurely white hair and jet-black eyebrows. Gazing blandly at the BADA personnel, he listened while Madame Nordstrom continued:

". . . Colonel Oblonski, who has been assigned because of unique qualifications," she said with a brilliant smile in his direction. "We've put an office at his disposal and no doubt he'll inform you how he plans to proceed."

Her own cooperation, it went without saying, would be unstinted, however delayed.

"Apparently, the premier of Poland is calling on my private line." She excused herself.

This bravura performance was impressive but, thought Thatcher with a glance at the impassive Oblonski, not necessarily effective.

"QUITE THE HIGH-HANDED lady, isn't she?" said Oblonski with the interior rumble that denoted amusement as he entered the office assigned to him.

His aide was more sensitive to international niceties.

"I suppose you could say she's one nation speaking to another," he suggested.

"Yes, but she talked to BADA first, didn't she?" Oblonski replied. "With pretty strong hints that there was a lot to say about Zabriski. Well, to give her credit that makes it easy to know where we should start. I want to talk to those foreign bankers who found the body."

"You mean you don't think this was a robbery that went wrong?"

"The wallet and the pockets were untouched, Alex," explained Oblonski. "Tell them to send down the Americans."

Everett Gabler and John Thatcher, overcoats in arm, duly appeared. Their testimony, a model of its kind, furnished Oblonski with an overview of Zabriski's movements in the delegates' lounge as well as their own. Oblonski did not seek more.

"A CLEAR STATEMENT, although not immediately helpful," he observed after Thatcher and Gabler had been dismissed with profuse thanks.

Subsequent segments of the parade past him made the Sloan Guaranty Trust shine by comparison.

". . . all I can tell you is that Zabriski had some kind of bee in his bonnet," said a witness with absolutely nothing to contribute.

". . . storming up to Bach at Andersen's table. But I couldn't hear a word. . . ."

Even congenital busybodies had been handicapped.

"No one had the courtesy to tell me a thing," said a still-resentful Lithuanian. "You'll have to ask Eric. Or that grubby little Estonian, Hroka. He was right in the thick of things. He and Leonhard Bach both, as if either of them has anything to do with BADA. Now, von Hennig I understand, he's a delegate.

And American bankers—well, that goes without saying. But you'll have to ask Annamarie why she chose . . ."

One by one the lounge upstairs was emptied. By the time the last important personage had been allowed to go home, Oblonski had become interested in the hours immediately preceding Zabriski's death.

"Von Hennig, this Bach, and the Estonians," he read from a list. "Andersen too. They all left before the body was discovered, so they'll have to wait. In the meantime, the boys downstairs have identified the tire iron as BADA property. Let's have a word with the parking attendant."

But the attendant had already departed for the day and in his place came a solid elderly man, quietly self-possessed.

"I'm the BADA mechanic," he explained modestly. "The only reason I'm still here is I had a job to finish. The real attendant left at six o'clock. That's when they lock the back gates and make people circle the building to the front drive."

He was not bothered by any linkage between the murder weapon and BADA.

"If you were working late, how could anybody take one of your tools?" asked Alex.

"Things took longer than I expected," said the mechanic placidly. "So I went to the cafeteria for something to eat. Must have been gone oh, a half hour or so. From about six forty-five to quarter to seven."

Oblonski consulted his map of BADA. "And access to your shop is through the bay doors facing the lot, or that door from the corridor inside?"

"Yep," said the mechanic.

"Couldn't an outsider have gotten into the parking lot from the front drive?" demanded Alex.

"No way," said the mechanic. "The whole area's floodlit and attended all night. He'd have had to walk or drive right past the guard out front."

Alex subsided but Oblonski was still reviewing geography. "So anybody inside BADA heading for the parking-lot exit had to walk past your shop."

"Yes, and some of them like to use it as a shortcut. Herr Zabriski, for example, and his secretary. They've done it when I've been working late."

"Zabriski wasn't always alone?"

"Sometimes he was, sometimes he wasn't," said the mechanic with indifference. "Of course, I lock up before I go home."

As soon as he left, Alex nervously blurted out, "Colonel, if we prove this is an inside job, they'll say we're causing an incident!"

"Oh, no," Oblonski assured him. "We're just finding out what happened so the brass can decide how to handle it." With that out of the way, he went on. "Now Zabriski and that German went up to the bar, didn't they? Let's see if the bartender is still around."

The emergence of a Spaniard speaking fluent Polish astonished the young assistant, but Oblonski, who had spent years on the mean socialist streets, would not have blinked to find a Tibetan mixing BADA's martinis. How well, he asked, did Pablo recall his patrons?

"Perfectly," Pablo boasted. "Herr Bach? Well, he was already at a table, but instead of waiting to be served, he came rushing up to the bar. That was because Herr Zabriski was in a hurry to talk to him privately."

"Is that what you assumed, or what they actually said?"

Pablo did not falter. "When they got to the bar I was setting up a tray, so they pushed further down to a clear spot. That's when Herr Zabriski said matters of such gravity couldn't wait. I definitely caught that snatch while I was passing."

"And then?" Oblonski asked.

There was a flash of white teeth in the swarthy face.

"After a minute or two, when I finished the tray, I went up

to them—and Herr Zabriski was saying something about evidence of a real BADA crime at the Kiel Canal."

"Ah," breathed Oblonski appreciatively. "Did you hear anything more?"

Pablo was enjoying himself. "No, they left right away, but Herr Zabriski looked as sick as a dog. Usually he was as sharp as they come but tonight—"

For whatever they were worth, his insights were interrupted. A policeman stuck his head in the door to announce that Madame Nordstrom was free to receive the authorities. The formulation was not lost on Colonel Oblonski.

"So off we go, into the presence," he said, rising obediently.

Madame Nordstrom did not let him forget the premier.

". . . after expressing our sense of loss, and welcoming his assurances of an intensive investigation," she said fluently. "Naturally, the resources of BADA are available to help clarify this tragic event."

Earlier, Oblonski had listened to her promises with the usual grain of salt. But now, thanks to the Spanish Pole, he was more fully armed.

"They tell me that Zabriski had stumbled upon something criminal at BADA," he said deliberately. "Do you know anything about that?"

Madame Nordstrom did not blanch.

"Very little—and only what I heard at second hand. Leonhard Bach—no doubt you'll be talking to him—could not or would not be more specific."

But Oblonski was not interested in Leonhard Bach at the moment. "Zabriski," he said, sticking to the point at issue. "What can you tell me about him?"

Again, Annamarie had little to offer.

"We are . . . *were* . . . professional colleagues, and I had the highest opinion of him. But otherwise, I know almost nothing about him. He was a widower with a grown son—but that's really all I can tell you."

The police, with other and better sources, were already digging into the background of Stefan Zabriski, so Oblonski nodded as if she had given him a nugget of great value and said, "But you can tell me about the man himself. About his judgement, for example."

She moistened her lips. "As you'll no doubt learn Stefan, in addition to his very great abilities, was sometimes overzealous. He could seem intolerant of quite venial offenses. Perhaps it would be more accurate to call him deeply committed to BADA. Ordinarily, when he got upset about some irregularity, I was inclined to think he was exaggerating."

"But not this time?" Oblonski pounced.

With limpid sincerity, she gazed at him. "*If* Stefan planned to write a report, and *if* he was murdered before he could do so— well, I for one do not believe in coincidence."

"Then you accept the possibility of a serious situation within your organization?"

"Believe me, BADA will leave no stone unturned to find out," she said forcefully.

"Because you're worried about the reputation of BADA?" he suggested.

"Naturally," she replied. "There will be no hint of scandal here if I have any say about it."

Wondering how she regarded murder he merely said, "Perhaps Zabriski's secretary will be able to help."

"Wanda!" exclaimed Madame Nordstrom uneasily. "But she isn't fit to talk yet, is she?"

WANDA WAS FIT and willing to the point of compulsion.

"Stefan would never do anything wrong," she insisted before Oblonski finished introducing himself.

96

The colonel examined his witness thoughtfully. Wanda had made an attempt to repair the signs of ravage; her hair was brushed and her lipstick renewed. But the great dark eyes, glazed with anguish, were sunk in a chalk-white pallor and she seemed unconscious of the vivid bloodstains on her blouse. Oblonski, drawing his own conclusions from these indications of grief, calculated that he had less than five minutes.

"Everybody says that he was very dedicated," he began warily.

"He cared too much about BADA, that was the trouble. That's why he was always annoying people."

"What people?" he asked, seizing the opening.

"Everyone," she said wildly. "Stefan wanted too much, too fast, and he was furious when the others insisted on prudence and delay."

This did not sound like the material of murder.

"He was bothered about something when he came back from his trip. Was it about BADA?"

"He was upset before he left. That's why he went away, to have time to think."

"Upset about what?"

"He wouldn't tell me!" Wracked by a dry sob, she covered her face with her hands, the incarnation of mourning. But the words still tumbled out. "I tried and tried, but no! He knew best . . . always knowing more than anybody about his ships, about his harbors, about everything except what was important. And what good did it do him? He's lying out there with his head . . ."

Before she could break down entirely, Oblonski dragged her back from the edge.

"He must have said something."

She clenched her hands over the arms of her chair, the knuckles showing white as she fought for control.

"Something was going to come out, something bad about BADA, and he was afraid they'd say it was his fault. But that wasn't so," she added fiercely. "He'd just been taken in."

Oblonski was keeping his voice as calm and emotion-free as possible. "Surely, as they all knew about his devotion, they wouldn't be so swift to blame him."

"Stefan had antagonized so many people. He knew they'd grab at the excuse to say he was incompetent."

Zabriski had been worrying about the wrong people, reflected the colonel.

The same thought had occurred to Wanda. "Oh, the fool, the blind fool," she moaned. "He was hoping things would calm down while he was away, or it would all turn out to be a mistake or some other miracle would happen."

It could now only be a matter of seconds before she would be useless.

"And when he came back this evening?" Oblonski pressed. "Did he say anything more?"

"Oh, yes. He said: 'Hello, Wanda, I won't want you until tomorrow morning,'" she replied scornfully. "Famous last words, no?"

Careful to sound sympathetic, Oblonski continued. "I don't suppose you heard what he and Bach were talking about."

Her lips twisted. "Stefan was saying his facts were right. They were always right!"

She closed her eyes abruptly.

Gently Oblonski persisted. "How did he sound—worried, anxious, angry?"

Her voice had become such a thin thread the colonel had to lean forward to catch her words. "He was beside himself. When they came out of the elevator I heard him raving about Eric Andersen. By the time he got to my desk he was muttering about Jaan Hroka and when the door closed he was going on to somebody else."

Suddenly her memories overcame her. "I shouldn't have left him; he was so helpless. But he said he didn't need me, and I didn't want to make things worse. So I just went downstairs to do some last-minute faxing before going home. Oh, damn them all. Look what they've done to Stefan!" she cried, her voice rising harshly. "Look what they've done to me!"

And without further warning she clutched her arms around her breasts and began rocking backwards and forwards to the tempo of her shrill wailing.

"My god," said Alex when they escaped from the infirmary. "I hate these sessions with bereaved women."

Oblonski had seen much more of this phenomenon than his subordinate. "That wasn't just grief," he announced. "She's scared to death about what her precious Stefan was up to. She's trying to establish his innocence before it becomes public. But then she's not very rational right now."

"What do you mean?"

"Somebody figured that, with Zabriski out of the way, it could be covered up. At least that's what the all-wise Madame Nordstrom thinks." His sardonic tone faded into dissatisfaction. "And if she's right, we've got one pretty mess on our hands."

11. Empty Net

A T NINE-THIRTY Colonel Oblonski decided to leave further inquiry at BADA to underlings.

"I'd like to get the story of what happened in that lounge from the ones who've gone missing," he said. "Before they put their heads together."

Alex was dubious. "If they've scattered we won't be able to get much done."

"There are only two likely hotels in Gdansk," Oblonski pointed out. "We should be able to get through one before they're all asleep."

His first and most important strike hit pay dirt. Leonhard Bach was hard at work in his room, rapping out instructions to some distant associate. Waving the colonel to a chair, he continued to focus on the phone.

"Then redirect her to Lisbon," he was saying. "The canal sure as hell won't be open this week, so there's plenty of time. And I want those freighters earning their keep."

"Shipping agents," he muttered when he finally hung up. Then, studying the card in his hand, he said, "What can I do for you, Colonel?"

Bach, in his present guise, was a far cry from the exuberant

Rostock booster. Already in an aged dressing gown and slippers, with a pair of steel-rimmed glasses perched on his nose, he was surrounded by a mountain of freight-forwarding documents.

When Oblonski briefly described Stefan Zabriski's death, Bach was aghast.

"Clubbed to death! It seems impossible," he protested. "Why, I saw poor Stefan only this evening."

"I know, and that's what I want to talk about."

"How will that help?"

"You must realize that Herr Zabriski's discovery of something amiss at BADA is now of prime importance."

Bach narrowed his eyes. "Now, wait a minute. Are you saying that's the reason he was killed? But that would mean . . . god in heaven, this could be a real stink."

"True. So, while you were very discreet when describing the situation to the chairman, it is now time to add the details."

"But I told her everything I knew. Didn't she explain?" Frowning, Bach went on. "Stefan wasn't giving me chapter and verse. If you've talked to Madame Nordstrom, you know as much as I do."

"Not quite."

The words were uttered so gently that Bach missed their significance.

"Didn't you forget Zabriski's anger about Eric Andersen?"

Taken aback, Bach thought for a moment. "I suppose that was Wanda," he decided. "I didn't mention specific names to Madame Nordstrom because they might be taken the wrong way—which is exactly what you're doing, Colonel. Stefan didn't make much sense, so it wasn't at all clear what he meant. He could have been saying that what Andersen did wasn't a hundred percent ethical but it was nothing compared to what someone else had done. Stefan wasn't pointing a finger directly at Andersen the way he did with Hroka—"

Bach broke off with a vexed exclamation.

"Hroka too?" asked the colonel.

"All right, I fell into that one myself. Stefan didn't like how some of the new boys in the East are doing business, and he said Hroka was a prime example."

"Of what?" Oblonski prodded.

"You may as well get it right," Bach growled. "Stefan said Hroka as good as tried to bribe him. But you've got to understand that the two of them didn't hit it off."

JAAN HROKA, ENCOUNTERED rolling into the hotel lobby behind a blast of alcoholic fumes, agreed.

"No, I didn't get along with Zabriski. Who could? He was against Estonians in general."

Oblonski remembered the same story Gabler had. "After the toxic dumping, maybe he had some reason."

With a wave so broad it almost toppled his balance, Hroka replied, "He started in before that. Stefan Zabriski was running BADA for the exclusive benefit of the Germans. His very first program was guaranteeing loans for new shippers. Over half those loans went to Germans. And as for the harbor grant, Zabriski meant to throw that to Rostock, no matter what. That's why his inspectors hit on an Estonian ship. He was setting us up."

Hroka splayed a gnarled hand on the reception desk for support and, thrusting his face close to Oblonski, was haranguing him at top volume.

Only when Oblonski was certain that no germane material would be forthcoming did he interrupt.

"Zabriski claimed you tried to bribe him."

"Not that old song," Hroka jeered. "You want to know what really happened? He was so dead set against Tallinn I asked him to stay with me and inspect the place personally. Little Mr.

Morality acted as if I'd offered him a bagful of money under the table. But Leonhard Bach flies government officials into Rostock for caviar and champagne and that just proves he knows how to run a business . . . unlike us poor peasants in Estonia."

Before the tirade could recommence, Oblonski asked if Hroka had overheard Bach's discussion with the chairman.

"Enough to know that, while Zabriski was playing games, someone had gotten his hand into the BADA till. And the great man was going to have to come up with an explanation for Madame Nordstrom even though she already wanted to get rid of him."

Without a flicker of reaction to this unexpected tidbit, Oblonski continued. "And you heard that he was planning to leave the building?"

"I heard he was spending the evening on his report." Hroka shrugged. "I didn't know where he was going to do it."

An uninhibited witness is always a find for investigators but, if only half of what Hroka said was true, Stefan Zabriski had created hostility on all sides.

"I understand you had wanted an interview with Zabriski. Did you try to catch him after he was through with Bach?"

"Hell, no. One brush-off was enough. I finished my drink with Herr Vigotis, the Estonian delegate, and then we left."

"Together?"

"Damned right!"

THE HOTEL NOVATEL summoned Eric Andersen from a billiard game somewhere in its depths. As a prominent public figure, the Dane cast his first response in the form of praise for the departed.

"Yes, they tell me Zabriski was central to BADA's operations," Oblonski said after the high-flown periods came to an end. "And that he had made a nasty discovery that Herr Bach discussed with you earlier this evening."

Andersen's eyebrows rose at this police interest, but he replied without hesitation. "Yes, Bach said it sounded to him like fraud. He then went over to relay the news to Madame Nordstrom."

"That seems an odd way for her to learn of the situation."

"I thought so myself. Particularly as Zabriski was going home to prepare a report. It probably never occurred to him that someone else would break the news first. But, then, he should have known better than to tell Bach."

Pleased to have acquired this knowledge of Zabriski's movements without specific questioning, Oblonski asked if others could have heard.

"We weren't whispering and the room was crowded. That's my point," Andersen argued. "Telling Bach was the equivalent of telling the whole building. He really should acquire some discretion."

"Perhaps he has . . . to a certain degree. Did he mention what Zabriski said about you? That the first instance of wrongdoing on your part was nothing compared to his recent discovery?"

The Dane's ruddy face darkened. "No, Bach did not. If he had, I would have marched downstairs and given Zabriski a piece of my mind."

So much for elevated sentiments about BADA's great loss.

"I'm afraid I must ask you what Zabriski was referring to."

"It's scarcely a secret. BADA's first undertaking involved cleaning up a toxic waste area and the council gave the job to a firm owned by my in-laws. Not only did I abstain from voting, but Zabriski himself endorsed the choice. His objections didn't come until he decided I was a threat to his hobbyhorse."

"Hobbyhorse? You'll have to explain."

Andersen smiled humorlessly. "Zabriski was hell-bent on having BADA participate in building a second Kiel Canal."

"A second Kiel?" Oblonski repeated, shaken out of his single-minded absorption. "But surely that would require incredible resources."

"Far more than BADA has, not to mention that the entire concept is insane. But, for some weird reason, Zabriski convinced himself that the Kiel disaster had eliminated all opposition to his pet project. He was running around, assuming everybody would vote the way he wanted. When I declined, he suddenly discerned impropriety in my relatives being employed by BADA. He went well beyond what is permissible, as I was forced to inform the chairman."

"And how did she respond?"

"She assured me there would be no recurrence."

With Hroka's words still fresh in his mind, Oblonski savored this confirmation of trouble brewing between the chairman and her chief of staff.

"And that satisfied you?" he asked.

For the first time Eric Andersen sounded amused.

"Madame Nordstrom is more than capable of maintaining her authority."

OBLONSKI WORKED LATE into the night, but he could not complete his collection. "Asking them to tell their stories after midnight would provoke howls of protest. We'll make an early start tomorrow."

Despite these precautions he found the Hevelius Hotel unrewarding. His call to Peter von Hennig's room went unanswered.

"A wasted trip," he commented. The Hevelius was located

in the heart of downtown Gdansk, but he was thinking ahead to the next item on his agenda. "We'll catch von Hennig later, Alex, but before we drive halfway up the coast to Sopot, call this man Vigotis and make sure he'll be there to receive us."

So the wheels of police routine began rolling toward Anton Vigotis although Peter von Hennig was actually within arm's reach—not in his own room but two doors down the corridor in John Thatcher's.

Peter was already well launched on a long, somber review. "Naturally when you informed me last night that Zabriski had been murdered, I was deeply shocked."

The situation was so grave that von Hennig had removed his jacket to reveal a pair of suspenders that, in some mysterious fashion, reeked of money. It had never before occurred to Thatcher that this humble item of attire could do so. Clearly these suspenders had not been picked up in any old haberdashery. Constructed of heavy-shot silk, they were probably the specialty of some little Italian boutique known only to the select few.

"Not half as shocked as Everett and I were," Thatcher said, setting the record straight. While some people were dining in comfort, others had been finding dead bodies.

But von Hennig, putting yesterday's horrors behind, was now focussed on their aftermath. "In fact, the more I think about it, the worse it becomes," he said. "Take this tale by Bach about Stefan Zabriski's ravings. At the time I instinctively discounted them."

Was it Leonhard Bach or Zabriski who had roused his skepticism?

"Oh Zabriski, always Zabriski," replied von Hennig, barely emerging from his internal stream of thought. *"De mortuis* and all that—but Zabriski was a fanatic. A clerk taking office stationery would be enough to set him off—and with a sympathetic listener like Bach he could really let himself go. But murder? That seems to imply he actually did uncover something serious."

Nobody was inclined to believe in coincidence, Thatcher noted. Did this argue a widespread subliminal cynicism about BADA? Von Hennig's next comment gave him more food for thought.

"And how are we supposed to launch a major bond issue under BADA's aegis if they're sitting on top of a financial irregularity of unknown proportions?"

Following this transition from crime to business, Thatcher said, "It's not as if we're operating against a tight deadline. And we haven't been trapped by any public statements. If BADA is not viable as an issuing agency, then it can be scrapped. That was only one possibility and I've never understood why you regard it as so much more attractive than a straight German issue."

"Poland," said von Hennig succinctly. "European integration requires the broadening of NATO and the European Union—and it's proving to be enormously difficult. The Russians are uniformly hostile, the so-called 'new Communists' are getting paranoid and attitudes in the West leave much to be desired. After generations of looking anywhere but East, we're locked into outmoded notions. We make allowance for the weakness of Greece and Turkey, then dither about Poland, which is absurd. BADA is one mechanism for returning attention to where it rightfully belongs."

"At least Madame Nordstrom—and Bonn—are taking steps in the right direction," Thatcher pointed out.

With the Kiel Canal closed, marine interests were affected all over the world. Shippers from France and Holland, from Spain and England, would all become necessarily aware of Poland in the forthcoming weeks. Their insurance claims would be processed in Gdansk, the conclusions of the accident investigation announced there.

"You could say you've already made your first moves," Thatcher concluded.

Von Hennig supplied the cloud for this silver lining.

"Yes, by turning world attention to BADA just as a scandal erupts, one that would never have been noticed otherwise. Damn Zabriski! The man was bad enough when he was alive. But he's managed to leave us this poisonous legacy. If he'd exercised a modicum of common sense, all this could have been avoided."

"Just how?"

"What would any normal chief of staff do upon discovering a fraud in his organization?" von Hennig demanded. "He'd go straight to his superior, that's what. You do realize that if Zabriski had marched over to Annamarie and spilled the beans last night, he'd still be alive and we'd know what we were dealing with. Instead he has to play games because he enjoys the melodrama of denouncing moral lapses."

If Peter was willing to overlook reality, Thatcher was not. "Come now, you've forgotten what Zabriski looked like in the doorway last night. Whatever was going on in his mind, he was not enjoying himself."

Stopped in midtrack, Peter reconsidered. "You're right about that," he finally conceded. "I'd forgotten that he's the one who established all the financial systems at BADA. This was a different kettle of fish than claiming all Estonia was responsible for Hroka's dumping. If Zabriski himself created a gigantic loophole that made BADA vulnerable to embezzlement, that would explain his reaction."

Thatcher nodded. "It might also explain his reluctance to speak to Madame Nordstrom."

"Together with that civil-service mentality Zabriski had in spades," Peter said contemptuously. "Anything important would have to be enshrined in a proper memorandum, particularly if it required a good deal of self-exculpation."

"And there's still another possibility." Thatcher advanced tentatively. "What if Madame Nordstrom were the embezzler? Bach said the report was going to the full council."

Von Hennig looked startled but he repressed the automatic protest that sprang to his lips. Only after due deliberation did he continue. "I scarcely think that's likely. Annamarie is quite wealthy in her own right and, god knows, she's ambitious. I don't think she'd endanger her future for personal gain."

The reserve in this assessment had not escaped Thatcher.

"Tell me, Peter," he asked curiously. "Do you like the woman?"

"She's a joy to work with. She's intelligent, reasonable, and, above all, capable of defining goals with a nice balance between prudence and progress."

"That scarcely answers the question."

"Oh, all right," Peter grumbled. "If you must know, she's too much all things to all men for me. Every delegate who goes to her gets a sympathetic hearing. She understands his particular difficulties, she appreciates his unique goals. Then, when the smoke has cleared, BADA is doing exactly what she intended all along. I favor a more straightforward approach."

"You don't have to tell me that."

Uncomfortably von Hennig felt obliged to continue. "I do realize that my position is indefensible. While I object to her methods I admit they are the only ones that would be so effective."

"At least you're on the same side at the present," Thatcher offered.

"We almost always are. In many ways," Peter said wryly, "that makes it even more irritating."

"For starters you both want the Kiel project delayed," Thatcher went on. "Then as a concomitant, you want the motive for Zabriski's murder determined."

"That would certainly be a help. But the killing was probably designed to prevent disclosure."

Here at least Thatcher could extend some comfort. "I don't want to raise false hopes, but Everett has agreed to establish himself in Gdansk for several weeks to go through BADA's records with a fine-tooth comb. If anybody can find an irregularity, it's Gabler."

Von Hennig looked up hopefully. "You think he'll pull it off?"

"If it's a fraud within BADA, that's quite possible. But Bach was not sure of that. If Zabriski came across something in which BADA's role was peripheral to the fleecing of someone else, then the odds are not so good."

Just then there was a perfunctory knock and the door opened to admit Everett Gabler. For once he came as a breath of fresh air.

"A very satisfactory morning," he announced robustly. "You know, von Hennig, although our discussions convinced me that the Sloan should open an office to monitor developments here, I had grave doubts about the feasibility of doing so. However, it has been easier than I expected."

"An office and a staff?" von Hennig queried. "Finding good help here is difficult. I make it a habit to bring my own with me."

Gabler went him one better. "That has been taken care of. You recall, John, that I hired Mrs. Gomulka to assist me? Well, she's proving to be invaluable. Indeed it was she who brought these quarters to my attention, and I think they will fit our needs nicely."

Tributes flowing from Gabler's lips were unusual and so was his omission of a formal request for Thatcher's approval.

"Perhaps we could drop by to inspect them on our way to lunch," said Gabler, bursting with pride.

"Lead the way, Ev," said Thatcher, wondering what to expect.

Minutes later, within two short blocks of the Hevelius, they contemplated a mini-skyscraper emblazoned with the name of its prime tenant.

"If it's good enough for Nissan, it's good enough for the Sloan, Ev," Thatcher congratulated him.

In the elevator Gabler continued to bask in his achievement. "Mrs. Gomulka assures me that we will have computer and fax capability within a day or two."

"Then she may not know as much about Poland as she claims," von Hennig warned.

Gabler was at his most nonchalant. "Perhaps, perhaps. Did I mention that she spent three years at the Bank of America?"

The two-room suite awaiting them on the eighth floor was reassuringly modern and Gabler discoursed happily on its advantages, breaking off only at the sound of a scuffle by the door.

"Ah, there you are," he said genially when it opened. "John, I'd like you to meet Mrs. Gomulka."

Thatcher blinked as the apparition deposited the packages with which she was encumbered.

"Carol," she amplified, shaking hands heartily. "Carol Gomulka."

Unconsciously Thatcher had pictured a gray-haired matron, wise in the ways of an alien society. Instead he was presented with a slip of a girl, still in her twenties, clad in blue jeans and running shoes, speaking in the unmistakable accents of Texas.

"This is just the first load," she announced, "but I managed to get everything. So Bill should have the equipment hooked up tonight."

Eyeing the mass of cables and connectors spilling onto the desk, Thatcher said that he understood finding technical equipment was difficult.

"You have to be a scrounger and none of this is new," she disclaimed with a gesture encompassing computer and ramifications. "But even if these things are used, they're in good working condition."

"I see."

A true daughter of the USA, she interpreted his expression at once. "Oh, it's not hot," she reassured him. "We rented it from people willing to do without for the price Mr. Gabler offered."

She and Everett beamed at each other in celebration of their team effort, then she plunged off to retrieve the rest of her loot.

"But she's an American," von Hennig said accusingly. "What on earth is she doing in Gdansk?"

It was, at least in one respect, an all-too-familiar story. Two years ago Bill Gomulka had lost his job in Silicon Valley, then inherited a farm from Polish grandparents. In the process of arranging the sale he had decided his talents had more scarcity value in Gdansk than in California.

"But while he waits for the computer tide to arrive," Gabler concluded, "they're both scratching a living with any employment they can find."

"Well, if the husband performs as well as the wife," Thatcher decided, "we are very fortunate."

Four hours with Carol Gomulka had succeeded in erasing reservations that Gabler usually entertained for years. After proclaiming that the Gomulkas could be relied on to fulfill their promises, he swept on to the general maxims so dear to his heart.

". . . always a mistake to lower reasonable standards. With sufficient fixity of purpose . . ."

DEMONSTRATING THOSE CARDINAL virtues, Colonel Oblonski and Alex had meanwhile slogged up the coast to the Mirador. It stood on a pebbly beach, an island of summer fun now shuttered against the icy Baltic breezes. After parking the car, they trooped into the badly lit lobby where Anton Vigotis stood waiting.

"Dreadful, dreadful," he said of the circumstances that

brought them together. "There is a small sitting room—or my suite upstairs . . . after you, Colonel."

But as he padded ahead of them, he demonstrated more concern than grief at Stefan Zabriski's sudden death. By the time he sat facing Oblonski, Vigotis's piety had disappeared altogether.

Leonhard Bach's exchange in the lounge with Chairman Nordstrom still rankled.

"We could hear every word. Bach didn't even bother to lower his voice," he said censoriously. "As if more scurrilous innuendos and allegations are in any way helpful!"

With everybody advocating a conspiracy of silence, Oblonski could only thank god for Leonhard Bach and his loose lips. Without them, Stefan Zabriski's last hours on earth would have remained a total blank. As it was, certain outlines were taking shape.

"I'm told that Herr Bach advanced an opinion about why Zabriski was so upset," he suggested slyly.

"That I cannot say," Vigotis rejoined. "We left the lounge almost immediately after Madame Nordstrom."

Like nearly everybody else, he showed a strong desire to disassociate himself from the whole sorry episode, but Oblonski had no reason to disbelieve him. " 'We'?" he said, consulting his notebook. "That would be you and Jaan Hroka who left together?"

"That is correct," said Vigotis, relaxing visibly. Then, with belated thoughts of hospitality, he rose and ambled gently around the room in search of something to offer his guests. Finding a box of cigars, he extended it to Oblonski, adding, "We didn't part company until I turned off in the lobby, to have the desk call me a taxi."

Oblonski stiffened. "And Herr Hroka did not?"

Vigotis remained placid. "Why, no," he said, fussing over his Havana. "He has a car so he used the other exit."

"To the parking lot?" asked Oblonski, grateful he had avoided specifying the scene of the crime.

With dawning reluctance Vigotis replied, "Yes, that door in the rear, past the mechanic's workshop. Why do you ask?"

When Oblonski told him, he winced.

12. Scuttlebutt

ARLY NEWS BULLETINS from Gdansk listlessly reported the murder of Stefan Zabriski. Then, through the magic of television, he was transformed into a prominent member of the international community, a world-renowned activist and, without explanation, a symbol.

"No comment," said Madame Nordstrom, running a media gauntlet.

When her example spread through the ranks of BADA, veteran reporters fell back on barroom philosophy and taxi-driver wisdom. Their satellite transmissions were strong on human interest and weak on specifics.

Nevertheless the coverage was followed avidly, especially in Copenhagen, where there was a personal connection.

"How I wish Eric were here to explain what's really happening at BADA," said the acting chairman of the Nordic Wildlife Coalition, one of Denmark's flourishing advocacy groups.

"Andersen misses a lot of our meetings," remarked a dissident, wearing his academic scruffiness like a uniform.

The chairman of NWC was Denmark's delegate to BADA and the list of his affiliations did not stop there. The luster of Eric Andersen's celebrity was much sought after.

"Sometimes I'm afraid he spreads himself too thin," quavered an elderly admirer.

But Andersen also had critics.

"Besides, what makes you think he knows what's going on?" demanded a young intellectual.

The implication that Andersen was a mere figurehead was heretical.

"A foolish remark, Hans," said the acting chairman like the schoolmistress she was. "Remember his last lecture. Eric proved that he knows all about BADA, down to the last detail."

"He also said that BADA's the only way we can encourage environmental responsibility in the East," said Hans, imitating Andersen's familiar accents. "A lot of crap. What is BADA actually doing? Damned little, if you ask me. They're just another bunch of concrete pourers."

Before the acting chairman could retaliate with every green achievement she remembered, a peacemaker intervened.

"International cooperation, Hans," said Reverend Dr. Jacobbsen. "Hands across the Baltic."

Hans was opposed to the established church too. "And sweetness and light, I suppose. But look at BADA. People are killing each other."

His exaggeration elicited sighs, but tolerance is a national characteristic. "You make it sound like mass slaughter," said Dr. Jacobsen. "It is one heinous crime, tragic indeed. But I agree with you, Hans, that it is a cause for anxiety, and I'm sure Eric feels the same. We can only hope and pray that it was the act of a madman."

"According to the internet," said Hans, stunning everybody with science, "that would mean somebody at BADA is the lunatic. Apparently the cops have been grilling all the delegates."

"Among others," said a TV viewer.

Ignoring this contribution, Hans swept on. "Well, if Andersen is sticking to his usual line, he won't be a lot of help."

Much as she wanted to get back to the agenda, the acting chairman could not let this pass.

"His usual line?" she asked sharply. "Do you refer to Eric's tireless campaigning to save the Baltic?"

"I refer to these fairy tales he peddles about BADA and all its promise," responded Hans impudently. "That wonderful, efficient staff! All those right-minded people dedicated to doing good. If Andersen's sticking to that garbage, the police will laugh in his face. Obviously there's something pretty rotten at BADA and apparently Andersen's never noticed. He's certainly never bothered to mention it."

"Then you haven't been listening," said the acting chairman. "Eric is much too wise to attack his colleagues in public, however much he may oppose them. But he certainly does not underestimate them. He is fighting the good fight for all of us and he will not let this brutal act interrupt his good work."

"Amen," said Dr. Jacobbsen with paralyzing sincerity while Hans rolled his eyes.

BADA WAS COMING under fire from another quarter, the Chamber of Commerce in Rostock. Their weekly luncheons were heavy affairs, with smoky portraits of bygone Hanseatic merchants looking down from the wall, and mountains of cholesterol on the table. The staple of all conversation among the members was the D-mark.

"So Germany sends them money, which is crazy in the first place," said a well-padded lawyer. "We could put it to better use here. And what do we get in return? Murder, for god's sake—and not much more."

That Rostock needed all the financial help it could get was self-evident to this group.

"BADA may help us renovate the harbor," said the mayor.

"And pigs can fly," retorted a constituent. "When you say things like that you sound as bad as our friend Bach. By the way, where is he?"

"He's in Gdansk, Magnus."

"Oh sure, right in the thick of things," Magnus grunted. "Probably having the time of his life."

Germans have a term for the joy to be derived from the misfortunes of others, but there is a reverse to that coin. In grubby, depressed Rostock, Leonhard Bach's prosperity stood out like a bright shining star, as eye-catching as the fresh paint on his spanking Valhalla vessels.

The mayor thoughtlessly compounded his error. "Leonhard's got a lot of faith that BADA can give Rostock a shot in the arm," he said, quoting from memory. "It makes sense to me."

The argument was familiar to them all. Promote Baltic traffic, construct modern facilities, revitalize trade, and some of the goodies would trickle down into local hands.

"But if you believe BADA can do that, you believe in miracles," Magnus insisted. "All they do over there in Gdansk is draw up rules and regulations, more forms to fill out, more make-work. Show me something I can take to the bank."

"Leonhard says—"

"Leonhard says that BADA is the White House, the Kremlin, and the Vatican all rolled into one—just because he wangled that loan out of them, god alone knows how."

With tongues loosed by beer and Bach's absence, his townsmen let fly. The mayor gave them five minutes, then called for order.

"Still, you've got to admit BADA does some good. Look at the Kiel Canal. This Pole who got murdered organized the relief efforts, and you can't deny they helped."

Magnus wiped foam from his upper lip with a vicious swipe.

"Who needed him? The German authorities could have coped very well. We don't need outsiders telling us what to do."

The Chamber of Commerce was no longer the only game in town. Other voices were being raised, advocating alien doctrines.

"Save the fish! Plant trees! Control emissions! Do they ever stop to think that people need protection too?" blustered the lawyer.

As soon as subversive precepts began to circulate in Rostock, Magnus attributed them to BADA.

"Stirring up trouble," he fulminated. "No wonder somebody got driven to desperation."

"Well, you can't accuse Leonhard of that," said the mayor to lighten the atmosphere. "When it comes to real priorities, he's got his head screwed on right. That's why he's over in Gdansk now, lobbying for the harbor, for a new and better canal."

"Pie in the sky," said Magnus, unwilling to give the devil his due.

But interest had shifted back to the troublemakers.

"Funny about this killing, though," said a stolid building contractor. "You'd think that, if someone was out to damage BADA, they'd go after Madame Nordstrom. She's the one who calls the shots."

Latent antifeminism surfaced. "She's the one who does all the talking—and too damned much of it too. But I understand Zabriski really ran the show."

"Besides, nobody could be anti-BADA enough to commit murder."

"Except Magnus!" quipped the local wit.

"Not me," said Magnus. "One of those back-to-nature nuts, maybe. You'll have to ask Bach about it. He's the big expert on BADA."

Somebody had seen Leonhard Bach on the late-night news

roundup. "And he didn't have much to say about BADA or any-thing else."

"That's a switch!"

LEONHARD BACH'S UNCHARACTERISTIC restraint and the discre-tion displayed by Annamarie Nordstrom won warm approval in Berlin. However, doubts were entertained about Colonel Oblonski.

"He doesn't look very intelligent," said one of the adminis-tration's spin doctors. "You know we offered our assistance to the Polish authorities, but they refused."

"That's not surprising, Heino. They're always so touchy, these Poles," said his counterpart.

The phone lines linking these experts had been humming steadily without effecting a true meeting of minds.

"Not only touchy, but inconvenient," said Heino. "This out-rage could not have occurred at a worst time, speaking in terms of public perception. Peter von Hennig was on the line to the minister just now—"

"Saying that Zabriski stumbled over something unsavory at BADA? Yes, he called here too."

"Which further complicates matters that are already com-plicated enough," Heino lamented.

All official spokesmen for all governments want to keep things simple. It was not for this pair to ask why their masters were worried about murder or any other crimes at BADA. Their job was to neutralize any troublesome fallout from the coverage in Gdansk.

"However, with the police trudging around uselessly and lit-tle hard information available, this unfortunate spurt of pub-licity will die down of its own accord. Who cares about what's happening at BADA?"

Wishful thinking had led him astray as his colleague was

quick to remind him. "Peter von Hennig, for one, and the finance minister. And the chancellor himself was recently photographed shaking hands with Madame Nordstrom."

Since a picture is worth a thousand words, this evoked a long-suffering sigh, then a revision. "Let me rephrase myself. How many people are deeply concerned with an obscure Pole named Zabriski? Frankly, I'm sure we can trust the forgetfulness of the general population."

Heino disagreed.

"Think of the land mines out there," he said fussily. "Think of the uproar if large-scale deliberate plundering is brought to light."

"Short of armed robbery, it will not matter a bit," said his comforter. "The only reason for all this negative publicity is the murder. And, I repeat, that will soon pass—unless of course Madame Nordstrom struck down Zabriski."

"Is that meant to be a joke?" yelped Heino.

"Of course it is. Compose yourself, Heino. There may be discoveries embarrassing to the people involved with BADA, but they can be contained. Once this immediate uproar dies down Stefan Zabriski will be consigned to oblivion."

NOT IF WARSAW could help it.

"An international civil servant who happens to be a Polish citizen! Murdered on Polish soil! How could such a thing happen?"

The minister's secretary was his liaison to Gdansk. By now Ignace knew more than he wanted to about BADA, but relaying that knowledge was uphill work.

"Serious dissensions have developed within the organization," he began again. "It is feared that Zabriski may have roused the enmity of one faction. Either that or he discovered serious wrongdoing—"

Jerzy Witzold had a short attention span and a politician's sensitivity to television. Buffing a manicured nail on his lapel, he ignored the backgrounding. "And Oblonski? Is he telling you more than the little he says to the public?"

Here Ignace had less to offer. "He is interrogating witnesses and looking into Zabriski's past. But it is early days, Minister."

"In other words, no progress."

Ignace agreed, then the minister went further. "And another black eye for Poland."

On one level his reasoning was impeccable. Viewers all over Europe were being treated to glimpses of run-down Gdansk neighborhoods as well as reconstructed historic mansions. But the minister was operating on a higher plane.

"Justice," he said reverently, casting Poland as a champion of human rights. "Swift, impartial, and conducted under the rule of law."

Unfortunately reality, in the form of Colonel Oblonski, was not cooperating. Until the police identified the perpetrator, Poland's reputation would suffer. And then, god forbid, Zabriski's murderer could turn out to be a fellow Pole.

"And it would be more than tourists who'd be turned off," said the minister broodingly. "Who wants to invest in a crime-ridden slum? Pride alone dictates that we cannot allow this to happen."

Appeals to Polish pride were not as effective as the administration liked to think but they were frequently made, often in the name of a martyr or a fallen hero.

"Hmm," said the minister, thinking aloud. "A martyr."

"Zabriski?" gasped Ignace.

With considerable exasperation Witzold rounded on him. "You lack vision, Ignace. A martyr to the cause of international harmony. A martyr to Poland's contribution to the free new world. A martyr to the rebirth of Baltic greatness."

It was Ignace's turn to vent impatience.

"And what exactly do we do for a Polish martyr?"

Smiling like the cat who swallowed the canary, Minister Witzold said, "Need you ask?"

13. Consigned to the Deep

O H, MY GOD, they're having a state funeral," Thatcher announced after scanning the hand-delivered message.
Gabler looked up alertly.

"Very proper."

Thatcher realized he should have expected this response. Funerals constituted the only known form of social gathering that Everett was willing—nay eager—to attend. All the atmospherics appealed to him—the sonorous voices, the decorous attire, the time-honored ritual. At the Sloan, unless obsequies absolutely demanded the tower suite, Gabler was regularly seconded for duty.

"But it's down in Warsaw," Thatcher said in a last bid for sympathy.

"Naturally we will wish to pay our respects."

As always this sentence sparked the desire to ask why. Until two weeks ago Thatcher had never heard of Stefan Zabriski, and in the interval since had only exchanged a few words with him. Unfortunately, with Finanzbank lurking in the shadows, this was the ideal time to stress the Sloan's sensitivity to all things Baltic.

"I guess we'll both have to go."

Everett nodded serenely. He had never contemplated any other possibility.

THE BADA PARTY that arrived in Warsaw was gratifyingly substantial. Nevertheless, when a program of the day's schedule was presented to Madame Nordstrom, she gasped with dismay. Recovering, she said apologetically:

"I think we should plan on being here longer than we expected."

Peter von Hennig took the bull by the horns.

"You'd better tell us the bad news, Annamarie."

Gallantly she complied. "Stefan's body is lying in state at the Royal Castle of the Kings. That's where we start. We then go to the Church of Saint Alexander for a high requiem mass. The funeral procession from church to cemetery runs along the Royal Road to Wilanowski Palace for the interment ceremony at Dowazki Cemetery. After that there will be a reception at the Palace Lazienkowski."

The drill sounded basically familiar to Thatcher. He and half of Wall Street had recently bade farewell to a governor of the Federal Reserve Bank in roughly the same way. Of course good old Gerry had departed without a backdrop of ancient castles, basilicas, and palaces.

Casimir Radan, as the resident expert, felt it necessary to amplify Annamarie's warning.

"These sites are not next door to each other. It will probably take most of the day."

And, as BADA soon realized, it was going to be one ordeal after another. Among the last to arrive at the castle, they found the proceedings well under way. The bier, guarded by four soldiers at rigid attention, stood under the vaulted ceiling of the great classical library. An endless line moved forward to one side of the casket for a last moment, then circled to the other side where a group of figures in deep mourning waited.

"The family," someone whispered.

Thatcher was relieved to see that Polish tradition did not require conversation with the bereaved. While some people murmured a few words of condolence, most simply halted in their tracks and sketched a ceremonial bow, thereby avoiding the awkwardness of speaking about the unknown to the unknown. It was a practice that Thatcher intended to adopt himself.

As it developed his precaution was unnecessary. Madame Nordstrom brought BADA's delegates forward as a unit, conveyed their solemn regrets and smoothly flowed on.

In her wake came Wanda Jesilko.

Instantly one of the women in the family group stepped forward with open arms. She and Wanda embraced, sobs emerged from the entangled long veils, and a man in a black armband took up a protective position at their side. In the confusion Thatcher shuffled by unnoticed.

With Wanda now incorporated into the Zabriski family the rest of the line passed without incident, until Leonhard Bach held things up by addressing lengthy remarks to the man with the armband.

"Herr Bach is speaking to Stefan's son," Madame Nordstrom murmured. "I don't believe they've ever met."

Being the last in, the BADA party was among the first to be ferried to the Church of Saint Alexander. As mere auxiliaries Thatcher and Gabler were directed to the rear amidst strangers.

"A sad occasion," said the roly-poly man at Thatcher's side, after ascertaining that English was the language of the day.

"Indeed, yes. My meetings with Herr Zabriski all took place at BADA where he was a very respected figure."

"Ah, I lost touch with Stefan when he moved to Gdansk, but we knew each other for many years in Warsaw where we were close neighbors. When the children were young our families often went on picnics together. Later there were the merry evenings we spent playing cards with him and Wanda. I was glad to see Pauline and Adam do the right thing."

Nodding agreement, Thatcher acknowledged the younger Zabriskis had gracefully handled a situation that many families fumble.

As they waited for the pews to fill with politicians and prelates, resident diplomats and emissaries from abroad, Roly-Poly continued his recollections of Stefan Zabriski through the decades. He did not fall silent until the first dolorous notes of the organ signaled the beginning of the mass. Thatcher did his best to remain attentive to the service—to the priests coming forward to greet the casket, to the disciplined responses from the congregation, to the soothing harmonies of the choir. But then, during two lengthy eulogies in Polish—one from the cardinal and one from the president—he had plenty of time to think.

Merry? Picnics and cardplaying? This was not the Stefan Zabriski of Gdansk, notorious for working late into the night seven days a week. Somehow BADA had transformed normalcy into obsession.

Once outside the church Thatcher saw that organizing the procession would be a lengthy business. In addition to the limousines for the official party there were military units, marching bands, and delegations from many civic groups. Gabler used the delay to report his own insights.

"The man sitting next to me was from the marine bureau and he remembered Zabriski as a fervent soccer fan."

Stranger and stranger, Thatcher reflected.

Even Everett, apostle of dedication and unremitting toil, compared the Zabriski of Gdansk unfavorably with the Zabriski of Warsaw.

"He didn't antagonize people at the marine bureau. Perhaps his power at BADA went to his head."

"Peter is convinced Zabriski was going crazy."

When they were finally summoned to their conveyance, they found they were sharing it with Eric Andersen, who was making the best of things.

"It's all running smoothly, isn't it?" he said as they inched forward.

"Do you happen to know where we're going?"

"The other side of the city. Wilanowski was the historic summer palace, out in the country once, but of course now it's all built up. My god, just look ahead. Now that is pageantry."

They had entered a broad avenue, straight as an arrow, that allowed them to assimilate the cavalcade of which they were the tail. Contingent after contingent marched to the muffled drums and muted brass of Chopin's *Funeral March* while the limousines crawled behind. For Poland's sake Thatcher was pleased to spot television trucks at strategic intervals.

"And some of those military units are well worth photographing," he remarked.

The sun was doing full justice to the occasion, reflecting off the polished brass buttons and buckles of soldiers, the gleaming jackboots of officers, the gold-threaded embroidery of regimental flags. In somber contrast, the casket on its low caisson was draped in unrelieved black. As it passed before the crowds lining the sidewalks, men bared their heads and many women crossed themselves.

"Now we're coming to an interesting area," Andersen offered.

Thatcher examined the stretch of ample, but ill-assorted buildings, many of them set in spacious grounds surrounded by fences.

"Embassy Row," he said, identifying it without difficulty.

Here the architecture of the twentieth century had displaced the reminders of the past. The American Embassy presented itself to the world wrapped in the usual glass and concrete. But, a block later, the French had done even worse. Their giant bunker had apparently been designed to withstand mechanized assault.

Everett, of course, was trying to turn the occasion to some educational use.

"Look at the Yugoslavian Embassy," he directed.

They were moving so slowly they could read the large signs posted by the republics into which that country had fragmented.

"BADA was wise to choose Poland for its headquarters," Everett continued. "No ethnic problems, no worry that the country will disintegrate."

Thatcher had to admit that Gabler had a point. Poland, in spite of constant partitions, in spite of losing national independence regularly for over a hundred and twenty years, remained one homogeneous people unified by one church and one history.

After what seemed like endless miles in second gear, even Gabler began shifting restively and Thatcher was near rebellion. The ornate churches, the high-rise office buildings, the modern apartments had long since been left behind. Now they were crawling through a residential landscape with detached single homes, terraced row houses, and more and more open space occupied by garden allotments.

"When you said 'built up,' Andersen, this was not quite what I expected," Thatcher observed.

The only onlookers now were small children, attendant mothers, and the odd pensioner. The children often downed balls and toys to prance beside the bands and soldiers.

They were if anything moving more slowly than before. While the military units marched inexorably forward, some of the civilian groups on foot were beginning to flag.

Time dragged. Thatcher was reduced to comparing one allotment with another. This one had been tidied up for the winter, while that one remained bedraggled. Some had brave displays of chrysanthemums while others eschewed anything but edibles.

Finally Andersen straightened.

"Here we are," he announced, peering ahead to the merger of their boulevard with another. "This is where Jan Sobieskiego and Wilanowski come together. We're on the home stretch."

And not a moment too soon, thought Thatcher, automatically adjusting his tie.

As he did so the sun disappeared behind a cloud and a biting wind came howling in from the east.

The graveside ceremonies, protracted by the assembly of so many groups, took place under arctic conditions. Nonetheless the mourners, with sensation rapidly disappearing from all digits, did their duty. They listened to a series of brief remarks in a motley of languages. They heard a last dirge performed by the band. They watched the traditional gun salute fired over the coffin. Finally the first symbolic handful of soil was dropped.

During the subsequent confusion Eric Andersen disappeared, his place taken by Peter von Hennig. It was to him that Thatcher made a suggestion.

"Surely we've done all that is absolutely required. We could give the reception a miss," he whispered, clapping together chilled hands. "If we slipped quietly away now, nobody would miss us."

But von Hennig was the German delegate to BADA and Everett was Everett.

"Impossible," said Gabler firmly.

"It would mean we've wasted all our efforts so far," von Hennig reasoned on a more practical note. "Besides, there is a bright side. We'll be seeing one of the city's showplaces and we'll be more comfortable than we've been all day."

Thatcher did not find these inducements compelling, but he knew when he was stuck.

"Onward and upward," he said gamely.

133

14. Dropping the Pilot

THE PALACE LAZIENKOWSKI was in the center of Warsaw surrounded by acres of woodland, which was one of the city's many parks. Despite the chill there were couples strolling about, women gathering beech leaves, and a surprising number of groups heading purposively along the footpaths.

When the funeral cortege swept into the forecourt, Thatcher realized there was some merit to von Hennig's decision. Summer lushness had faded but the Palace glowed—a renaissance mansion with terraces on a river graced by swans. Beyond a small bridge they could see an outdoor amphitheater crumbling into picturesque ruins.

"Very impressive," said Everett.

Thatcher was not ready to commit himself.

Indoors, however, he encountered not only staterooms with rich furnishings but life returning. Even the Zabriskis were no longer presenting a tableau of unnatural grief. When Thatcher carelessly placed himself next to Wanda Jesilko at the refreshment table he found he had nothing to fear.

"No, it's kind of you to invite me, Pauline," she was saying, "but I've got to return to Gdansk. Stefan's work has to be organized for transfer. That's the least I can do."

When Pauline appealed to her husband, he commended Frau Jesilko.

"Of course you're welcome any time, Wanda, but I think you're making the right decision. You're at a loss right now and some kind of occupation will be best for you," he advised pompously. "Come to us later."

There were no tears and, within minutes, Wanda was claimed by an old acquaintance.

Beyond the immediate vicinity of the family, spirits were also rising. Travel schedules, impressions of Warsaw, and weekend plans provided fodder for small talk, but many of the guests reverted to more pressing concerns.

By the fireplace Thatcher came upon Leonhard Bach cross-examining a German official about conditions at Kiel.

"They're still treating the water and clearing away the sunken hulls."

"God! That means they still have to get the navigable ships out."

There was a sober nod.

"It will all take time."

And Eric Andersen was huddled with an unknown, discussing the choice of a replacement for Zabriski.

"Of course, there are certain advantages to employing a Pole. In the interests of a fair rotation, however, BADA is unlikely to choose another one."

Probably the most intense conversation was that engrossing Madame Nordstrom, Peter von Hennig, and a representative of the ministry of justice.

"The sooner the police investigation is successfully terminated, the better for BADA," she was saying crisply.

"We understand your anxiety and rest assured, Madame, that Colonel Oblonski has his instructions. He is an officer noted not only for his competence, but his discretion as well."

"At the moment I am more interested in results," she replied with a militant gleam.

Von Hennig supported her. "There's no point trying to cover up things," he declared. "We have over two hundred employees at BADA, with the world press camped out in Gdansk wining and dining every file clerk. They're probably doing the same with the police force."

All government agencies cling to the illusion that their doings are guarded by impenetrable security.

"I scarcely think that is possible."

"Perhaps not," von Hennig conceded diplomatically. "But if there is a scandal in BADA, somebody will tell them. Ah, there you are, John."

The ministry man seized on the presence of a stranger to terminate the discussion.

"This has been a sad day not only for BADA but for Poland," he declaimed, bowing over Madame Nordstrom's hand in farewell. "But at least we have the comfort of knowing that Herr Zabriski would have appreciated this recognition of his invaluable services."

As soon as he was gone Annamarie's lips twitched.

"This isn't what Stefan would have wanted. The way he felt about the Baltic, nothing short of a Viking funeral would have sufficed—with a burning pyre pushed out to sea and the rest of us following in barges."

"Then we have much to be thankful for," said Thatcher, glancing out the window at the steel-gray sky.

"Hard as that is to believe?" she challenged.

Everett Gabler joined them; he had been looking outdoors to more purpose.

"There's an enormous crowd waiting in front," he told them.

"Yes, the environmentalists. Didn't you see them gathering as we arrived?" Annamarie asked. "They smell a plot. All they know about Stefan is that he cracked down on toxic dumping, helped clean up the Kiel Canal mess, and now he's a bloody corpse."

"They're making speeches and the police presence is growing," Gabler continued.

"If those people outside knew how Stefan really felt about ecological improvements, they wouldn't be so enthusiastic about adopting him as their fallen hero," she said tartly.

Reality, Thatcher reflected, has nothing to do with staged events. By transforming Zabriski into a martyr, the Polish government had in effect encouraged this miscasting.

Peter von Hennig was less interested in the vagaries of public perception than in what was happening at the other end of the room.

"The president is saying good-bye to the cardinal," he announced with satisfaction. "That means they'll start bringing up the cars."

As soon as the guests began to leave, the constant activity at the door admitted a whole new spectrum of sound. There was somebody exhorting the faithful through a bullhorn; there were official barked commands; there were jeers and catcalls.

By the time Madame Nordstrom's car pulled up the disturbance was escalating.

"In a few more minutes their audience will disappear. They're working up to a grand climax," von Hennig predicted.

"Then it looks as if we're going to be part of it," Thatcher reasoned as von Hennig's name was called.

Emerging onto the portico, they glimpsed the familiar protest scene—a semicircle of angry faces, a sea of placards, a straining police line.

"The signs are in English," said Everett, always the acute observer.

"They want international coverage, Ev," replied Thatcher.

"And they should get it," said von Hennig, reminding them of the media in attendance.

138

But when a decaying orange sailed through the air, the three of them abandoned their detachment to hurry down the steps towards the driveway. At the same time an angry command sounded and several mounted police swerved into position to press the crowd further back. The response was immediate. The bullhorn blared defiance, the front row of demonstrators linked arms, and one enterprising young man whipped out a handful of marbles that he scattered across the courtyard.

The horses deftly sidestepped these hazards but Everett Gabler, eyes on his goal, failed to see the polished agate in his path. His foot slipped, he crashed to the gravel, and his head skidded into the limousine's wheel.

After that it was pandemonium. With the first casualty hitting the ground, the mob's blood lust was roused. Protesters broke through the lines, additional police rushed into the fray, and a barrage of missiles flew overhead, while Thatcher and von Hennig scrambled to form a protective barrier around Gabler.

"Everett, are you all right?"

". . . what? . . . what's that?"

The reply was not reassuring, nor was the sight of Gabler clutching his head and groggily trying to focus his eyes. Fortunately the limousine immediately preceding their own squealed to a halt and Thatcher saw the agitated countenance of Casimir Radan protruding from the rear window. Then the door flung open and, disregarding the banshee wails that rose as the enterprising young man was plucked from the crowd, Radan trotted back down the driveway.

"Thank god," breathed von Hennig. "A Polish-speaker."

"Is he badly injured?" Radan asked anxiously as soon as he reached their side.

Everett rolled over, began to rise, then sank back with a moan of pain.

Raising his voice to a thunderous pitch, Radan managed to override the background noise level. Two stalwart policemen hurried to take up guard duty while another sped to a radio car.

"There will soon be an ambulance."

Trips to the emergency room are the same all over the world. The afflicted disappears and his companions wait . . . and wait . . . and wait.

"But Everett was beginning to sound a little better, didn't you think?" Thatcher asked, searching for confirmation.

"In his own inimitable way," von Hennig replied.

Once in the hospital Gabler had recovered enough to direct a flow of incoherent instructions to his stretcher bearers, sublimely indifferent to the fact that not one word was understood.

With the victim safely in the hands of medical personnel, Casimir Radan had departed.

"Unfortunately that means now we can't even talk to the desk," Thatcher said gloomily.

"It never does any good anyway."

But Radan had continued his efforts on their behalf and these bore fruit an hour and a half later in the shape of a new arrival. After a brief exchange at the desk he made a beeline in their direction.

"Mr. Thatcher? I'm Dr. Norris Butler. The American embassy got hold of me after Mr. Radan called."

Succinctly Thatcher explained the situation.

"Well, I'll see what's going on," Butler said before he too disappeared into the inner bowels.

"I should have thought of the embassy," Thatcher reproached himself.

"While I dislike adding to your troubles, there's something else you might consider," von Hennig said. "With all those television cameras at the palace this must have been picked up and

140

no doubt dramatized. By now the news has probably reached New York."

Grimly Thatcher acknowledged the accuracy of this statement. After the usual calculations about the time difference, he realized that it was the middle of the working day at the Sloan. George Lancer, the chairman of the board, and Charlie Trinkam were probably frantically on the phone, trying to reach him, trying to locate Gabler, trying to get action from the state department.

"They'll just have to wait," he decided. "I'm not leaving until Butler has some news for us. Apart from everything else, this may not be the best place for Everett. It certainly doesn't fill me with confidence."

He glanced around their stark surroundings with deep misgiving.

"Be reasonable. What hospital does?"

Thatcher had more than enough time to contemplate imagined deficiencies in Polish health care before, at long last, Dr. Butler reappeared.

He was clutching the usual sheaf of X rays.

"There is a broken bone in one ankle," he began, pointing vaguely to the film. "But we've got a first-class orthopedic surgeon lined up. There shouldn't be any nasty developments there."

He then came to a full stop, still holding unexamined X rays.

"And?" Thatcher asked tightly.

"There is no fracture of the skull, you'll be glad to hear. But there is a concussion and when the patient displays signs of disorientation and bewilderment, precautions are advisable. They'll want to keep him for observation. Between that and the ankle, he'll be here for over forty-eight hours. Then, assuming concerns about the concussion have been allayed, he'll be ready to leave."

Thatcher expelled a pent-up breath. Those glassy eyes and that thin thread of a voice had made him fear the worst.

"That's a relief," he admitted.

"You won't be able to see him until tomorrow at the earliest, maybe not until the day after. They'll want to keep him as quiet as possible. But I'll be monitoring the situation and you can always reach me through the embassy."

Dr. Butler than added to his good works by offering the facilities of the embassy for calling New York, a piece of hospitality that Thatcher and von Hennig were glad to accept.

When the connection was made, George Lancer sounded ready to dispatch a search-and-destroy mission. The first garbled accounts to reach New York suggested that the mob had made a dead set at Gabler, crushing every bone in his body.

"Relax, George, it was just an accident. Everett slipped on a marble somebody threw in front of the police."

But even the medical prognosis failed to appease Lancer's wrath. He was still breathing fire when Thatcher had himself transferred to Trinkam's office.

Here the reaction took a different form.

"Poor old Ev," Trinkam responded with sympathy. "He'll hate it in the hospital. They'll try to tell him what to do and they won't have that health food he likes."

But this was mere preamble. While Lancer thought in terms of institutional expeditions, Charlie itched for personal action.

"Now this will leave you shorthanded, John. I've got a bag packed and there's a plane for Frankfurt I can catch. I'll wing it from there to Warsaw."

"No!" Thatcher exploded.

After the day he had put in he was in no mood to indulge a desire for theatrics.

"I'm not having the entire sixth floor diverted to BADA," Thatcher continued on a more moderate note. "Nothing's happening there until Monday anyway. We'll see how things go. If necessary you can dispatch Ken Nicolls to hold a watching brief in Gdansk."

"With Everett on the wounded list that still leaves plenty for you to do."

"I'll manage," Thatcher said stoutly.

15. Running Aground

O THERS COULD TAKE time off for funerals; not so Colonel Oblonski, who had far too much to do.

"All right, so I didn't like Zabriski. Have you found anyone who did?" said a sullen Jaan Hroka for the third time.

It was a home question. So far only the Finnish delegate claimed brief glimpses of a sunny side to BADA's chief of staff.

"Zabriski was usually abrasive and exigent," he had declared. "But you should have seen him the night we were all in Kiel. When he was playing the accordion, he seemed like a different man. I didn't think he had it in him."

This was the first that Oblonski had heard of BADA's assault on the oppressive gentility of the Maritim. It might not illuminate the internal contradictions of Stefan Zabriski, but it did explain something else.

"So he was not worried that night in Kiel?"

"Worried? He was in roaring good spirits."

"And the next day? Was he still happy?"

"Oh, yes, he was all smiles on the plane back."

At least that established a framework. Zabriski had not been troubled until he reviewed the computer readouts in Gdansk. Unfortunately the police experts had drawn a blank from this same material. Oblonski returned to Jaan Hroka with a growl of dissatisfaction.

"Disliking Zabriski is one thing. But your whole future was imperiled by him."

"Listen, he was shafting a lot of people besides me. Just ask around."

"Maybe. But what was Zabriski doing just before he was murdered? Not only had he studied your application for a BADA loan with all the details on your fleet, he was also checking insurance claims for ships stranded in the canal. If yours was phony, he would have nailed you."

This random shot fell short of its mark.

"Not unless he had second sight," Hroka retorted.

"What do you mean?"

"I haven't filed yet. I'm still waiting for the engineers to examine my hull."

Cursing himself for not having verified this point, Oblonski hastened to recover the offensive.

"Then why did you lie about your movements at the murder scene? Because you hoped to hide the fact that you were walking down the corridor to the parking lot at just the right time to grab that tire iron."

Hroka's moment of victory had been short-lived. "That was just a misunderstanding," he muttered. "You asked if I left BADA with Anton Vigotis. I thought you meant the lounge, not the building."

"A very natural error," the colonel purred. "But now we have that cleared up, you admit you could have gone through the workshop, taken the tire iron, and waited for Zabriski in the parking lot."

Alarmed by this sudden affability, the Estonian remained silent.

"Come now, we have Vigotis's statement. You have no choice."

"Oh, yes, I do."

Remorseless in his logic, Oblonski swept on. "You said good-bye. Then Vigotis turned right, you went to the left. It is really quite simple."

Squirming under the attack, Hroka refused to make eye contact.

"I didn't leave BADA right away," he admitted.

The black eyebrows arched eloquently. "So now we have it! Perhaps you went upstairs for another crack at Herr Zabriski. Perhaps you accompanied him through the shop and out to the lot."

"I did not! I was with someone else."

Hroka was manifesting restlessness, evasion, defiance. Unfortunately, in Oblonski's experience, these were signs of shamed reluctance rather than deep-rooted fear.

"You've got to understand that all the delegates act as if they're real big shots," Hroka began on a note of self-justification. "You ask them for the simplest information and they start yapping about confidentiality. Christ, even Vigotis won't talk straight to a little guy like me, and I needed to know what the hell was going on. But Vigotis faxes a lot of stuff back to Tallinn. So, when I said good-bye to him, I wasn't leaving BADA and I wasn't heading for the parking lot. I did what anybody else would do. I tracked the fax girl to the cafeteria, then walked back upstairs with her."

To speed things up Oblonski said, "You were offering her a bribe to get a peek at Vigotis's correspondence?"

"Why shouldn't I see it? Whatever high and mighty games he likes to play, he's supposed to be representing Estonians, and that's me."

"Never mind about that. What happened?"

"At first she pretended she wasn't interested but she was just trying to jack up the price. I was arguing with her when we heard Zabriski's secretary calling out to someone that she'd talk to them after she finished faxing. Well, I didn't want her to see me there so I ducked into the supply room."

Those mobile eyebrows had snapped down but Oblonski's voice was neutral. "Go on."

"Instead of just dumping her papers, the Jesilko woman picked up some incoming stuff and started reading. God, I thought I'd be there all night, the time she was taking. But finally she went next door and I took the chance to beat it. That's when I went out to my car."

"Why did you have to slink around that way? Couldn't you just pretend you were faxing something?"

"Be serious, Colonel. If the girl got rattled into spilling the beans, Zabriski would have raised holy hell. I figured I was doing everybody a favor by lying low."

Adopting an air of profound skepticism, Oblonski said severely, "We will of course check this latest story you've come up with."

"You do that!"

THE FAX OPERATOR was a dumpy girl with heavy makeup and a sharp, calculating expression. After five minutes Oblonski was inclined to agree that she had been bargaining with Hroka about price. But now she took full advantage of her initial refusal.

"I told him it was out of the question," she said righteously. "But I was still trying to get rid of him when we heard Frau Jesilko. And that made him so nervous he simply dived into the storeroom before I could do anything."

"You didn't feel it necessary to tell Frau Jesilko?"

The girl shook her mane of bushy hair.

"Oh, no, I wasn't going to get involved. It was a big relief to have her finally go next door. That was when Herr Hroka sneaked off."

* * *

THERE HAD NOT only been witnesses in the cafeteria, there had been speculation there as well.

"I wondered who he was and why he was hanging around the doorway," testified a clerk from the mailroom.

"And then we saw Marie go off with him so that explained everything," chimed in a telephone operator.

"It did?" Oblonski asked amiably.

"Well, we all know what Marie's like. She'll go off with anything in pants."

"Particularly if she thought there was something in it for her," added the clerk slanderously.

Far more interesting, however, were the observations of the auto mechanic. He was not familiar with Jaan Hroka but he recognized a photograph instantly.

"Oh, him. He was ahead of me in the corridor to the cafeteria. I wouldn't have noticed him except that he didn't go inside, just stood looking in. And then, once I'd gotten my meal and started to eat, the girls at the next table were talking about him."

"Did you see him leave?"

"Yes, it turned out he was meeting that little tart from the fax station." The elderly man sniffed. "Right inside headquarters. Disgraceful!"

JOHN THATCHER UNDOUBTEDLY had his burdens, but at least he had avoided being part and parcel of the long haul back to Gdansk. Others at BADA were not so fortunate.

"God, I'm glad that's over," Annamarie announced upon entering her apartment and dumping gloves and purse on the nearest surface.

Her husband emerged from the bathroom.

149

"That bad, eh?"

"You wouldn't believe it," she said grumpily, going on to detail the dramatics in Warsaw. "I sometimes wonder whether any of this is worth it."

Nils Nordstrom was an easygoing man who had long since accepted his wife's driving ambition. "You don't mean that, and you know it. Why not just collapse while I get you a drink?"

Taking him at his word, she kicked off her shoes and yanked at the black half-moon clip that was doing service as a funerary hat. By the time her husband handed her a glass she was propped against the pillows on the sofa. With the first sip she began to recover.

"You know, one of the New York bankers got himself carted off to a hospital. I wish I'd thought of that one."

He looked down at her. "Don't worry, you will."

She grinned. "Well, it's worth thinking about. Anytime one of our delegates bites the dust, he'll get the full cathedral treatment back home. So a well-timed sprained ankle would pay for itself."

"Busy, busy, always thinking," he teased her. "Look, tomorrow's Saturday and I don't have to be back until Monday morning. What about spending the weekend in the fresh air? We could go sailing."

"That sounds wonderful. I could use a breathing space."

"How bad are things going to be?"

Reaching for a pillow at the end of the sofa, she stuffed it behind her head and, cradling her drink, fell into reflection. "It's hard to tell. As far as what's foreseeable, it's six of one, half of a dozen of another. We'll probably have a god-almighty brouhaha selecting a successor chief of staff. But while everybody is busy politicking I can select the panel for the Kiel inquiry and polish off the vote on the harbor project."

"I suppose you'll tank right over them on that one."

"It won't be hard. Giving thumbs-up to Tallinn will be a relief to almost everyone now. And, long term, we'll be able to handle the canal proposal on a rational basis."

They both knew the heart of the problem remained.

"And what about the unforeseeable?" he asked briskly.

"Oh, lord, Nils, how can I tell? Stefan's murder means there are all sorts of wild cards out there. For starters, there's whatever mess he stumbled onto. I'm not going to have that hanging around like a time bomb. Then, there's the identity of the killer. If it's some anonymous computer expert who found an ingenious way to transfer funds, that's one thing. But if it's a delegate . . . God, I seem to have been talking nonstop since I came through that door," she said, leaning her head far back to stretch her neck muscles.

"And now you've got it out of your system, forget about BADA for the weekend," he advised kindly. "Monday is a long way away."

UNLIKE THE NORDSTROMS, the Eric Andersens were not spending the weekend together. Andersen had been in the forefront of the disturbances at Lazienkowski Palace and had barely made it to the last car of the convoy returning to Gdansk. Feeling considerably battered, he was in no mood to undertake a round-trip to Copenhagen before the council's next meeting.

"She's convened the session for nine o'clock on Monday, Clara," he explained to his wife over the phone. "There just isn't enough time."

Clara lamented the important events he would miss, emphasizing in particular a joint session with the Danish branch of Greenpeace. The entire Andersen tribe was committed to ecological reform.

"They'll just have to get along without me," he grunted.

It went without saying that the family presence would still be felt.

"What a shame. Since Frieda's out of town too I'll have to try getting hold of Christian."

"It might be better if you went alone. You've got some sense."

Andersen had learned to voice disapproval of his wife's nephew in terms of a flattering comparison.

"There's nothing fundamentally wrong with Christian. He's just young, Eric," she said indulgently. "They're impatient about everything at that age."

Among the things Christian was impatient about was the legalistic, legislative, pettifogging approach to a cleaner environment favored by his elders. At the ripe age of twenty-two, he reveled in demonstrations, traffic pileups, daring incursions into military zones, and vivid abuse of all and sundry.

"It would help if you could shut him up for once," his fond uncle suggested. "This is not the best time for him to be talking about throwing bombs."

At first she did not understand.

"Christian is simply voicing his convictions. I admit he tends to exaggerate, but that's because he enjoys the excitement of direct confrontation."

"He enjoys going to jail!"

Clara bristled in defense of her young.

"He has been arrested twice for blocking entrance to a chemical facility. In other words, he was lying down in a road. There's no need to make it sound as if he's an apostle of mayhem and destruction."

"I'm not talking about what he does," Andersen growled, sensibly retreating a few paces. "I'm talking about the way he sounds. Given the canal disaster and my position at BADA, the family should not be associated with extremist factions."

"Ah ha!" she pounced. "So you're really talking about yourself. But you're not responsible for what your nephew says. Why should it embarrass you at the council?"

Recent developments had altered Eric Andersen's list of priorities.

"We have a murder investigation going on here at BADA," he reminded her.

"But what does that have to do with you, Eric?"

His voice had deepened to a basso rumble.

"Nothing so far. And I'd like to keep it that way."

16. Sea Wolves

OLONEL OBLONSKI, WHEN summoned to a meeting with his superiors on Saturday afternoon, realized far too well that he had only negative findings to report. As so often in the past he would belabor the theme that clearing away underbrush is a valuable exercise.

But the harassed men around the table barely gave him an opportunity to deliver two sentences.

"I'm afraid we're going to have to scratch Hroka and Frau Jesilko," he began apologetically. "They both have alibis for the critical period."

The news was not received in the manner he expected.

"Who cares about them?" demanded a ministry of justice official. "Now we have real problems."

Oblonski contented himself with projecting polite receptivity.

"This is what we're talking about," the ministry's adviser snarled, thrusting a communiqué from the German government into Oblonski's hands. "It will be on the news this evening. I can hear them now. Kiel Canal sabotaged by eco-terrorists!"

Blankly Oblonski read the text of a letter received by the *Kiel Beobachter* from a group claiming responsibility for the disaster.

"Good god!" he exclaimed. "But this can't have anything to do with Zabriski's murder."

"Oh, no?" barked the official. "Just wait until tomorrow. After that disgraceful riot, every newspaper in Europe will make a connection. The ecologists stage a catastrophe, then one of their heroes is murdered in revenge. Naturally that makes them go berserk at his funeral."

The colonel was shaking his head firmly. "Zabriski was the last man in the world to be sympathetic to environmentalists. This business about his being a martyr is simply journalistic nonsense."

"All right," said the official, reversing smartly. "You said he found out something that made him look sick, didn't you? He probably discovered who caused the disaster, and they killed him to shut his mouth."

Oblonski sympathized with the passions dominating the room. The last thing the ministry wanted was a roiling stew of foreign interests, continent-wide manhunts, and television spectaculars. From their point of view a lowly Estonian shipper as killer would have been good; a sex-driven secretary even better.

"What does the German government say about this?" he asked cautiously. "It is certainly not characteristic of terrorist groups to wait a week before revealing their role in an attack. Particularly if they've just murdered somebody to keep it quiet."

The official looked even more annoyed than ever. "They think this may possibly be a hoax. Apparently they know all about the group signing the letter and doubt their participation."

Oblonski nodded. "And their police keep very close tabs on the greens who are violence-prone. Furthermore it's not unknown for one of these groups to claim credit for a disaster whose cause has not been determined."

"You're missing the point, Oblonski!" growled the adviser. "What matters is that there's going to be a media carnival. For god's sake, they're already here in Poland."

Far too tactful to remind anyone that the media were in place because a pageant had been staged for them by the same all-wise authorities now deploring their presence, Oblonski returned to his own concerns.

"The thrust of my investigation cannot be greatly influenced by this development. Even if there is some connection between terrorists and Zabriski, that would simply go to motivation. The physical parameters of the murder remain. He was killed at BADA, with a BADA weapon, by someone who knew his movements and probably his intentions. The crime remains BADA-centered."

The ministry's adviser was still seeking a reasonable substitute for the humbler suspects that Oblonski had cleared.

"Some little runt of a clerk there," he suggested. "All you have to do is find an environmental enthusiast."

This was no time to explain that the little runts had left for the day long before Zabriski's murder had been committed.

Instead Oblonski prepared his listeners for the shoals ahead as diplomatically as possible.

"It is true that there are dedicated ecologists at BADA," he intoned somberly. "Unfortunately some of them occupy very important positions."

TRUE TO BONN'S forecast, the news was delivered to the waiting world that night, and by Sunday Wanda Jesilko had planned her tactics.

"You'll want the books too," she said as she carried a tea tray into Stefan Zabriski's sitting room.

She had set aside the day to help Adam Zabriski. He was dividing his father's belongings into those to be retained, those to be sold, and those to be thrown away.

Adam was in a corner, lost in reverie as he absently stroked the ancient leather case of his father's much cherished violin. Shaking his shoulders to rouse himself, he moved forward, glancing around the unadorned walls.

"It's pretty bare, isn't it?"

"Stefan never noticed pictures or flowers," she said tolerantly.

"I'm surprised you didn't live together."

Spooning sugar into their cups, she used his remark to further her ends.

"At first it was because of Katya," she said, referring to her daughter. "And then, by the time she went off, Stefan had really begun to change."

"I haven't seen much of him since I got elected to the legislature," he admitted.

Wanda and Adam had not only known each other for years, they were practically coconspirators. Stefan Zabriski's wife had spent her existence smoothing his passage through life. When she died Zabriski expected his son to fill the void. Adam had been only too happy to step aside for Wanda Jesilko.

"Coming to Gdansk was not good for Stefan," she continued deliberately.

In the act of choosing a pastry from the plate, Adam paused. "But Father said he loved his work here," he objected.

"That was the trouble. For the first time, Stefan had a say in what was going to be done. As a result, he became hypnotized by what he thought he could do at BADA. He was growing more and more autocratic."

"Come now, he wasn't that bad."

"Not before, no." She shrugged. "In Warsaw he never questioned that the government was all-powerful. After all, who could? Here it wasn't like that at all."

"Well, naturally."

Wanda ignored the interruption. "In case you received the wrong impression from the funeral, the council members usually aren't here. They just fly in for business and then go home. Stefan didn't take them seriously. What's more, he didn't bother to hide his attitude."

"That is a mistake for anyone in his position," Adam pontificated.

"Stefan made a lot of mistakes," she said evenly.

Adam thought he knew what was coming. "Are you telling me that Father was wrong when he claimed there was some kind of fraud?"

"Just the opposite."

Raising his cup, Adam examined her over its rim. Wanda was notoriously lavish with words and gestures. Never before had he seen her so constrained.

"Go on," he said uneasily.

For a moment she did not reply. Instead she poured more tea for both of them and halved a pastry for herself.

"The police are returning Stefan's files to the office tomorrow morning. They haven't found anything. But I plan to go through them myself in case there's something they missed."

Disturbed by her manner, he said, "What's troubling you?"

Still she hesitated, then she chose an oblique approach. "Stefan was a very honorable man."

"Of course, of course."

From Adam's point of view, Warsaw had more than satisfied the need to eulogize his father.

"I'm trying to phrase something difficult," she said, sensing his impatience. "Stefan had convinced himself he knew what was best for BADA. He was absolutely sincere in his belief."

A sudden cold prickle skating down his spine warned Adam, too late, what she was about to suggest.

"And therefore Father might have done something improper?" he finished for her incredulously. "That's absurd."

"It wouldn't have seemed improper to him. It would have been a shortcut to a desirable BADA goal."

"I can't imagine how you picked up such a lunatic idea," he snapped.

She answered him literally.

"Partly because of the way Stefan looked the night he was killed. He seemed absolutely overwhelmed. And he usually enjoyed ferreting out irregularities. You should have seen him when he found out about the toxic dumping."

"So it was not like him to be so depressed. Maybe he was coming down with an illness."

Serenely disregarding his bleat, she went on. "A lot of people thought Stefan was pro-German, but that wasn't it. He was simply determined to push through a Kiel Canal project. When the disaster didn't produce the backing he expected, he was so bitter that I wondered what he had been up to."

Adam looked at her in dawning horror.

"You're asking me to believe that he'd engineer an accident in the canal?"

"No, but I do think he might have become involved with elements that were simply using him. He hadn't been choosy about his allies lately. If he found out what they'd done and threatened to go public, they might have killed him."

"He can't have changed that much!" Adam choked.

Staring straight into his eyes, she went on remorselessly. "Remember, he was murdered. That means somebody was desperate to get him out of the way. I think we'd better find out why, Adam." Scooping up the tray, she bore it toward the tiny kitchen. As she passed from sight she spoke over her shoulder. "Because if it's what I'm afraid of, we may have to do something about it."

Adam thought of his father's reputation, of all those tributes in Warsaw, of his own political aspirations. Only then did he address the kitchen doorway.

"If you learn anything, Wanda, you must come to me first."

Two DAYS OF blissful insulation on a thirty-two-foot sailboat with her husband had been sufficient to return Annamarie Nordstrom to fighting trim. Even the blaring stories about sabotage at Kiel that awaited her on Sunday night failed to ruffle her. She accorded them exactly the amount of attention she felt they deserved, then got on with business. By Monday morning she was dispatching her agenda with vengeance.

"Good morning, Colonel, I was half expecting you," she said.

"I am fortunate to find you available. I thought you were voting on the harbor project today," he replied.

But he had underestimated the speed with which BADA was proceding.

"We awarded the grant to Tallinn at ten o'clock this morning after a very short session."

"So you won?" said Oblonski.

Her smile was rueful. "In a manner of speaking. But the delegates are in an uproar at the idea of somebody deliberately causing that night of havoc in Kiel—and so am I."

"Does BADA have anybody who can tell me whether it was physically possible for radicals to do it?"

She was ahead of him. "I have asked one of our experts who's just back from the canal to join us. But there's something else you should consider."

"What's that?"

"This letter to the *Kiel Beobachter* was not the only one. There was an earlier message from a different group. That one went to the Kiel Canal authority."

An angry red tide rose above the colonel's stiff collar.

"And you did not feel you could confide in the Polish police?" he asked with savage irony.

She lofted a placatory hand. "I am as annoyed as you, Colonel. The German government decided to hush it up and only informed me this morning. The point, however, is that we have two separate groups getting into the act."

"So one of the notes, at least, must be a hoax," he said.

"And I can tell you which one. The first message says they used a small pleasure boat."

Their conversation was cut short by the arrival of BADA's expert.

"No perpetrator could have anticipated the chemical consequences. That was due to the reaction between two separate cargoes later on," he explained. "All they could have expected was physical damage and perhaps some comparatively harmless leakage."

"Then they would have been aiming at a minor disruption of the canal—maybe for a day or so," Oblonski reasoned. "It was sheer accident that they caused a major spill, not to mention a chain collision."

"Yes."

"But surely you can tell us which terrorist letter fits the facts. The pilot on the first ship to be hit must know the approximate size of the other vessel."

Before the chemical expert could answer, Annamarie cut in.

"That's not how things work in a fog, Colonel. When you're dependent on sound you can easily be misled. Many small boats, including the one my husband and I own, are equipped with very loud foghorns. When one of those goes off under the bow of a freighter, they assume they're dealing with a big vessel. My assistant and Wanda Jesilko have the roster of ships in the canal. Let's check with them."

She rose and headed for the corridor so energetically that Oblonski had difficulty reaching the door in time to open it for her. Without breaking stride she continued her argument.

"The canal records show the order in which vessels paid their tolls. My bet is there won't be any pleasure craft."

"Why do you say that?"

She was emphatic. "The weather conditions were frightful, Colonel. Commercial shipping must continue under those circumstances. But someone out for recreation—if he has any sense—finds a safe anchorage and waits for the fog to lift."

Annamarie's assurance lasted only as long as it took to reach Stefan Zabriski's suite, where Wanda and the assistant were crouched over a computer monitor.

"Well, Richard?" Annamarie asked impatiently.

"There are two possibles," he replied.

"Two?" Annamarie faltered. Then, recovering, she snapped, "The idiots!"

"So in the fog one of them could have charged around, starting the trouble that then snowballed."

Richard paused, pleased with his analysis.

"Absurd!"

Richard looked deflated, but Colonel Oblonski had no fear of the chairman. "Why?" he asked stolidly.

"Because it would be suicidal. They haven't fished any bodies out yet, have they? Here, let me see the specifics on those two boats," she demanded.

As soon as Wanda's agile fingers had punched up the details on the screen, Madame Nordstrom snorted.

"Just as I thought. One of them is four tons and the other is three. They're both midgets compared to a commercial vessel. Someone didn't just head for a freighter, rev up the engine and charge in!"

Richard's imagination soared to another peak. "What if they were in it together? The first one was aimed at a target. Then the crew jumped off and were picked up by the second!"

The only experienced sailor in the group was dismissive.

"Sheer folly!" she said curtly. "Leaving aside the impossibility of aiming accurately at the sound of a foghorn, you're saying that they jumped into a sea of propellers, relying on another boat to thread its way through dense fog to pick them up."

Her blast of scorn was followed by a cool interjection from Wanda Jesilko.

"But the reason you're here, Colonel, is that Stefan was murdered because of something he uncovered. And that couldn't have had anything to do with pleasure boating. BADA doesn't keep records on holiday sailors and Stefan wasn't interested anyway."

Oblonski was momentarily silenced. Belabored on the one hand by Annamarie, the authority on small boating, and on the other by Wanda, the authority on Stefan Zabriski, he could not refute their arguments. But he distrusted their vehemence. Five short days ago Wanda had been incoherent. And Annamarie, this morning, was a far cry from the drawn, harassed woman who had set out for Warsaw. It made him wonder exactly how many problems had been solved by Stefan Zabriski's death.

At least Wanda Jesilko's last remark, Oblonski finally decided, was vulnerable to attack. "But Herr Zabriski was concerned with insurance recoveries. Maybe that was it. One of the small boats could have put in for suspiciously extensive hull damage."

Glancing at her keyboard, Wanda scored again. "I've already looked and there is no such claim."

"To hell with that thing!" Oblonski erupted, flicking a contemptuous finger at the monitor. "We don't need it. The ships are still in the canal, aren't they?"

Happy to be back on firm ground, Richard assured him that they were.

"Then an examination of the hulls should settle it."

Madame Nordstrom was not yielding an inch. "Possibly."

"Well, right now I'd like the two national registrations."

"The sailboat with auxiliary is English out of Ipswich," Richard replied obligingly. "And the power cruiser is Danish."

Oblonski rolled on. "I'll need the names of the owners and operators as well, so that police investigation into their backgrounds can start."

This continued rejection of informed advice finally made an impact. While Wanda took refuge in careful impassivity Madame Nordstrom, less accustomed to opposition, glared balefully.

For whatever their reasons both women, Colonel Oblonski suddenly realized, were dismayed by the course he was taking.

17. Shore Leave

John Thatcher, a confirmed landsman, had not spent his weekend bouncing around the Baltic in a small sailboat. Nonetheless, for purposes of keeping abreast of world events, he had been just as isolated. Like so much that had contributed to his recent discomfort, it had all been von Hennig's fault.

"You can't be planning to stay here when they won't even let you see Gabler," Peter had protested after they left the embassy on Friday night. "You'd do much better to join me."

"And what are you proposing to do?"

Peter regarded the decision as made. "We'll go to Janow Podlaski for the horse auctions. I'm planning an anniversary present for Heinrich and Trudi."

Dimly Thatcher remembered there was a connection between the von Hennigs and horses. Peter, who cantered around the countryside for pleasure, had produced a son who was a competition rider. Heinrich, in turn, had been outclassed by his young wife.

"That's right," said Thatcher. "Trudi rode in the Olympics, didn't she?"

"And came away with the silver," was the prompt rejoinder.

There remained an unanswered question.

"But why buy in Poland of all places?"

Von Hennig was shocked.

"This is a major international auction. It's famous around the world."

Still dubious about his own role in these proceedings, Thatcher pointed out that he knew nothing about horses.

"That doesn't matter. You will discover many other points of interest."

THE DISCOVERIES BEGAN with their trip the next morning. As nearly as Thatcher could tell he was heading into the land that time forgot. Tucked away to the east—smack against the Russian border—the area was devoid of industry, serviced by abysmal roads, and populated sparsely.

The first sign that there was a jewel tucked away in these unpromising surroundings came with passage through the town of Janow Podlaski where serried ranks of gourmet restaurants—rivalling anything available in Warsaw—suggested that there were deep pockets to be picked somewhere.

Indifferent to such amenities, von Hennig enlarged on their immediate schedule.

"Tomorrow we'll attend the auction. This afternoon we're visiting some of the farms I know. That way you can learn the general layout and meet some of the other buyers."

They were soon engulfed by a scene Thatcher had never expected to see in Poland. Although a novice at livestock auctions, he had more than once visited a client with a breeding farm in bluegrass country. The atmospherics here were very familiar. In the pastures brood mares grazed tranquilly, most of them only three or four months gone in their eleven-month period. The foals they had dropped the previous spring frolicked in fields of their own. And in more than one paddock, muscular stallions were being paraded before critical observers.

The variations that were apparent merely emphasized the underlying similarity. The stables might be constructed of masonry, but their sparkling whitewash evoked the fences of Kentucky. The grooms wore tunics and cavalry boots but they were doing and saying the same things to their recalcitrant charges.

There were, however, two fundamental differences. The first took some time to impress itself on Thatcher's untutored eye. These animals were not American Thoroughbreds.

"Arabians," von Hennig replied to an inquiry. "Some of the finest in the world."

But there was no escaping the second distinction. This landscape was redolent of ancient privilege and ancient preoccupation. The stables were not stripped-down functional buildings. Rich in period detail, topped with crenellated towers, they spoke of an age that lavished time and money on architecture. And those semimilitary uniforms were merely the contemporary equivalent of the retainer's livery. Here, Poles had been breeding horses before Kentucky saw its first white man. It all put the mint julep in its proper place.

"I can see that they've been doing this steadily for a long time, including the last fifty years," Thatcher remarked. "It must have been a wonderful source of hard currency for the commissars."

"Yes, what's more, it's an old Polish tradition and they didn't succeed in uprooting all of them. Oh, good, we've arrived at Tadeucz Pilch's place."

Past the gateposts was a quarter-mile allée lined on both sides with parked cars.

"People certainly pour in," said Thatcher as they trudged toward the courtyard. "Is this a once-a-year invasion?"

"God, no! This bunch is here for the auction. But the government arranges tours for horse clubs and they come from all over for a full six months."

That explained the restaurants of Janow Podlaski.

As they proceeded Thatcher's spirits were insensibly rising. No matter how much pomp and circumstance surrounds a funeral it remains an acknowledgment that all flesh is mortal. And hospital waiting rooms tend to reinforce the same theme. Stud farms, however, are a celebration of life.

The best, however, was still ahead. Von Hennig made directly for one of the many groups huddled together in earnest discussion and introduced Thatcher. Then, with a murmured apology, he sped off toward the stables, leaving Thatcher to the horse fanciers.

But within fifteen minutes he discovered that these people had more in common than Arabians. This was not only a gathering of wealth, but wealth of a particular kind. Oh, there might be a few jaded specimens of the idle rich, but for the most part they were swashbucklers. Regardless of whether they rampaged through manufacturing, real estate or currency exchanges, they formed a fraternity whose common mind-set obliterated race, creed, and color.

For men such as these, Janow Podlaski was more than the site of a horse auction; it was an impromptu marketplace. Preliminary overtures were commonplace while, in a few instances, actual deal-making was in progress. Totally absorbed, Thatcher moved from one clutch to another, barely conscious of the moment when he slipped from being part of the audience to part of the action.

"Well, John, did you manage to occupy yourself?" von Hennig asked when he reappeared over an hour later.

"I seem to have acquired a client for the Sloan."

"I thought you might," said von Hennig smugly. "You'll find it's the same everywhere."

And so it was. By the time they left their fourth and final stop, the sun was beginning its descent and Thatcher's little black book was filled with notes. Next month at the bank he would be receiving a heavy-construction firm from Rio de Janeiro and an electronics manufacturer from Taiwan. The appointments were conventional enough. The only oddity was that they were being made in a stable.

Thatcher found himself marveling at the persistence of the horse as a status symbol. It was all too obvious why the medieval knight on his charger, both caparisoned for war, struck awe into the simple peasantry. And, even in the milder climate of the nineteenth century, the gentry sweeping by in carriages would have been objects of envy to a weary, foot-slogging population. But why, at the birth of the twenty-first century, did these adventurers still gravitate to stud farms? Probably because in their freewheeling world the image of success was everything.

Only hardheaded bankers like John Thatcher preferred more solid collateral.

THE NEXT MORNING von Hennig was all business.

"Enough fooling around," he announced as soon as the last drop of coffee was down. "Now, the auction."

Obediently Thatcher rose. He had always realized that, sooner or later, he would be required to study a horse.

They, along with many others, were at the grounds early enough to watch the trailers being unloaded. Thatcher recognized some of his new-made acquaintances, but this morning there was no idle chitchat. Barely a sentence was exchanged as horses balked and swerved, spectators scampered out of harm's way, and handlers cursed nonstop. To Thatcher it was simply an immense sea of confusion.

But once the auction began order emerged. Viewed individually these animals were spellbinding. With coats gleaming like silk, hard muscles rippling smoothly, heads held high, they compelled admiration. Finally a sable-brown stallion with four snowy-white stockings pirouetted into the ring and took Thatcher's breath away.

"Magnificent," he murmured involuntarily.

Von Hennig was so busy with his heavily annotated catalog that he had rarely looked up, but now he cast a measuring glance at the subject of this praise.

"You've chosen well," he congratulated Thatcher.

"But you won't be bidding on him?"

"Not unless I want to bankrupt myself. He'll probably be going to another stud farm."

The sums then elicited by the auctioneer proved his point. Thatcher was not surprised. Plenty of rich men buy paintings and statuary, jade and crystal, because of the sheer aesthetic pleasure derived from these lifeless objects. Was it any wonder that beauty allied to animation should produce the same itch?

It was a full hour before von Hennig bestirred himself. After riding four price rises, he shook his head firmly.

"Just testing the waters," he explained in a brief aside.

There was nothing experimental about his second foray forty-five minutes later. It was a full eight rounds of bidding before he finally retired with the bitter observation, "With a world trade recession you'd think prices would be depressed, not inflated."

"Too bad," said Thatcher perfunctorily. Yesterday his lack of response would have been owed to the maxim that rich men's follies always were—and should be—outrageously expensive. But too many horses had come and gone. Now John Thatcher was a critic. He had not cared for the chestnut with the dramatic blaze streaking down his nose. Too garish, he thought disapprovingly. Better to wait for something more deserving.

It did not come until midafternoon when a majestic gray entered the ring as if he owned it. Arching a magnificent neck embellished with a mane that was almost black, he placed each hoof with the balanced precision of a gymnast as he circled the ring.

Without a word spoken Thatcher knew that Peter was now in deadly earnest. Poker-faced, he was jerking his rolled-up catalog a scant inch to signal his readiness to meet each new price level. In spite of this unnatural impassivity he had managed, by some mysterious form of ESP, to identify his chief competition.

"That damned Spaniard is serious," he hissed from between motionless lips.

Many rounds were necessary to prove him right. Bidder after bidder fell by the wayside until only Peter and the Spaniard were left. To the outside world von Hennig remained unimpressed by the ongoing duel. But Thatcher, conscious of the tension at his side, watched the white-knuckled grip on that improvised baton, and saw that auction fever had struck.

Ten minutes later the gray officially belonged to von Hennig, who slumped back, heaving a vast sigh.

"A splendid purchase," Thatcher said sincerely.

Slightly self-conscious, Peter eschewed all reference to extortionate prices, instead dilating happily on the power, speed, intelligence, and spirit of his acquisition. Thatcher agreed as wholeheartedly as if he had discerned every one of those attributes. And when they moved on to an unfavorable comparison with the flashy chestnut, he was amused to find himself growing quite heated.

Peter, maintaining his reputation for sangfroid, insisted on remaining for the final sales. Only then did he sweep Thatcher off, first to a desk where the mundane details of payment and transportation were arranged and then, triumphantly, to a hands-on inspection of the gray. Running his palm along the mighty rib cage, fondling a hock strong enough to crush a tank, caressing that rich, burnished mane, he gave grunt after grunt of satisfaction.

"Just the thing for Trudi," he finally announced.

But his day was undeniably capped that evening when they were having drinks in the lounge before a farewell dinner in

Janow Podlaski. Surrounded by aficionados, Peter was the target for a rain of felicitations about the gray, about Trudi's delight, about forthcoming Olympic victories.

Thatcher's reward, on the other hand, came when they seated themselves at a large, convivial table and he found himself next to a world-renowned Greek shipping tycoon.

"Perry, I didn't even know you were here," von Hennig greeted him. "Why weren't you bidding?"

With a small, satisfied smile, Pericles Samaras said he had done his buying yesterday. Then he politely tried to include Thatcher in the conversation. When Thatcher explained the real reason for his presence in Poland, the Greek frowned thoughtfully.

"Ah, BADA. I'm joining my lawyers there next week. Let's hope this new program of theirs actually does streamline claims. I have three of them and that oil tanker stuck in Malmö will cost a bundle."

"You'll see more than that," von Hennig said. "Some of our more ambitious plans at BADA could impinge on your own activities."

Samaras shrugged. "Revitalizing Baltic harbors? Making those Eastern shipyards competitive? It will be a long time before that comes to pass."

"As a matter of fact, our chairman agrees with you. Madame Nordstrom thinks the immediate gains will come from forcing growth among the private shippers."

"That too is not on the immediate horizon," Samaras said comfortably.

Peter grinned.

"Not impressed by Leonhard Bach's publicity, Perry?" he challenged.

There was a moment's blank silence.

"Bach? Oh, yes, he's the one with four or five medium-sized

freighters, isn't he?" asked Samaras, making this inventory sound like a pocketful of candy bars.

While Peter continued his comments, it occurred to Thatcher that Samaras's career had probably familiarized him with every conceivable motive for Stefan Zabriski's death. Accordingly, at the first break, Thatcher seized the opportunity to describe the murder at BADA and its context.

"And of course," added von Hennig, "that leaves the police speculating about the criminal activity that Zabriski might have unearthed."

Samaras was censorious.

"BADA should never have appointed a Pole to that position. Or anybody from the Eastern Bloc. How could they deal with something like this?"

For one dizzy moment Thatcher thought Samaras was implying that the instinct for larceny was unknown under communism. The next words were reassuring.

"The main feature of a socialist state is that there's only one entity really worth stealing from."

"Ah, I think I understand," Thatcher murmured.

"It doesn't make any difference whether it's some workman appropriating a plant truck for his own moonlighting or a commissar diverting millions from a state-owned enterprise. After fifty years it's all standardized. But in a free market," Samaras said cogently, "there are fresh opportunities opening all the time."

"For inspired improvisation to suit changing conditions?" Thatcher suggested.

"Exactly."

Peter wanted more concrete detail. "But what kind of improvisation would be called forth by the canal closure?"

Pericles Samaras did not even pause to reflect.

"Any number. Of course, there are all the changes that can

be rung on insurance fraud. There will certainly be people try-ing to exaggerate damage to their hulls. There could be people forging manifests to recover for cargoes that never existed. I'm not at all sure that you couldn't expand that concept to include ships that were never in the canal in the first place."

"Come, come, Perry," von Hennig protested. "You're letting your imagination run away with you."

"Don't be so hasty. With the right documents, with the right contacts, I could do it."

There was a muted relish in Samaras's voice that hinted he was deriving positive pleasure from his imaginative efforts.

"Ships, after all, can be moved," he went on, dreamily elab-orating his scheme. "A clever man might be able to show an ad-juster the same one twice. Not normally, I grant you. But with this big a disaster, with that many hulls lying over a space of miles, with harried and overworked inspectors, you probably could pull it off."

"Anything else?" asked a fascinated Thatcher.

"Accidents can always bring strange things to the surface. Not all cargoes are what their documents say. Your Zabriski could have stumbled on to gunrunning or the illegal export of antiques. Maybe a ship that was severely damaged didn't file a claim. Nobody wants an insurance adjuster finding a major ship-ment of cocaine."

Thatcher was beginning to be depressed by this glib recita-tion.

"In fact, there are no limits."

"That's about it. I find it a safe rule to assume that anything I can contemplate, somebody will have figured out how to do."

Far from helping, Thatcher thought, this man was stretch-ing the list of possibilities to infinity.

Peter, meanwhile, had been overcome by his official position as delegate to the general council.

"And that doesn't even get to the problem of chicanery within BADA," he said ruefully.

"Now there's a field!" crowed Samaras. "Without knowing anything more about Zabriski, I know he wasn't a hotshot accountant. He probably set up a system for fund withdrawals that required a simple signature."

The two bankers knew about the safeguards customarily shoring up those simple signatures.

"God, you're probably right," groaned von Hennig.

"Letting this man deal with Danes and Swedes and Germans was like letting an innocent wade into a pool filled with sharks."

Thatcher had reached a decision. "I think it would be more useful to concentrate on the forms of skulduggery that Zabriski was capable of recognizing. That at least would narrow things down."

Before Samaras could reply an unknown man sitting nearby succumbed to the temptation to join this intriguing conversation.

"Lots of crooks around," he announced brightly. "Let's face it. Everybody here in this room has a healthy sense of acquisition."

"But strictly within the limits of the law," said Samaras piously.

Only courtesy prevented Peter von Hennig and John Thatcher from arguing the point.

18. Still Afloat

JOHN THATCHER'S FORAY to Janow Podlaski had exposed him to a spectacular anomaly in contemporary Poland—opulence flourishing in a hardscrabble countryside. It was only fitting that his excursion should end with the offer of a lift back to Warsaw in a private plane, while von Hennig was similarly wafted to Gdansk.

The medical report that he received over the phone as soon as he checked into the Marriott was encouraging. The operation had gone splendidly, Mr. Gabler's recovery had been robust, and a late-night visit would be permitted. With this breathing space in hand Thatcher allowed himself a cup of coffee in the mezzanine lounge outside the gambling casino. Here he fell into the maws of a chatty Pole, obviously prospering under present conditions and only too willing to expand on his newfound wealth.

He had spent ten long years in the ministry of culture, he explained, sending Polish symphonic ensembles anywhere in the world that would receive them with hard currency. Nowadays he was working the other side of the street.

"I book big-name rock groups into Poland," he said proudly. "It's a gold mine."

"And you have no problem filling halls?"

"Anywhere there are students or young people I can produce a capacity crowd," the happy impresario boasted. "I'm damned if I know where they get the money."

It was, Thatcher had retorted, a phenomenon familiar to the West.

But as he walked to the hospital, Thatcher was forced to conclude that there were so many anomalies visible to the naked eye that life in Warsaw seemed composed of them. The swarm of noisy little cars choking traffic had to park on crumbling sidewalks. Street vendors peddling blue jeans from rickety folding tables powered their modern cash registers with electric cords snaking to distant doorways. Across from a department store hordes of Russians conducted an open-air market in an attempt to sell something—anything—to their now wealthier neighbors. And, in a world characterized by rising entrepreneurial sap and restricted capital, every street corner housed clutches of young men busily negotiating into their cellular phones, a pale shadow of their mightier brethren at Janow Podlaski.

Moods of quiet reflection, however, never survived long in Gabler's presence. He was sitting up in bed, his eyes gleaming.

"Ah, John," he said, laying aside the *Financial Times*. "Isn't this business in Kiel shocking?"

It was typical that, flat on his back and under sedation for half the weekend, he should be more current than his colleague.

"I've been out of touch, Ev," Thatcher said briefly, waiting for an explanatory lecture.

But Everett had other fish to fry.

"Tut, tut, then you'll have to bring yourself up to date," he said dismissively. "Now, John, I've discussed my condition at some length with the doctor and there is no cogent reason why I should not accompany you to Gdansk tomorrow."

The word *cogent* said it all. That alert gleam was the result of an invigorating set-to with his medical advisers.

"Your ankle seems to be in a cast," Thatcher said mildly.

"A mere trifle!" Gabler replied at his loftiest.

"You haven't forgotten that Poland is the land of nonfunctioning elevators?"

"Those at the Hevelius and our office are fully operational."

It was clear what was going on. Everett had cast himself in one of his favorite roles, that of the ideal Sloan officer. In this capacity he was ready to brave all discomforts. Thatcher was far too canny to raise any of the problems so grandly ignored. Instead he tried awakening the soldier to a different duty.

"But you will inevitably be delayed longer than you expected. I know that you have the Mersinger agreement scheduled for final negotiation."

"That's been very much on my mind. So I called Charlie Trinkam several hours ago and he's agreed to be my proxy," Gabler reassured him. "He now understands all the points I intended to raise."

Poor Charlie! Yanked away from his weekend to be coached on the responsibilities of a pinch hitter.

Everett was on a roll, knocking down opponents like so many ninepins, and he soon received an ally. The orthopedic surgeon, stopping by on his rounds, enthusiastically endorsed Gabler's program. The ankle injury was minor and another night of observation would take care of the concussion. As for the cast, that was the lightweight variety obviating the need for crutches.

"Those two canes will be adequate," he said, waving to the corner, "and Mr. Gabler has already practiced with them."

Thatcher had witnessed this kind of surrender before. The surgeon simply wanted to see his patient's backside. Indeed the only oddity was that Gabler had not been released on the spot and that was explained when the surgeon moved to the door.

"I'll say good-bye now, Mr. Gabler. I'm going off duty and you will have left by the time I return tomorrow."

Everett followed up the doctor's departure by announcing that the nurses would have him ready to leave first thing in the morning.

"I'll bet they will!"

Anywhere in the United States, mused Thatcher on the steps of the hospital, Miss Corsa would be addressing this predicament for him. She could, however, scarcely be asked to work her magic in Eastern Europe.

But to think of secretaries was to think of Carol Gomulka. Thus far her typing had proved adequate. Maybe the time had come to test for more immediately useful skills.

At least she did not object to being called at her home on Sunday evening. Her first cheerful greeting soon modulated into sympathetic clucking as she heard of Everett's mishap.

"He'll need help getting about," Thatcher explained. "So, first of all, we'll need a bigger car. That's the easy part. Then we'll have to find somebody who can drive, somebody who can speak fluent English as well as Polish and then, as the two of them will be cheek by jowl all day, somebody who . . ."

He paused as he searched for a tactful rendition.

"Somebody who can handle Mr. Gabler," Carol supplied kindly.

"Exactly."

Carol fell into a pensive silence and Thatcher could supply only one form of incentive.

"We'll pay through the nose."

"Well, that always helps. I can't promise anything yet, but I may know just the right person."

BY LUNCHTIME THE next day Thatcher devoutly hoped so. In spite of distracting headlines about letters to the Kiel Beobachter he had managed to lay on a chauffeured limousine for portal-to-portal transport. And all had gone well until halfway to

182

Gdansk. But the four steps up to the restaurant and the long narrow corridor to the rest rooms had provided a grim preview of things to come. Everett, tottering on his two sticks, was about as independent as a newborn babe.

He, of course, still had plenty to say about the morning's lead story.

"It is outrageous that a decent concern for the environment should be perverted into criminal violence."

"If, in fact, they really were responsible. There seems to be some doubt on that point," Thatcher remarked.

Trying to capitalize on misfortune was, in Gabler's opinion, as despicable as causing it.

"Well, it's not the sort of action I'd expect from even extremists," Thatcher continued. "After all it resulted in the kind of toxic damage they vociferously deplore."

"Ah, but we seem to be dealing with singularly inept and ill-informed people. Look at this elevation of Stefan Zabriski into one of their martyrs when the man was basically on the other side."

It was only natural that Everett should take a dim view of the protests at Zabriski's funeral. Thatcher had no quarrel with that but he did have another objection.

"There's no reason to suppose that the same group was involved on both occasions."

"Not on the surface," Gabler acknowledged. "You cannot, however, ignore the fact that they both sprang into action at the same time."

Thatcher frowned. "If we're talking about the timing of dramatic acts, aren't you overlooking the biggest one of all?"

Everett, still picturing roiling mobs and sinking ships, was caught off guard. "What do you mean?"

"Zabriski's murder."

"But that had nothing to do with environmentalists!"

"How do we know? So far we've learned that Zabriski was a

man of strong convictions ready to use unconventional methods. He was willing to bring down the government of Estonia without a second thought. In his position he could have been useful to many special interests—including radicals of all sorts."

"He was also a lifelong civil servant."

"Oh, come off it, Everett. They've gone crazy before and the easiest way to do it is by mindlessly embracing a fuzzy ideal."

Gabler was not happy with this line of thought but he nodded soberly.

"I have to admit that Zabriski displayed erratic judgement. But his bias seemed to be towards economic expansion," said Gabler, his eyes widening as he considered the implications. "John, you're not suggesting that protest in Warsaw was a diversionary feint?"

"I'm not suggesting anything. I just wish I knew more about environmental groups."

His wish was about to be answered.

IN THE COURSE of hauling Everett into the Nissan building, Thatcher forgot everything but the prospect of two chairs. Nonetheless the sight that met his eyes when he flung open the office door stopped him in his tracks.

Carol Gomulka and a man were facing each other across a desk embellished with a bottle of champagne and an array of plastic glasses. While she quaffed her drink, the unknown was saying heatedly, "It's all a lot of garbage. That Eighth Day crowd may have written to the *Kiel Beobachter* but they never took direct action in their lives."

Carol, noticing the new arrivals, was exuberant.

"You're here! Great! This is my husband, Bill, and he's going to be Mr. Gabler's driver. We were just—"

She broke off, overcome by sudden misgivings about the signs of debauchery.

Her husband, however, suffered no such qualms.

"We're celebrating. They accepted my proposal and I've got the job," he sang out.

Everett, carefully lowering himself, went straight to essentials.

"What job? And how can you drive me if you've accepted other employment?"

Bill Gomulka was only too happy to tell him. A small, privatized razor blade company in Poland had done well enough to be bought by a foreign firm. Computerization was the first order of the day and Gomulka's bid to run a training program had been chosen over sparse competition.

"Being bilingual has finally paid off. And the course will last for six months with payment in hard currency. But the reps from IBM won't come for two weeks so I'm free until then."

"And now that Bill has his foot in the door," Carol chimed in, "he'll be able to get more contracts."

He had even bigger ideas. Gazing mistily into a golden future he said, "It doesn't have to stop with Poland, honey. This is happening all over Eastern Europe. We might end up with offices in Budapest and Prague." Exhilarated by these possibilities he hoisted the bottle. "Have some champagne."

"At this hour?" Gabler replied primly. "I'm not sure I want—"

"I do," Thatcher interrupted. While he appreciated the details that made this new attendant available, he was more impressed by Bill Gomulka's physical contours. Carol's husband was built like a wrestler. His broad shoulders and thick chest suggested that, in a pinch, he could gallop up a flight of stairs with Gabler tucked under his arm.

A preliminary cough from Everett alerted Thatcher.

"Never mind about that now, Ev. You'll have plenty of time to talk to Bill about his business problems later. I'm interested in what he was saying about the Eighth Day radicals. You're familiar with them?"

"Bill knows all about environmentalists. He was active in Greenpeace," Carol said proudly.

"Only for summers while I was in college."

Today she was not letting him hide his light under a bushel.

"He went to jail. In Russia!" she added impressively.

Faced with two startled glances, Bill felt obliged to explain. Many years ago he had set sail with a group determined to harass Russian whalers. They had been so effective that the Soviet navy had appeared on the scene.

"I was scared shitless," Bill confessed. "It looked as if they were going to blow us out of the water."

Instead the miscreants had been escorted to a cell on land where they were severely lectured for a week before being handed over to their respective embassies.

"Of course I was a kid then," Bill apologized with all the gravity of the young. "My thinking has changed in the last ten years."

While still firmly committed to the cause, Gomulka had redirected the focus of his attention.

"I've learned a lot from living in Europe. Confrontation is fun but it's a game for dummies. To make progress like Denmark, you've got to work through the establishment."

Bill's transformation, it seemed, had entailed membership in a succession of organizations.

"By now you must have a fairly accurate overview of the entire movement," said Thatcher. "Do you think it's likely that any of them, not just these Eighth Day people, should attack the Kiel Canal?"

Asked for a serious opinion, Gomulka became cautious.

"First off, there are hundreds if not thousands of organizations worldwide. That means you're dealing with a cross-section of the population. So nothing's impossible. Still, I wouldn't expect the canal to be a target. It's not an obvious source of danger like

186

a nuclear reactor, so you wouldn't have popular support. Then there's the risk of causing casualties and, if you ask me, the people ruthless enough for that like to do it up close and personal. That's what turns them on. Finally, it would be damn tricky to arrange. You'd have to hang around the locks day after day waiting for a sudden thick fog."

This lucid analysis was not enough for Everett Gabler. "Obviously some of them did not mind causing casualties at Lazienkowski Palace," he said acidly. "Who do you think was responsible for that?"

While her husband debated his choice, Carol recalled the duties of a hostess. Producing a dish of salted nuts, she bent over Thatcher to whisper, "Is it all right about hiring Bill?"

"Better than all right."

She had, indeed, found the perfect driver. Instead of being rendered captious by his dependence on a stranger, Everett would seize the opportunity to instruct young Gomulka. By the time the two weeks were over he would have covered everything from creating a small-business plan to going public. In return for all this tuition, the Sloan would have an environmental expert on tap.

It was a marriage made in heaven.

19. Home Port

ETWEEN POLAND AND Germany lies a shifting border that
has always raised hackles. Normally a query from an unknown Gdansk policeman would have been relegated to the
bottom of the pile at Kiel. But the harassed Canal Authority,
enraged by the specter of terrorism, was in a vindictive mood.
If Colonel Oblonski had reason to suspect two small boats in
particular then—come hell or high water—Kiel would cooperate.

Energetically they began to search for a location along the
canal that could accommodate a giant crane. While this mon-
ster was being maneuvered into position, boarding parties
achieved feats of navigation, disentangling the *Brigitte* and the
Pelican, then threading them past every obstacle to a site near
the massive concrete pad.

The *Pelican*, a thirty-foot ketch out of England, arrived first,
and it was a sorry sight. The bowsprit had disappeared, leaving
the ripped jib to lie in tattered folds over the bow. The vessel's
two-masted silhouette was now wildly out of proportion, with
the top third of the mizzenmast canted over the smashed dinghy.
And the rain of debris that had pockmarked the superstructure
of the cabin littered the deck.

"It certainly looks as if it's been through the wars," remarked one of the workmen.

The moment of truth was fast approaching. The crane was in the center of the pad, the *Pelican* had been swaddled in batting and cables, and the experts had found themselves a coign of vantage. They were, of course, not the only spectators. As all these activities were taking place in the middle of a weekday, the adjacent community could not produce its full complement of residents. But there were at least twenty gray-haired couples, a number of women with baby carriages, and the usual collection of deliverymen whose rounds had put them in the right place at the right time.

"Do we know anything about the people who were on board?" an expert asked.

A local official pointed unenthusiastically at the water. "That's them. They're from Oxford."

Four young men had managed to clamber down the steep incline to line up at the very rim of the canal. Clad in grimy jeans and sweatshirts each clutched a large stein. They had watched the swaddling process critically and now they awaited the climax.

Movement was perceptible as the hull was raised inch by inch. Then the virtuoso at the crane controls applied power with an ever-so-delicate touch until at last the vessel swung free with water streaming off its sides. The four students raised their beer and, as the *Pelican* swiveled through the air towards the waiting flatbed truck, produced a ragged cheer.

"That hull is as clean as a whistle," said a disappointed expert after a preliminary scan. "They were lucky, damned lucky."

Far different was the scene later that afternoon when the same crew and the same crane addressed the *Brigitte*. A chill, dank drizzle had sent the bystanders back to their homes and only one solitary wayfarer on a bicycle had halted to watch the ascent.

The official who had identified the Oxford contingent now watched the trim cabin cruiser being coaxed into position and nodded approvingly.

"At least these people believe in polishing brass and renewing paint. Who are they?"

There was no approval at all from the canal inspector who was flourishing a clipboard.

"The registered owners are a Mr. and Mrs. Hans Rasmussen of Copenhagen. But the vessel was being piloted by a Miss Dagmar Rasmussen and she had a boyfriend with her."

"Then where are they?"

This time there was a significant pause.

"They boarded a plane before the smoke cleared, leaving instructions with a local boatyard."

Now all eyes shifted to the *Brigitte*. Wallowing low in the water, she had miraculously escaped the rain of debris that had pelted the English sailboat. And the hull, when it was winched upward, appeared unblemished until the final two feet were exposed.

"Well," breathed one of the experts softly, "will you look at that?"

He was pointing to a long, raking gash along the port side of the bow.

COLONEL OBLONSKI BEGAN by paraphrasing freely.

"Kiel says *Pelican* is in the clear," he told Alex. "That leaves the *Brigitte*. And *Brigitte* is Danish."

But long before he had finished pages of nautical detail, the BADA rumor mill was humming.

Downstairs Wanda Jesilko listened with apparent indifference, then headed straight for Stefan Zabriski's office.

"Sure, take what you want," said its current occupant. "I think the police have brought everything back."

"Just as well or we'd never get anything done around here," she said lightly.

Among the delegates to BADA the response took a slightly different form.

"The *Brigitte* you say?" observed Eric Andersen when his secretary relayed the latest. He waited until she left before adding, "Goddamit to hell! Now what am I supposed to do?" But he knew there was only one option open to him.

"Lili," he said, striding to the door. "Something unexpected's come up. I'm spending the night in Copenhagen but I'll be back tomorrow afternoon."

COPENHAGEN WAS MORE than Eric Andersen's hometown. It was his base of operations, efficiently maintained by his wife no matter how far he roamed.

Clara had been busy since his phone call from Gdansk.

"Christian's landlady says he's away," she reported the minute Andersen set foot in the front hall. "He left a couple of weeks ago, and she doesn't know when to expect him."

"Just what I was afraid of," he said, depositing his overnight bag. "Your precious nephew—"

"*Our* nephew!" she insisted.

"All right, *our* nephew," Andersen conceded. "But I am right, aren't I? About Dagmar Rasmussen and *Brigitte?*"

Lowering her voice she said, "The children are upstairs. Come into the kitchen so we can talk. I've kept some things hot."

Following her, Andersen drew the only conclusion he could. "So the missing boyfriend may well be Christian. My god, how many hours have we wasted talking to him?"

Clara did her best for the dearly beloved son of a dearly beloved sister. "I still don't believe it," she declared. "It's not like him at all."

"For god's sake, Clara," he said, goaded by an old argument. "Neither of us knows what Christian is capable of! Relying on him was always a big mistake. But now, with all those casualties and millions of dollars of damage, it's beginning to look as if we were blind. If Christian's involved . . ."

If Christian were involved it would be tragedy for the whole Andersen family. Clara could foresee weeping parents and stricken relatives. Andersen's crystal ball showed legions of his supporters fleeing from the taint of disgrace.

"I suppose you want to talk to Christian," Clara said dully.

"That was the general idea," he replied. "I thought maybe he could convince me that the *Brigitte* wasn't involved. But now that he's disappeared into the blue . . ."

His shrug acknowledged defeat.

"There must be something we can do!" Clara said fiercely. "Anything's better than sitting here, waiting for the worst!"

He barely heard her.

"At least go talk to the Rasmussens," she said. "Find out what they know. Maybe they can tell you where Christian is. And if you can talk to Christian before anybody else does . . ."

"Talk is the least I'll do with Christian once I get hold of him," promised Andersen. "Still, you're right. The Rasmussens are the only place I can start."

As a result an hour later he was reversing out of a cul-de-sac.

"Trust the Rasmussens to live in a hellhole like this," he grumbled to himself.

He was lost in an outlying suburb that was a world apart. The sole reason for its existence was a small cove whose shoreline was so corrugated that almost every home had water frontage. The boating enthusiasts forming its population did not care that this geography required a bewildering jigsaw of sandy tracks. Furthermore, the inhabitants seemed incapable of giving accurate directions. He had already stopped twice.

"Let's see," the last gasoline station had pondered. "You go straight for about one kilometer and there's a fork. Take the left and then it's . . . oh, the third or fourth right."

It had been a full three kilometers to the fork and the lane had dead-ended before any turn at all.

"I need native guides," Andersen said with bitter humor.

But his third stop was fruitful. The door opened on sounds of cheerful babbling, explained when two small boys and a shaggy dog spilled into the driveway.

"Oh, the Rasmussens!" exclaimed the comfortable matron behind them. "Why, you're practically there. Just keep on going to the top of the hill and they're the first house down on the other side. But I don't know if they're back yet. They were loading suitcases into the car when I drove past yesterday."

"Many thanks," he said, firmly suppressing all assumptions. For better or worse this dismal search was coming to an end. Following instructions he crested the hill to sink into a layer of dark ground fog. Even crawling at a snail's pace he almost missed the looming black shadow barely distinguishable in the surrounding murk. Not a single light shone from the Rasmussen residence. Nonetheless Andersen pulled in and got out. After searching the front porch for any notification about deliveries or mail, he futilely repeated the process at the kitchen door.

Stubbornly he continued to the garage. But the doors were locked and the window blacked out. He was still debating further action when the brow of the hill was outlined by approaching fog lights. As the orange glow broadened Andersen experienced a chill of apprehension. It could of course be a late commuter. But there was something about the competence of those probing lights that alarmed him.

"Christ, that's all I need," he thought, hurrying to his car. Then, with more speed than prudence, he backed out of the driveway and swept forward.

By the time the police cruiser slowed for the entrance, Andersen's car had been swallowed by the fog, leaving behind only the muffled red glare of his taillights.

"I WONDER IF you might help us. We're trying to contact the Rasmussens and they're not at home," the policeman said.

The same cheerful woman had answered her door. With a clear conscience she could think of only one thing.

"I hope it's not an accident that has you all looking for the Rasmussens."

"All?"

"Yes, there was a man here a few minutes ago asking the way to their house."

The two policemen glanced at each other as the image of those disappearing taillights took on new significance.

"Did you happen to get his name?"

No, of course she had not asked his name. But there had been something familiar about his face.

"I don't pay much attention to cars," she admitted, in reply to the inevitable question. Then her face brightened. "But Freddie does and he was in the driveway. That's my little boy."

"I realize it's late but would you mind if we questioned him? We wouldn't frighten him."

She grinned broadly. "No, I don't mind and Freddie's always game for anything that puts off bedtime."

When Freddie appeared, still pink from his bath and wearing a natty bathrobe, he justified her confidence on both counts.

"Of course I noticed the car."

Then, with a sideways glance at his mother, he came to a full stop. Freddie was going to drag this out as long as possible.

A good deal of give-and-take was necessary to establish that the car had been a 1991 Volvo, a dark green four-door sedan.

"And the model?"

After Freddie reeled off the specifics the policemen beamed at him.

"I'll bet you collect license plates," the older said invitingly.

But this was a serious mistake. The soft, rosy features collapsed into a disdainful pout. Collecting license plates was only fit for babies, according to Freddie. But when his mother began to rise, he pushed on. Stickers, on the other hand, were a worthy study and he had one of the best collections in the third grade. He always looked at stickers.

"Tell me about those on the Volvo."

At first they had not seemed hopeful. Slogans about saving the reindeer were common as dirt. Why, even Hansi Brutel had those. But in the lower corner of the rear window Freddie had struck pay dirt.

"I'd never seen one before."

It had been a circle emblazoned with BADA HEADQUARTERS, GDANSK, POLAND.

"Thank you, Freddie," the policeman said sincerely. "Thank you very much."

20. Slipping Anchor

HEN HE RETURNED to Gdansk the following day, Eric Andersen encountered a welcoming committee.

"Just a few words, Herr Andersen," said Colonel Oblonski's deputy.

With masterful affability, Andersen smiled at Alex. "Then let's get it over, whatever it's about," he said. "There's important work waiting for me at BADA."

His escort remained stolid and, when they reached police headquarters, Oblonski genially greeted his guest.

"I knew you'd want to cooperate."

"Well, here I am," said Andersen.

If anything, Oblonski was pleased by this reserve. "Just let me review some facts. You had several exchanges—acrimonious exchanges—with Zabriski. Then he made some charges about your business ethics. Do I have that right?"

"Surely I've explained all this before."

"Yes, but I want to be sure I've got it straight. In general, you and Zabriski were opposed to each other."

"There has never been any secret of that," Andersen replied, indicating boredom.

"He wanted more and more development," Oblonski drove on. "You're for protecting the environment."

When Andersen let this pass, Oblonski's ingratiating twinkle disappeared. "To be more specific, you locked horns over his big ideas for the Kiel Canal."

"Quite right, Colonel," said Andersen, tensing.

"So you must be concerned about eco-terrorists getting into the act," Oblonski continued.

"I've read the papers. Nothing seems to be proven yet."

Oblonski sidestepped the matter of proof. "So, you heard about *Brigitte*. Now, I don't suppose you happen to know anything about the *Brigitte*, do you? Something, for example, that made you suddenly decide to visit Copenhagen?"

"The *Brigitte*? No, I never heard of it before. As for my hop to Copenhagen—it was a spur of the moment desire to see my family."

"Then why were you nosing around the Rasmussen home last night?" Oblonski shot at him.

Since celebrity always carries the danger of recognition, Andersen had been braced for this one. He heard his own voice, calm and disdainful. "Nosing around is a strange way to put it, Colonel. My wife happened to mention that the Rasmussens owned the *Brigitte*. It seemed only courteous to call on them, both to express my sympathy and to offer any assistance I could."

"By bumbling around their backyard, knocking over benches?" Oblonski demanded.

Without a quaver, Andersen said, "I don't know what you're talking about. I rang the doorbell. When it appeared that no one was home, I left."

Oblonski balanced a pencil between two forefingers. After aligning it perfectly, he looked up at Andersen. "But you do know the Rasmussens."

"They are acquaintances of my wife," said Andersen. "Now, if you're finished . . ."

"Perhaps we could go over your trip a little more thoroughly, if you don't mind. I realize you can refuse. After all, you're here quite informally. And I'm sure that's the way we both want to keep it."

Andersen first made sure that he was settled comfortably in the hard wooden chair provided for him. Then he gave Oblonski permission to proceed.

"Go right ahead," he said evenly.

TWO HOURS LATER, Andersen reached the Novatel. His room was neither warm nor welcoming, but it was a haven.

He poured himself a stiff drink, then took a greedy gulp before he sank onto the bed. Propping himself against the pillow, he tried reviewing his performance but, as fatigue weighed his eyelids, Oblonski gradually disappeared, to be replaced by phantoms—Christian as a bright-eyed child of angelic innocence, Clara white-faced in her kitchen, Stefan Zabriski mouthing obscene accusations. Then the darkness at the window overtook him and he slept.

Minutes later—or was it hours?—he was jerked awake. Convulsively sweeping glass and contents to the rug, he sat up and listened again. The tapping on the door was gentle, almost apologetic. For a moment Andersen remained motionless. Then he swung his legs off the bed.

"Just a minute," he muttered, shuffling to the door and flinging it open.

"May I come in?" asked Annamarie Nordstrom.

In a long raincoat and a floppy hat, she could have been in disguise. But there was nothing furtive about her request and Andersen, trying to clear the cobwebs from his brain, gestured an invitation.

"Good heavens!" she murmured, two steps in. "Perhaps opening the window would help with that smell."

The frigid blast that aired the room led her to keep her coat on. It also reminded Andersen that he and Madame Nordstrom were not on terms close enough to justify unannounced visits.

As if she read his thoughts, she flushed slightly. "I got worried about you, Eric. When you didn't turn up this afternoon, I was afraid that something might have happened."

The effort was not up to her usual standard, but Andersen fastened on his own interpretation.

"You mean you thought I'd been arrested, don't you?" he inquired.

This was too much for her.

"Look, Eric, yesterday we found out some Danish cruiser is under serious suspicion. Then you take off for Copenhagen saying you'll be back today. And you don't show up. I just want to know what's going on."

"All right, if you must know, I got hauled in by Oblonski. Somehow he found out that I went to see the owners of the *Brigitte.*"

"Why did you do that?" she asked baldly.

"That's nobody's business but mine," he said. "Not yours or Colonel Oblonski's."

The rebuff had its effect.

"I have no desire to intrude on your personal affairs," she retorted. "However, the police seem to be tying all this to Stefan's murder. That, you have to admit, *is* my business."

For a moment they glared at each other. Then, shrugging his irritability aside, he began pacing the room.

"You can see what's happening, can't you?" he said over his shoulder. "Zabriski uncovers something about the canal before he's murdered, and then these notes come out of nowhere. Suddenly a lot of good, decent people are getting a black eye."

"Everybody knows the radicals, even if they did do something crazy, are just a fringe group," she interjected.

"But their activities can be used to discredit the rest of us."

"Including me?" she asked wryly.

"Especially you," he said, diverted from his own preoccupation. "If they decide that Zabriski was murdered by environmentalists—of any sort—you're going to see BADA turn into a trade association. You know, Annamarie, you ought to start taking steps to protect yourself."

Her mission was taking a turn she disliked. "Believe me, I will," she riposted. "But, in the meantime, it won't do for either of us to become paranoid, will it?"

"Paranoid my foot," he said crudely. "Wait until you've got Oblonski on your tail."

Although she realized there was nothing more to say, Annamarie could not leave in silence.

"I see no reason to be alarmed," she said, rising decisively. "However, I did want to be sure that you were all right. You are, aren't you, Eric?"

"I'm fine," he said. Then, in a slightly different spirit: "And you, are you fine too?"

"Yes," she said curtly.

That made two liars instead of one.

ERIC ANDERSEN AND Annamarie Nordstrom were not the only pair holding discussions away from BADA. As John Thatcher crossed the hotel lobby the next morning, he was flagged down.

"We should talk, John," said Peter von Hennig.

But the Hevelius did not suit his purposes.

"There's a place down by the embankment," he said. "We can be private there."

The Café Polonia was small and cheerless. In one dim recess, a student read his newspaper. Behind a long counter, the proprietor was deep in conversation with the lone waitress.

"This will do," announced von Hennig after careful scrutiny.

"If you say so," said Thatcher dubiously.

"It's all these stories about terrorism at Kiel," von Hennig began as soon as they were seated. "They've thrown Bonn into a panic."

Observing that he had Thatcher's undivided attention, he grew more expansive. "They've totally revised their policy, John. The German government now intends to start the canal project as soon as possible."

At this juncture the waitress drifted up. While von Hennig busied himself with the ordering, Thatcher considered the implications of this about-face. On the one hand, it revived the possibility that heaven was going to shower gold on the Sloan and other foresighted banks. But appearances are often misleading.

"As soon as possible?" he repeated when von Hennig was available. "Exactly what does that mean?"

"Next spring, for god's sake," von Hennig snapped. "And they haven't even thrashed out which proposal they'll adopt."

"Even though these letters may be a hoax, as the German police seem to think?"

"Now they know the canal is vulnerable, they've gone hysterical. With all this publicity they're afraid of copycats. You wouldn't believe the security precautions they're taking."

Right or wrong, this decision raised certain other difficulties.

"And what about BADA's role in the financing?" Thatcher asked.

"Scrapped," von Hennig announced bitterly. "Unless we get some kind of miracle in the next two weeks we can kiss BADA good-bye. Nobody is including them as long as they're knee-deep in an unsolved murder and suspicions of embezzlement."

If Peter was this upset, how did the chairman of BADA feel?

"What would you expect?" von Hennig answered Thatcher's question when it was voiced. "She's white with fury."

No wonder, thought Thatcher. A five-year opportunity to restore BADA's respectability had just shrunk to two weeks. And all because of a couple of letters, quite possibly faked. Either Madame Nordstrom was the victim of a very unfortunate coincidence, or somebody had been remarkably clever.

NEITHER NATURE NOR life had prepared Annamarie Nordstrom for the role of supine victim. Peter von Hennig would have been astonished to learn that he had been permitted to witness only a carefully calculated fraction of her anger. After his departure, she took the unusual step of returning to her own apartment, ostensibly for lunch. Actually it was to place a secure call to her husband, the only person in the world with whom she could not only vent the full measure of her bottled-up rage, but use language never heard in the office of BADA's chairman.

"Somebody's screwed me," she snarled at the end of her account of Germany's turnabout. "You can see what's going on, can't you? A couple of phony notes are mailed and those assholes in Bonn stampede like a bunch of mindless cattle."

Like most working politicians, Madame Nordstrom harbored an opinion of her professional confreres even lower than that of the general public.

"Now wait a minute, honey. Sure things haven't turned out right. But that doesn't mean some evil genius is behind them. There's the accident at the canal, there's a lot of brouhaha about terrorists and then the government responds, maybe not intelligently but predictably. That could be all there is to it. You yourself said the disaster couldn't have been deliberately rigged."

"Like hell that's all there is to it. What about a murder smack in the middle of BADA? And why do I have the feeling that, in some weird way, Stefan Zabriski is responsible for everything?"

"Even if he was, he's dead now."

"And that's supposed to make him a saint?"

"No, but it does mean two things. First, he can't be pulling strings any longer and, second, he's out of reach."

While grumpily acknowledging the force of at least his second point, she was not mollified.

"Whoever it is, isn't going to get away with this," she promised.

"Use your head, honey. Once the Germans have announced their decision to go forward at once, they're through listening to people advocating delay. You'll just be wasting your time; there's nothing you can do."

Her reply came like a whiplash.

"Don't bet on it!"

She was not through by a long shot. It took several different formulations of her indignation before she managed to discharge her accumulated spleen. But all good marriages are based on some form of quid pro quo. Nils Nordstrom had his own complaints against the world. He had just discovered the duplicity of his South American distributor and was ready to boil over himself.

". . . playing fancy games with the Baccarat people behind my back . . ."

". . . a warehouse filled with stuff that was never shipped for the holiday season . . ."

". . . canned him this morning and told him where he could put his rake-offs . . ."

For ten minutes Annamarie heard about iniquities stretching from specialty shops in Caracas to department stores in Buenos Aires. This wifely docility paid for itself. By the time the phones were grounded in Gdansk and Stockholm she had regained the power to think dispassionately.

Nils, of course, was absolutely right. The German government was no longer interested in suggestions for delay. They would be too busy planning their progress.

Suddenly the light of simple wickedness beamed from her eye. Then let them hear from those supporting immediate action. Once again she reached for the phone, this time to dial an important personage in Germany.

"Good afternoon, Herr Keppel," she began. "I've just learned of the decision about the canal."

"Yes, isn't that wonderful news. Sad, of course, that it took a catastrophe to bring the cabinet to its senses. But at least they've come up with the right response."

"Naturally everybody in the Baltic is interested and all sorts of rumors are flying around. But I realized that you, with your long commitment to this project, must know exactly what is happening. Can it really be true that the government is already conferring with Herr Schmidt about his proposals?"

Herr Keppel's satisfaction evaporated on the spot.

"What?" he thundered. "But that man's suggestions could be ruinous. His over-elaborate program would take forever."

"I confess I am somewhat concerned," she murmured. "It almost seems as if they are rushing things through in order to present a fait accompli without any consideration of more moderate approaches."

Annamarie had never studied the differing schemes for modernizing the Kiel Canal. But, as Herr Keppel's anxiety overflowed, she learned all that she needed to know for her second call.

"Good afternoon, Herr Schmidt. I've just learned of the decision about . . ."

Every call produced new names and new material. She did not cease her efforts until she had spread alarm throughout six groups, all powerful enough to demand the attention of their government and all dismayed at the thought of the opposition stealing a march. With any luck they could mop up cabinet attention for months to come.

"Time," she told herself with weary contentment. "This is all about time."

*   *   *

ERIC ANDERSEN RETAINED enough of his Calvinist upbringing to accept the hangover stabbing at his temples that morning as an appropriate penalty for past sins. Nonetheless it added to his woes upon hearing the morning's news and impaired the efficiency of his reaction.

His first impulse was to press the red button to every environmental organization on the continent. Second, and more painful, thoughts obtruded.

"No," he was saying ten minutes later. "The memorandum from the Nordic Wildlife Coalition should go out over your name. In view of the lengthy absence my work at BADA will entail, your position as acting chairman should be recognized."

Entirely misreading the situation, the schoolmistress was overcome. "Oh, Eric, I appreciate the honor and I'll see that it gets out tonight."

She was not the only acting chairman to be similarly acknowledged that day.

"We have to think of the greater good," Andersen told his wife several hours and several aspirins later. "Right now the use of my name could be counterproductive. We'll have to stay behind the scenes as much as possible."

"I suppose that goes for my family too."

"Even more so."

Neither Andersen nor his wife wished to discuss the obvious reasons for this strategy.

"It won't be easy," Clara said sadly, thinking of the many organizational letterheads prominently featuring one of those names. "But I'll warn Frieda."

FOR THE POORER members of BADA the decision could have only one consequence. The more Germany and BADA diverted

206

funds to the canal project, the less money would flow into their own coffers. Looking around for a scapegoat, they found one. Anton Vigotis was their unlikely choice.

"It's fine for you," they lashed out. "You've got your harbor. They enlarge the canal, bring in a lot more shipping, and Tallinn's sitting there with modern, new facilities ready to suck the lifeblood from its neighbors."

The charge was led by Casimir Radan, his white moustache bristling with ferocity.

"We could have won the next grant and competed with you," he declared, unaware of Madame Nordstrom's plans to perpetuate Gdansk as a symbol of regional decay. "Now you'll get rich on the traffic diverted from us."

Vigotis was not lacking in diplomatic skills but he was suffering from stupefaction. For the first time in recorded history Estonia was being labeled as another one of the fat cats.

21. Pushing Off

B UT NO MATTER how varied reaction was to Germany's revised plans in some quarters, Leonhard Bach saw only victory, pure and simple.

"This calls for the biggest party Gdansk has ever seen," he declared exuberantly.

Since his employees knew what was good for them, they scrambled to meet his deadline. As a result, two days before the great night—with photo crews arriving to capture every moment—the props were all in place.

After inspecting the best that the city had to offer, Bach finally chose a historic mansion strategically located in the heart of Old Town. To reach it, his guests would retrace the steps of many a feudal grandee. They would enter under a massive Renaissance portal, within shadows cast by an ancient church. Then, proceeding past a double row of tributes to fifteenth-century greatness, they would find their goal within sight and sound of the lapping waters of the River Motlawa.

"I am surprised," said Peter von Hennig, hearing of the preparations under way, "that Bach doesn't plan to have the waiters wearing jerkins and leggings."

Thatcher's only anxiety about this predilection for the antique had centered on the disabled Everett Gabler. But it had been easy to expand the invitation to include the Gomulkas. So on the night of the party, there was a strong right arm assisting the invalid through architectural hurdles.

Fortunately Leonhard Bach had selected a building that had undergone discreet modernization. The heavily paneled walls and the richly carved furniture—all almost black with age—would have been oppressive had it not been for lavish lighting reflected by arrays of crystal and silver.

Thatcher surveyed the scene with some approval. "At least Bach has leavened the BADA mix," he said. "He's invited outsiders and they've brought their wives—or whatever."

Dilution, he always maintained, helped. Tonight Carol Gomulka, in bright red silk, was far from the most colorful woman present. In an anteroom, furs were being doffed to reveal midthigh skirts, regal ball gowns, and gauzy harem pants. There was even one spandex sheath.

"Wow," said Carol reverently. "He's got everything here."

It was another advantage that they were occupying a space that was human in scale. Instead of a vast great hall, Bach's party was unfolding in a series of medium-sized salons that offered the opportunity for congenial encounters or, in a pinch, escape.

Depositing Gabler on a settee with Bill Gomulka in attendance, Thatcher took Carol by the arm and set off in search of their host.

They found Leonhard Bach nearby, holding forth to the Polish delegate to BADA and to Adam Zabriski. He broke off when Thatcher greeted him.

"The reason I'm not at the door is that I've been trying to persuade Adam and Casimir to join me there. But they're being shy about it."

Bach's companions did not look shy to Thatcher. They looked resentful.

"No, no," Zabriski's son protested. "This is your party, Herr Bach."

Following his lead, Radan agreed fervently.

Their refusal struck Thatcher as eminently comprehensible. But Leonhard Bach, inspired, was beyond stopping.

"It's a terrible shame Stefan isn't here to see this day," he said, shaking his head at life's tragedies. "But we should recognize his contribution to the cause of a new canal."

Before anybody could reply there was a distraction.

"Ah, Madame Nordstrom," said Bach. "This is a great moment for BADA, isn't it?"

Annamarie skilfully finessed the issue.

"Let me congratulate you, Herr Bach. It seems to me that everybody who is anybody is here tonight—from every corner of the Baltic. I wouldn't have thought such a gathering possible."

Her flattery not only made Bach purr, it also distanced BADA from the celebration. To complete the good work, she added, "Didn't I see the finance minister over there?"

"Where?" Bach demanded, searching for another illustrious guest. "Ah, there he is!"

Making hasty excuses he darted off.

"Thank god!" said a disgruntled Adam Zabriski. "That man wants to turn tonight into a wake for my father." Then, recovering his public manner, he added, "If you'll forgive me, I'd better see how Frau Jesilko is doing."

He marched off, leaving Casimir Radan plunged into confusion.

"I don't understand Bach," he complained. "Is he maintaining that Zabriski had anything to do with Germany policy?"

Madame Nordstrom was acid. "Everybody revises history, Casimir. In Warsaw, Stefan was a martyr for the environment. Tonight, he's the man who single-handedly fought to build a premature canal."

"Do I gather, Madame Nordstrom, that you're not pleased with this new timetable?" Radan asked.

The blue satin shoulders of her gown twitched before she confessed, "Frankly, I think it's a rotten idea."

But she was still fighting a rearguard action. "Or rather that's what I'd say if I hadn't seen this sort of thing before. The Germans may have ordered a blitzkrieg, but it probably won't work out that way."

"You think that bureaucratic inertia will be in your favor?" Thatcher suggested.

"I'd prefer some luck," she replied. "The first break would be dispelling these clouds of suspicion. When I should be thinking about BADA's future, I have to deal with the Polish police instead."

Casimir Radan resurfaced. "Rest your mind about the police, dear lady. Oblonski is no fool."

"Perhaps not," said Madame Nordstrom ambiguously. "Nevertheless, the fact remains, Casimir, that just now he is causing Eric—and all of us at BADA—considerable inconvenience."

When Thatcher came upon Eric Andersen a half hour later, the Dane was not visibly hagridden. Perhaps he had lost some of his healthy glow, but he was holding his own against a circle of antagonists.

"Oil spills? Oh, the Americans blamed Exxon, but it happens everywhere. Yet you shippers oppose regulation."

A rebuttal, citing the cost of double hulls, continued the debate. Andersen countered arguments effectively by himself until fortuitous support arrived.

"What about passenger carriers?" Bill Gomulka demanded, attracted by a subject he could not resist. "Remember that Polish car ferry that capsized? The only survivors were crew members. That's pretty damning."

They were still slugging it out when Thatcher decided to find out if Everett Gabler had been abandoned. But the Gomulkas, he discovered, covered for each other. Carol, who had procured two heaping plates from the buffet, was ensconced on the settee listening to a sermon about the virtues of seafood.

"Good idea," said Thatcher. "I'll get myself something to eat and join you."

"I've never seen so much caviar in one place," Carol told him.

She could have mentioned other delicacies as well. Leonhard Bach's caterer, exhorted to hymn the Baltic, had supplied an array of regional specialities. Ignoring Gabler's strictures, Thatcher swept past herring and salmon, mackerel and eel, to the roast beef. There he found himself face-to-face with Jaan Hroka.

"I just had a few words with Mr. Gabler," the Estonian said. "Too bad he's still laid up."

Forking slices onto his plate, Thatcher agreed. He was about to inquire into the current status of Hroka's ship at Kiel, when Leonhard Bach passed, steering somebody to the bar.

"Good party," Hroka grunted at him.

Bach halted. "Glad you're enjoying yourself. You've got to admit, Hroka, that we've finally got something to cheer. I always said that the only future for people like us was a new canal."

The cordiality between the two of them seemed to be as skin deep as ever but, with Tallinn now in his pocket, Hroka felt magnanimous. "I never said you were wrong. I just said other things should come first."

"There isn't a port in the Baltic that won't benefit," Bach persisted.

"Plenty of people seem to think so," Hroka replied. "I was just talking to one of the big boys from Hamburg—"

"Aha, you'd better watch it," said Bach. "Let me give you a tip. Don't trust every Westerner with a spiel."

"And what's that supposed to mean?"

"Face it," said Bach. "They've got the modern equipment,

they're cozy with their banks, they know how the system works. They sure as hell don't intend to share the pie."

"So?" Hroka asked.

Tonight, Bach saw any resistance as something to beat down.

"You don't think you're going to get much help from Estonian banks, do you? Or Western banks? Ask Mr. Thatcher . . ."

But Thatcher had already ducked his opportunity to play chorus to Leonhard Bach. He was on his way back to Everett.

By the time he polished off his roast beef, he had been joined by two Finns, Bill Gomulka, and the Latvian delegate to BADA.

"I think I'll see what's going on upstairs," he murmured.

The sounds drifting downward prepared him for the disco he discovered at the rear of the second floor. Once again he had to give high marks to the party's organizer. While only festive strains assailed guests in the main salons, up here the younger generation could enjoy an overpowering decibel level. As he looked on, Thatcher sighted a flicking red skirt. Did Carol Gomulka realize that her energetic partner was Germany's latest king of software? If not, he would have to enlighten her before the evening was over.

Thatcher gave the frenzied cavorting a full ten minutes before he was driven to seek refuge. But at the foot of the stairs he ran into a bottleneck. Wanda Jesilko, clutching the banister, was delivering a speech to an audience of two.

"The nerve of Leonhard Bach," she declaimed, loudly and clearly. "Because things have broken his way he throws a big, fancy party and claims it's a memorial to Stefan."

"Would you lower your voice?" pleaded Adam Zabriski, casting anguished glances behind him.

Waving a glass of vodka grandly, she said, "Why should I be ashamed? Stefan died for BADA and do any of these delegates care? Just look at them! They might as well be dancing on his grave."

Since several of the delegates were within earshot, Madame

Nordstrom remonstrated. "Now Wanda, they're simply carrying on with the job. After all, that's what Stefan would have wanted."

"Oh sure, that's easy enough for you to say. Your problems are solved. He's gone and without any tricky power struggles."

In the same reasonable tone Annamarie continued to protest. "You know perfectly well I valued Stefan, just as you also know he could sometimes be difficult."

"All you care about is BADA's reputation," Wanda flashed back. "With all your talk about carrying on."

"As if you haven't been doing exactly the same thing. Rummaging through his files, coming here tonight."

The counteraccusation was too much for Wanda. Hostility evaporating, she sank limply onto the convenient step.

"You're right," she wailed. "I'm as bad as the rest of you. Look at me! Putting on a party dress and dancing! How could I?"

As far as Thatcher was concerned, she should have put drinking front and center in her self-indictment.

"This has all been too much for you," Adam announced heavily.

She ignored him. "I thought the important thing was to protect Stefan's reputation," she began.

Hastily Adam tried to lay this theme to rest. "But Father's conduct was irreproachable. The police have proved that."

"As if they could tell anything." Wanda was staring into her glass, talking more to herself than to her companions. "What if Stefan did do something wrong? Who cares? This party has made me realize his killer is probably here, having a good time, looking forward to the future. It's not right, I tell you. Murderers shouldn't be allowed to run around enjoying themselves."

"I'm sure the authorities are doing everything possible," said Adam, clearly fancying himself their representative.

"Nobody cares what happened to Stefan, nobody but me," moaned Wanda, growing more lachrymose by the moment.

Since nobody was budging an inch Thatcher remained an unwilling witness to Annamarie's next attempt.

"Wanda, you shouldn't have come back to work so soon," she said kindly. "Why don't you take off for a few weeks? Go somewhere that doesn't have all these reminders."

Wanda's bold features fell into the clown's travesty of a smile. "The widow going on a cruise to forget her sorrows?" she asked sadly. "Maybe you're right. Maybe I should take a last look at all those dinky little ports and then the hell with the Baltic. All those places Stefan was so crazy about—Riga and Lubeck and Malmö and . . ."

"If that's what you want," said Annamarie, trying to end the drunken litany.

But it was Leonhard Bach's tireless bustle that did the trick. Hovering at the chairman's shoulder, he said, "Madame Nordstrom! I've been looking for you. There's somebody you should meet."

WHEN THATCHER FINALLY reached Everett Gabler, he was pleased to discover a newcomer had joined Peter von Hennig by the settee.

"Perry!" he exclaimed. "I didn't expect to see you so soon."

Pericles Samaras explained that with insurance claims, wise men did not dawdle.

"Well, you're lucky," said von Hennig. "You've arrived for the biggest bash Gdansk has seen in years."

Unimpressed, the Greek replied, "Why do you think it's so big? Look at that bunch of shippers tackling Eric Andersen. They all had to come here anyway. I'll say one thing for BADA's handling the insurance program. You run into all your competition."

"It had to be something more compelling than an invitation from Leonhard Bach," von Hennig remarked sagely.

Everett suspected there might be another lure. "And Germany's announcement had nothing to do with bringing you all here?" he asked keenly.

"Oh, that!" said Samaras. "Of course there's plenty of gossip about this wonderful new canal. But some of us think it's not exactly around the corner."

Thatcher summoned up an earlier conversation. "You haven't been talking to Chairman Nordstrom, have you?"

Samaras chuckled complacently. "Better yet, I had the privilege of dancing with the lady."

Repressing images of these two formidable figures in the disco, Thatcher asked, "Business or pleasure?"

"Both," Samaras conceded.

"As if you didn't pick up everything you could, Perry," von Hennig accused him. "You were fishing to find out how she's taking the news, and I'll bet you got an earful."

"Come, come, Peter. She may be disappointed but she's a sensible woman," said Samaras reproachfully. "Now that Germany has made up its mind, she knows that she either swings into line or stops being the head of BADA."

Samaras had something to say about other women on the dance floor too.

"But who was that gypsy creating a scene up there?" he continued. "I know Poles like their vodka but she was a real embarrassment."

Peter von Hennig and Everett Gabler were at a loss but Thatcher, to his regret, was in position to make an informed guess.

"Ah, Wanda Jesilko, going from strength to strength."

BUT WANDA, WHO knew the limits to her alcoholic courage, had decided to call it quits. One more drink and she would be weeping in a corner. And that, she decided, must not happen here.

Choosing her moment, she slipped into the small anteroom. It was a raw, chill evening with a brisk wind. The same impulse that had caused the shippers' wives to don their furs had impelled Wanda into high, lined boots and her thickest coat. The small stir she made collecting her belongings was enough to produce a servitor on the lookout for early departures.

"May I call you a taxi, Madame?"

"No, I live close by," she said, impatient for him to let her out and close the door on all the merriment behind her.

Wanda was one of the few BADA personnel who actually lived in Old Town. She had come to the party on foot and looked forward to the sobering walk home. Pausing on the step she rejoiced in the sudden blast of cold air. Head down and shoulders hunched, she plodded into the stinging sleet. Her path took her along the river, with sullen black water on one side and shuttered gaunt brick warehouses on the other. At some remote subterranean level, Wanda felt that for the first time this evening her surroundings were in harmony with her emotions.

Wrapped in her own world, buffeted by the wind so that she swayed unsteadily, she never heard the footsteps gaining on her and never sensed the club rising to deliver a vicious blow.

Then, blackness closed in.

22. Scraping Bottom

ER BODY WAS hauled out of the river early this morning,"
Oblonski's assistant explained at the mortuary. "As soon as
I saw the report, I knew you'd want to know."

Without reply, the colonel followed Alex down the corridor.
This was not an inspiriting way to start the day.

In any city that has a river winding through it, the police are
hardened to the unpleasant consequences of drowning. Nonetheless, Oblonski kept his inspection to a bare minimum.

"Any signs of violence?"

The examining doctor pointed to Wanda Jesilko's temple.
"One bruised depression here. But with the stone embankment
and the junk churned up by passing ships, she could have banged
up against anything. Probably the autopsy will just tell you
whether or not she was alive when she went into the water."

Oblonski had already averted his gaze to a sodden mass on a
nearby table.

"Are those the clothes?"

"Yes. She never had a chance once she was in the river. The
boots and that coat would have turned into lead weights."

"Well, do the best you can," directed Oblonski, moving to
the door. "And send me your report as soon as possible."

Outside he paused to suck in great healing lungfuls of air and to glance appreciatively at the brilliant blue sky and the frosty mantle of sleet that had not yet melted. Alex, meantime, was eager to demonstrate his initiative.

"The Jesilko woman lived only a block from the river and last night was that big party in Old Town. So I called BADA and they say she was invited."

The traffic arrangements for Leonhard Bach's gala had been so complex the entire police force knew about it.

"Which means Andersen was there too. Not to mention the rest of that bunch." Reviving, Oblonski decided that this time he would consult outside sources before tackling the unhelpful BADA cast. "Find out who catered the affair and tell him to collect the people who worked among the guests."

Several hours later he faced a motley crew of waiters, barmen, and busboys. Even the complaints of the traffic detail had not prepared him for the scope of the festivities.

"You were all on this job?" he asked incredulously.

Their nods represented almost their last contribution. The colonel had the foresight to equip himself with photographs but, even so, his witnesses were hazy about Wanda Jesilko.

"There were so many people," they explained. "All moving around, all jabbering."

"And there was so much to do," their employer added. "Herr Bach was on top of me all the time. He wanted the buffet and bar restocked constantly, he wanted trays circulating. He was checking on the kitchen and the deliveries. My god, you'd think it was the end of the world if someone had to wait five minutes."

But finally one middle-aged man slumped in the rear and giving every evidence of a hangover emitted a grunt when the picture of Wanda reached him.

"I remember her. She left early."

"Aha! And did she leave alone?"

"That's right, she was all by herself."

"Now we're getting somewhere. Did she say anything?"

The waiter rasped a hand down his unshaven jaw. "She'd taken off her shoes and put on her boots by the time I noticed her. So I helped with the coat and offered to get a taxi. When she said she didn't need one, I let her out. That was all there was to it. She was standing on the step tying a scarf around her head the last I saw."

"Say, I'll bet that was the woman I saw going towards the river," a younger man exclaimed. "I was changing the ashtray on a table in the front window. While I was there I looked to see if we were in for a real storm. The only person outside was this woman in high boots and a scarf just getting to the corner. She didn't look any too steady on her pins to me, but of course there was a lot of wind."

With no more information about Wanda forthcoming, Oblonski flourished the photograph of Eric Andersen.

"Sure, he was the one with a bunch of rich Germans," someone said instantly. "They were all arguing with him about something."

The group was recalled by the waiters because of its constant inroads on the supplies.

"Every time you took a tray over to them, it was wiped out," they reported waspishly.

As this was the extent of their recollection, Oblonski returned to the hangover victim.

"If you were monitoring the cloakroom, you know who else left early."

He was speedily disabused. Everybody working in the front half of the main floor had been instructed to offer taxis to departing guests.

"All right. Then at least you can pinpoint the time of Jesilko's departure."

At first even this seemed beyond the powers of his informant. The man would only say that the party had gone on for hours after Wanda departed. But by dint of wheedling and bullying, by appealing to the others, Oblonski did finally succeed in extracting an approximation.

"Now, does anybody remember when other people left?"

The confusion produced by this question seemed unresolvable. They agreed that Wanda must have left near eleven o'clock, and that the party broke up between one and one-thirty. But a thin trickle of departures during the intervening hours was described in completely useless terms.

Three or four anonymous men had been placed in taxis, one of whom sounded to Oblonski like Peter von Hennig.

"And there was a gray-haired couple about fifty," someone volunteered. "From their accent I thought they were Finns, but they might have been something else."

The main thing that Colonel Oblonski took away from the caterers was a vivid impression of the function they had serviced. Masses of faceless people had spent hours in a timeless void—constantly changing partners, ranging from room to room and even floor to floor.

It was probably futile to hope for exact details from anybody. Nonetheless there had been one man trying to oversee all this frenetic activity. Without high expectations the colonel next descended on Leonhard Bach.

"I just heard the news," the German said at once. "My god, I never thought my party would end this way. It's awful."

Oblonski, after agreeing it was a sad end to the festivities, asked what Bach had noticed about Wanda Jesilko—who she was with, what she was doing, why she left early.

"You don't know what you're asking, Colonel," Bach protested. "I was busy as hell. You know it takes work to get a party like that swinging. Between keeping an eye out for the ones who needed to be introduced around, making sure people knew about the dancing, hustling the caterers, I didn't pay much attention to the BADA crowd. I don't think I even saw . . . but wait a minute! I did see her. Someone wanted to meet Madame Nordstrom and I found her talking to Adam Zabriski and Wanda Jesilko."

"And about what time would that have been?"

Bach flipped his palms upward in a helpless gesture.

"God, I don't have the slightest idea. It wasn't anywhere near the end of the evening. But then it couldn't have been too early because Frau Jesilko was already—" He broke off for a moment before blurting out, "I suppose you could say I should have watched out for her. But, hell, it never occurred to me that anyone would be walking home."

Puzzled, Oblonski said, "Why should you be watching out for her?"

"Look, I'm not sure, I only saw her for a second. But it did seem as if she'd been drinking a lot."

According to the waiters, Oblonski pointed out, this was far from a unique instance.

Bach was only too happy to accept the excuse.

"Besides, it was just a fleeting impression. I could be wrong."

He was at least certain that he had not noticed Wanda leave.

"I knew I was going to be on the move all night and your people wouldn't allow any parking in front of the building. There were limousines scheduled to take the out-of-town crowd to the airport. Besides that I had a fleet of taxis stationed a couple of streets away so one of the waiters could call a cab whenever one was needed. I didn't have to worry about transport. A couple of people did search me out early to say good-bye. I can't remember who offhand, but I didn't plant myself at the door until everything was winding down."

It was all unsatisfactory. Precise time would now never be established and, absent a miracle, the medical report would leave Wanda Jesilko's death a toss-up. A tipsy woman staggering by the side of a river could so easily have had an accident. But Wanda's death had not occurred in a vacuum. Only a few weeks ago Stefan Zabriski had been murdered; last night his secretary perished in the Motlawa. It was too much to believe that the two incidents were unrelated.

On the principle of attacking where a breach had already been effected, Oblonski decided to single out Eric Andersen. He found the Dane in the BADA lounge where most of the delegates, coffee cups in hand, were discussing the tragic news.

"Herr Andersen, I would appreciate a few minutes of your time," Oblonski broke in without any pretense of apology.

"Good," Andersen replied surprisingly. "I was hoping for a chance to speak with you. Let's go to my office."

As he led the way towards the elevator, he confined himself to conventional remarks about Frau Jesilko. Nonetheless Andersen's entire demeanor had changed. Instead of tight control there was now open relaxation. Of course, the removal of Wanda Jesilko might also spell the end of some potential threat.

"I suppose you want to talk about my trip to Copenhagen," Andersen said, as soon as they were private.

"No, we will confine ourselves to more recent events."

"What does that mean?"

"Come now. First Stefan Zabriski and then, as my investigation intensifies, his secretary?" Oblonski asked as ominously as possible. "You don't find this significant?"

Instead of protesting Andersen wrinkled his brow in thought. "Put that way, of course it's suggestive," he admitted readily. "It just hadn't occurred to me."

Less and less pleased with the interview, Oblonski tried to keep up the pressure.

"Are you saying Frau Jesilko struck you as a woman likely to fall into a river by accident?"

"You know I did wonder about that, but I didn't see her last night."

"What difference does that make?"

Andersen shrugged indifferently. "Casimir Radan was just

telling me that she was putting down the vodka like water. But wait a minute, are you saying she was killed?"

"It is a possibility we are not overlooking. I must therefore ask about your movements last night."

"You mean you think I murdered her? In god's name, why?"

"If Frau Jesilko discovered any complicity on your part in Zabriski's death, she would have been merciless."

Andersen remained unshaken. *"Pfui!"* he said calmly. "That's a lot of bullshit. First, I had nothing to do with Zabriski's murder. As for my movements, you know about them. I was at Bach's party, just like everybody else."

"Of course." Oblonski's eyebrows rose in a sinister black arch. "Moving about, changing companions, unobserved for great stretches of time?"

Andersen was shaking his head. "It wasn't like that, at least not after the first hour. I was with the same people all night. In fact, I had a great time showing those shippers some of the facts of life."

"And when did you leave?"

Oblonski finally received a definitive answer, but it was not the one he wanted.

"I guess I was among the last to go. We didn't realize how late it was until the place had half emptied. Then somebody said it was after one, so we took the argument back to the hotel and kept it up for another hour."

"We?"

"Yes, a lot of them are staying in Gdansk on business."

"And you can give me their names?"

"I sure can. So just forget about trying to pin anything on me."

Normally Oblonski would not have credited any statement about being under constant observation. People were always fading away for a few minutes—to visit the men's room, to make an appointment with someone in a far corner, to pick up another drink. But Andersen had not merely been a member of this

225

group, he had been the focus of its attention. Furthermore, he had stayed late and returned to his hotel accompanied—and Wanda Jesilko had not loitered by that river for hours. Finally, even if Andersen had managed to slip away for fifteen minutes, how had he reentered the building? The front door had been locked with a bevy of attendants nearby.

None of these reservations, however, were visible on Oblonski's face as he said flatly, "I can scarcely forget about you, Herr Andersen. Not when you persistently misrepresent your actions."

This time Andersen took a deep breath.

"That's what I was hoping to speak with you about, Colonel." He produced a half-shamed smile. "I am afraid that I've been pretty foolish."

Not the most optimistic policeman could interpret this as a weird confession about two deaths.

"You're damn right you have," Oblonski retorted in a spasm of annoyance. "First, you claim you didn't know the Rasmussens. Then you refuse to explain—"

"Stop! It wasn't quite as bad as that. Actually it is true that I don't know them. I did, however, meet their daughter, Dagmar, when she was running around with my nephew, Christian. But I see that I'd better explain about Christian."

"Why don't you?"

Andersen smiled wanly. "Christian's in the environmental movement and he's a real hothead—always getting himself arrested at some protest. You know the type, Colonel. When I heard the *Brigitte* had been piloted by Dagmar Rasmussen and a boyfriend, we tried to call Christian. But he'd been missing from his lodgings for two weeks. At that point I really got worried. He could have been sucked into something crazy by the girl. So I decided to find out from the Rasmussens if he'd been aboard. When they disappeared too, all I could do was sit tight."

"In spite of the fact that you could have been withholding vital information?" Oblonski thundered.

"That's right," was the unrepentant reply. "I wasn't going to see the boy destroyed because of a single act of folly."

Still simmering, the colonel grated, "Are you telling me it was all a false alarm?"

"My wife says I should never have taken Christian's threats so seriously," Andersen replied obliquely.

"I suppose he claims he's innocent."

Now Andersen was positively cheerful. "Oh, it's better than that. His roommate is getting married so Christian and some others spent the last two weeks getting the new cottage ready— in front of a lot of witnesses. The Rasmussens were going to Jutland for the wedding."

"So everything ends happily," Oblonski snarled.

No policeman likes to lose his prime suspect. But if Andersen's story checked out, it made more sense to treat him as a possible source of information than to cling to a hopeless cause.

Grudgingly the colonel began the process by sharing a recent report. The Danish authorities found it hard to cast any of the Rasmussens as buccaneering terrorists. The parents were conservative to a fault and the daughter was unofficially described as a birdbrain.

"Trust Christian to pick one," said Eric Andersen.

IT IS NOT only the young who can be tiresome. Politicians can outscore them any day.

Adam Zabriski, back at his Warsaw office, absorbed the announcement of Wanda's death in silence.

Patiently waiting on the other end of the line, Oblonski anticipated the usual clichés about a sad loss.

Adam, however, decided on a different approach.

"Surely there is no need to cause unnecessary distress by making the facts public, Colonel."

"I beg your pardon?"

"Now that it is too late, I blame myself," Zabriski continued ponderously. "But I did not realize how unbalanced Wanda was, and, as my presence seemed to irritate her, I did not follow when she stormed off."

Adam was irritating the colonel too, but Oblonski had no desire to cut short their exchange.

"We have not yet ruled out accident," he said, trailing his bait enticingly.

There was another calculating pause before Adam decided to hedge his bets.

"Under the circumstances it would appear only considerate to stick to that explanation."

"But you yourself feel that Frau Jesilko committed suicide?"

"Unfortunately, yes."

"I would be most interested to learn why."

Adam had been marshaling his arguments. "You must understand, Colonel, that my father was Frau Jesilko's entire life. To have him brutally killed was a horror from which she was incapable of recovering."

"That she was grief-stricken at first is undeniable," Oblonski conceded, "but she seemed to be returning to normal."

"Only on the surface," Adam said firmly. "Poor Wanda had no reason for going on."

"So you think she had not been behaving characteristically?"

"It was certainly not characteristic to throw herself into misguided activity," Adam rejoined tartly.

At sea, Oblonski pretended to weigh this statement. "I don't know whether I'd describe it that way."

"What can you call it when she rifles my father's files for no good reason and goes out of her way to insult the BADA delegates? I tell you the poor woman was spinning completely out of control."

"And I expect all that vodka didn't help," Oblonski suggested.

Adam was not rejecting any helpful material.

"That too," he said at once. "She could barely hold a glass. I suppose you heard how she was spilling vodka all over the place. I thought Mr. Thatcher was going to be drenched."

The notes that Colonel Oblonski had been jotting now received an addition. *Question John Thatcher,* he wrote clearly.

"I didn't realize the American had been there."

"It was very embarrassing. Even Madame Nordstrom realized that Wanda needed a good long vacation."

Automatically Oblonski added Annamarie to the list that could provide him with a more objective view.

"Our talk has been most informative," he concluded on a formal note. "I must thank you for your candor."

"Not at all. I hope I have been of some help."

More than you realize, Oblonski thought to himself.

23. Taking Bearings

"SUICIDE? ABSOLUTELY ABSURD."

Annamarie Nordstrom's response was delivered with even more than her customary decisiveness.

"It does happen, you know," Colonel Oblonski pointed out. "Why not with Wanda Jesilko?"

"Wanda was a practicing Catholic who attended Mass every Sunday."

"Even so, she had just lost the man she had been with for years."

Annamarie shook her head. "You didn't know them, Colonel. Stefan was not the great love of Wanda's life."

"You can't deny that she was upset when he was killed."

"Of course she was upset. All I'm saying is that she was not unhinged. I do hope that you're not being deflected by this suicide suggestion."

"I'm not being deflected," he assured her. "We are making inquiries about people's movements last night."

She produced a wry smile. "And now you want mine?"

Annamarie's account was a model of ideal testimony, including a list of everyone she had spoken to prior to her meeting with Wanda Jesilko and Adam Zabriski.

"Very well. After you left Wanda Jesilko, what did you do?"

"I spoke with Herr Pfleugel for about fifteen minutes. By then it was after eleven so I found Herr Bach and made my farewells."

Oblonski frowned. Gdansk was proud to be the site of BADA headquarters and Madame Nordstrom was a familiar sight on local television. It was inconceivable that her departure should have gone unnoticed.

"But the waiters don't remember getting you a taxi."

"That's because I didn't take one. I drove myself to Old Town and parked a block over. With the weather so bad, I asked Herr Bach to show me out the back way."

"The back?"

They stared at each other with the same incredulous frowns.

"You do know the traffic situation, don't you, Colonel?" she demanded. "Parking was not permitted on the street. As I was directly behind the building, it was much easier for me to use the rear alley than to walk down to the river, over one block, then back up."

Thinking furiously, the colonel murmured, "I see."

His questions to the catering staff had been based on the assumption that all guests had departed from the main entrance. How many others had chosen a different route?

THE CATERER'S SECOND roundup was composed of his backstage crew and Colonel Oblonski was now a beneficiary of the passing hours. The journalists infesting Gdansk had fallen on Wanda Jesilko's death with gusto, busily creating a Romeo and Juliet tragedy in which the caterer's employees were thrilled to play a role.

Every single one of them remembered Madame Nordstrom. Her progress through the kitchen quarters had been a triumphal march.

"I've seen her on television, but she looks even better in person," enthused a dishwasher.

"And she was wearing such a lovely fur," chimed in a younger woman.

But real glory had touched the lady who concocted Baltic specialties.

"Madame Nordstrom complimented me on the herring salad," she plumed herself. "Said it was the best she'd ever tasted."

"And when she opened the door and saw the sleet, she stopped to tie a scarf around her hair. Just like you or me," the younger woman marveled.

Oblonski, who had kindly made no attempt to stem these recollections, was rewarded.

"Oh, that one! If she was the lady coming from the kitchen in a fur coat and a scarf, I met her. I was wheeling a dolly from the truck and she passed me in the alley," said one of the men who had been carrying in crates during the evening.

Queries about additional departures from the rear were answered more vaguely. All agreed that there had been several others but these were ordinary mortals, unrecognized at the time and probably unrecognizable in the future.

"It's bad enough normally with just the boss on our tails," explained the deliveryman. "But this time we had Herr Bach too, nagging about every little thing."

With a sigh Oblonski returned to Madame Nordstrom.

"She drives a black Saab. Did you happen to notice when it left?"

Pushing his cap back, the deliveryman plunged into heavy thought. Then his face cleared.

"My god, I think I did. There was this Saab with its nose parked right up against my truck. It was there when I passed her in the alley but next time I went out, it was gone. I noticed because that made it easier to unload and Herr Bach was at my shoulder yelling for me to hurry."

"How long between your two trips?"

"Who can tell? Five or ten minutes." Then, remembering an illicit cigarette, "A little longer, maybe."

And that exhausted the kitchen's contribution.

Determined to share his dissatisfaction with someone, Oblonski tracked Leonhard Bach from hotel to BADA switchboard to delegates' lounge. While the eastern German clearly remembered escorting Madame Nordstrom to the back door, he was surprised to learn that other guests had followed suit.

"They probably asked a waiter for a shortcut to cars out back," he suggested.

"That must be it."

Unappeased by this conversation, Oblonski growled at Alex. "We'll take that American banker next—the one who was with the Jesilko woman and Madame Nordstrom."

"I UNDERSTAND YOU met Frau Jesilko during the party," the colonel began after assimilating the splendors of the Sloan's new office.

John Thatcher admitted as much but could only hazard a guess as to the time.

"Somewhere between ten-thirty and eleven-thirty, I'd say."

"And what did you discuss?"

"Nothing," said Thatcher firmly. "When I came downstairs I ran into Frau Jesilko, who was with Zabriski's son and Madame Nordstrom. I was merely a spectator."

"Better still. That makes you impartial. How much had she been drinking?"

Thatcher tried to be accurate in a gray area.

"Too much. But, she was not dead drunk."

Oblonski recognized a witness who was being meticulous and appreciated it.

"So much for her alcoholic condition. What about her mental condition?"

"You mean was she suicidal?" Thatcher translated.

Oblonski considered this. "You did not think she was suicidal?"

"I'd only met her briefly, but she didn't sound that way to me."

"Perhaps you could tell me what you remember of the conversation."

During his brief recapitulation Thatcher was conscious that the colonel was scribbling industriously in his notebook. Trying to ignore this silent editorializing, he was glad to finish.

"And after Herr Bach took Madame Nordstrom away? Did Frau Jesilko say anything more then?"

"I have no idea," Thatcher said thankfully. "I didn't intend to be stuck with the remaining two and I left immediately."

"Then let's go back to these travels of hers. Frau Jesilko said she was going on a cruise? That would be difficult now. They are common in the summer and even during Christmas season, but not during autumn."

"I'm sorry if I misled you. That was my choice of word. She spoke merely of visiting a string of Baltic ports for the last time."

"And even the idea of a sentimental pilgrimage did not suggest suicide?"

"Not to me," said Thatcher.

Accepting that bald denial, Oblonski rose and formally thanked Thatcher for his time.

One courtesy deserved another.

"Please don't hesitate to call me, Colonel, if I can be of any further help."

But before he left the Nissan Building, Oblonski decided to seek assistance elsewhere.

"We're talking to the wrong people," he announced to Alex. "These BADA delegates and their illustrious visitors are too grand to know the real dirt. Get some men over to BADA to find out what the clerks and messengers are saying."

Bill Gomulka already knew.

"Talk to the ones who know what's going on and you hear the real story," he reported not long after Oblonski left.

Everett Gabler deplored gossip in all its forms until it had been elevated to the level of fact-finding; Thatcher had to emulate this excellent example. Only Carol suffered no inhibitions.

"Tell us," she urged, eyes dancing with anticipation.

"It all started with a bust-up between Annamarie Nordstrom and Zabriski," Bill began. "By now so much Technicolor has been added that it's hard to say what really happened. Apparently she threatened to fire him if he didn't straighten out his act. Then he said he had so much on her she wouldn't dare try."

"No wonder it had the place buzzing." Carol was savoring every word. "When was all this?"

"Right after they got back from Kiel."

"But surely there are more details than that," Thatcher reasoned.

"Hundreds of them." Bill grinned. "For starters, Zabriski chased her out of his office, foaming at the mouth. Or he talked about blowing the whistle on her and she clutched her heart and nearly fainted. Personally I like the one about Zabriski later sobbing heartbrokenly in his office. Want more?"

"Let's dismiss the flights of fancy," said Thatcher austerely. "Do you have any facts?"

"Some," Gomulka said obligingly. "It seems that Madame Nordstrom went through Zabriski's files."

Everett had been listening with patent disapproval. "I fail to see how that can be regarded as significant. She has made no secret of her determination to find out the nature of Zabriski's discovery."

"Sure, if that was the way it happened." Bill deliberately let the suspense mount, then continued. "But it turns out she called for those files before Zabriski was killed. Actually right after their fight."

There was a brief silence.

"That could cut both ways," Thatcher began slowly. "She could have been trying to find out what ammunition he really had."

"Or," Gabler ended for him, "she had decided to dismiss Zabriski and was planning to use his performance as an excuse."

"That was my other interpretation, Ev."

"Of course nobody at BADA cares about files," Bill went on chattily. "What they want is a sensational scandal at the top. That's why they've fastened on what Bach said in the delegates' lounge."

One member of his audience had not been there.

"What did he say?" Carol demanded.

"Bach talked about a really big scam with lots of money at stake. So it wasn't Zabriski going ape because somebody was just stealing office supplies or siphoning gas. The BADA cafeteria claims that, with millions of dollars involved, it had to be pulled upstairs."

"No!" Thatcher and Gabler said simultaneously.

When Gabler yielded the floor, Thatcher continued. "That was simply another Zabriski exaggeration. It was probably on the order of . . . well, Ev, you're the one to tell us; you've been looking at the financials."

"Five-hundred thousand maximum. BADA simply could not support losses in the millions."

When Everett Gabler spoke the subject was supposed to be concluded. To everybody's surprise Bill Gomulka produced an addendum. "One U.S. dollar buys you fourteen thousand zlotys."

Everett was affronted by this superfluous information but Thatcher said, "I see what you mean, Bill. Since inflation, everybody in Poland talks in terms of millions."

"And this guy Bach is a German who deals in deutsch marks," said Bill, warming to this theory. "They could have been talking about totally different things."

Everett disagreed vigorously. "If Zabriski was speaking in zlotys, then the defalcations were too small to justify a report to the council."

"It was a nice point, Bill," Thatcher said encouragingly, "but it doesn't really make any difference. Zabriski certainly gave Bach the impression that he was talking about something big, and that is why these suspicions center on the upper echelons."

"If they have any substance at all." After this ringing correction Gabler rolled on. "Apart from Zabriski himself, Madame Nordstrom virtually *is* the upper echelon at BADA. Any substantial embezzlement implies her participation or her inefficiency. The first is ludicrous. She would never endanger her own future for sums that are paltry to a woman of her wealth. As for this so-called incompetence, my research at BADA suggests quite the contrary."

If he had done nothing else, he had effectively silenced both Thatcher and Bill Gomulka. Unfortunately Carol was inspired to say, "I didn't know you felt that way about her."

Gabler was rigid with steely disapproval.

"That," he proclaimed, "has absolutely nothing to do with my evaluation."

COLONEL OBLONSKI WAS also being accused of bias.

"Of course I realize that you don't like Madame Nordstrom," Alex said hesitantly.

"I admit that I am not favorably impressed by *femmes formidables*, but that has nothing to do with it," retorted Oblonski, sounding exactly like Everett Gabler. "She was on bad terms with Zabriski, he had accused her of irregularities, and he was taking his report to the general council rather than to her."

In fact, the colonel was still smarting from his just-completed exchange of salvos with Madame Nordstrom.

"Slipped away through the back door?" she repeated ironically. "I could not possibly have made a more public departure."

Each and every question had been received as scornfully.

"Certainly I was planning to fire Stefan. In view of his recent record, very few chairmen would have considered any other course of action."

As for Zabriski's accusation . . .

"Your investigation must be even more incomplete than I imagined, Colonel, if you have not learned that Stefan regularly ascribed moral delinquency to all methods other than his own."

Even the absence of an alibi had been dismissed as inconsequential.

"No, I was not at home to receive the first call about Stefan's death. I was expecting my husband, so I stopped at the street stalls to buy flowers and some of the cheeses he particularly likes."

With those icy tones still ringing in their ears, Alex knew he had his work cut out for him. But action against Madame Nordstrom was so lined with pitfalls for innocent policemen, he thought it his duty to encourage second thoughts. "She knew that everyone in the kitchen would remember her."

"So she herself observed. That woman has an answer for everything."

"And it seems to me quite natural that a wife should welcome her husband with special treats."

"Ha! She's probably the reason he spends so much time on the road."

This was not promising, but Alex, seeing his own career go down in flames, soldiered on.

"We have discovered over ten occasions on which Zabriski described other people's behavior—apparently without justification—as venal, corrupt, immoral, and unprincipled."

"The boy who cried wolf finally did see one. Then *he* ended up dead too."

The discussion had carried them back to headquarters where a patrolman charged with questioning Wanda's neighbors had produced a witness. He was not preening himself on his find.

"I think she's just one of the curious kind," he said apologetically.

But Frau Bremer saw herself as the center of the investigation.

"Of course I knew her well," she proclaimed. "We lived on the same floor and saw each other all the time. I can tell you all about Wanda."

Patiently Oblonski extracted details of the acquaintance. On Sundays Wanda and the Bremers usually attended the same Mass, walking to church together.

"And we marketed in the same place so we'd often meet there. She was always ready for a chat."

But the foundation of the relationship, oddly enough, had been laid by the previous tenant of Wanda's apartment, who had been a regular fourth in card games with the Bremers and a retired widower on the floor above.

"Wanda wasn't available all that often," Frau Bremer said regretfully, "but, when she was, she liked to join us. She was a good player."

When Oblonski asked if there had been any interaction with Zabriski, she drew herself upright.

"Well, hardly. They weren't married. And it's not pleasant having to explain that sort of thing to your little daughter."

Moreover, thought Oblonski to himself, Wanda on her own had been more useful for those card games.

"Can you remember if you saw her in the period immediately before Herr Zabriski's death?"

Brow wrinkled, Frau Bremer struggled to organize fleeting thoughts before nodding. "It must have been about two days before that when we had our last game. I remember Wanda was free because he was out of town. But she was terribly distracted, making so many mistakes that she finally apologized. She said there was some trouble at the office, but I wasn't deceived for a minute."

"You weren't?"

"I wasn't born yesterday, Colonel," Frau Bremer explained unnecessarily. "When a woman is so bothered she can't think of anything else, then it has to be her children or her man, doesn't it?"

Reflecting that, in this instance, the office and Zabriski were the same thing to Wanda, Oblonski nodded.

Frau Bremer was now shaking her head dolefully. "Wanda was such an enthusiastic, lively woman. I can hardly believe that she's gone."

But accompanying these conventional exclamations of sorrow there was an avid lust for detail in Frau Bremer's eyes. Nothing this interesting had happened in her world for a long time.

"And that's all she said?"

"Yes, but she must have been really absentminded because the next morning she borrowed some coffee from me. And she was very orderly in her shopping. I was the one who ran out of things."

"And I suppose after the murder she was simply grieving?"

"That's right—until she went to Warsaw for the funeral. And my, wasn't that something! We saw it all on television. But I must say," she continued, her voice tinged with resentment, "I don't know why Wanda never told me what an important man Herr Żabriski was."

"You knew he was chief of staff at BADA, didn't you?"

"Yes, but I didn't realize that was anything special. The cardinal and the president were there. And that parade!" For a moment Frau Bremer was speechless, reviewing the magnificence of the obsequies.

Oblonski had a shrewd suspicion that she was regretting lost opportunities. If Zabriski, his sins condoned, had been welcomed to the Bremer household, Frau Bremer would now be in the happy position of boasting about her familiarity with the fallen great.

"What about when she came back from Warsaw?"

"That was funny. On Friday night when she returned she was just the way you'd expect—exhausted but pleased with all the tributes and eulogies. Usually after the funeral a woman is more subdued and accepting, if you know what I mean. But on Saturday evening when I took in some stew she had turned feverish and irritable, really almost impolite. She was making an appointment on the phone with somebody called Adam. Would that be Herr Zabriski's son, the one I saw as chief mourner?"

"Yes," the colonel grunted grimly.

"And they said he's a politician in the government. The Zabriskis seem to be a very important family. I suppose that's why Wanda did it."

Oblonski wrenched his mind back from considerations of trouble at BADA. Was Frau Bremer another proponent of the suicide theory?

"Did what?"

"Committed adultery. Of course I knew it would end badly, it always does. I've explained it all to my Grete. No matter how persuasive the man is, no matter how honeyed his words, it's still a sin. And it's always the woman who pays."

Stefan Zabriski as a veritable Lothario was difficult for Oblonski to swallow.

"This time both of them seem to have suffered a considerable penalty," he said mildly.

But his witness was not departing from the script. Wanda, she informed the colonel, may have tried to hide dissatisfaction with her lot, but Frau Bremer knew better. Beneath that cheerful, bustling facade there had been a woman suffering all the inevitable torments of her situation.

.

24. Uncharted Waters

"THEY WERE VERY happy together," the next lady to sit across the desk insisted.

"From what I have heard about Herr Zabriski, he could be difficult at times," the colonel ventured.

Wanda's elder sister was red-eyed but composed, the predominant expression on her pleasant, sad face one of overwhelming bewilderment.

"Oh, there's no denying he was a man who had to be handled, but Wanda had learned to do that while she was still just his secretary. She was not only good at it, she enjoyed it. Besides after her husband . . ." Sofia Niemcewicz's voice trailed away in embarrassment. Then she said hopefully, "But perhaps you already know about him?"

Silently Oblonski nodded.

Relieved to have the sordid facts provided by others, she went on. "Well, after Tadeucz, almost any man would have been an improvement. But even apart from the fact that Stefan was not an alcoholic and a gambler, he and Wanda got along well. He was musical, you know, and Wanda liked that. Then we always enjoyed having them over and I know Wanda was welcomed by his old friends. On the whole they had a very pleasant life in Warsaw. Of course there were hardships involved in coming to Gdansk. She left her family and he left his own circle. That was the only thing Wanda complained about, and then she'd laugh and say Stefan was spending such long hours at work they wouldn't have much time to see other people anyway."

This picture of a perfectly normal relationship with perfectly normal drawbacks was not a great deal of help, but Oblonski was merely establishing the general background against which the events of the last few weeks had taken place.

While he had been silent Sofia Niemcewicz's confusion had spilled over.

"I still don't understand it!" she burst forth. "That someone should murder Wanda. What could anybody have against her? She wouldn't have hurt a soul."

"It has been suggested that her death might be suicide," he murmured deliberately.

She bristled instantly. "How wicked! Who would dare say anything like that?"

"Actually the suggestion came from Adam Zabriski."

"That one," she almost spat, two angry red spots blossoming on her cheeks. "He's doing exactly what Wanda predicted. Trying to brush things under the rug."

Oblonski did not make the mistake of pouncing on this gratifying statement. Instead he activated his intercom to order coffee. Then he leaned back, intent on creating a relaxed, leisurely pace.

"So you'd been in contact with your sister recently?"

"Oh, yes, I saw her at the funeral. Mostly she was the way I expected her to be—very tired and drawn as if she'd been sobbing nonstop for days. The thing that surprised me was that she also seemed relieved. She said she was so grateful that nothing happened to stop the funeral, that Stefan had been laid to rest just the way she wanted. Naturally I wondered why she should have expected anything to interfere, but it was no time to say so. I even put off urging her to move back to Warsaw. I thought I'd give her a few more days."

Oblonski nodded understandingly, then seized the opportunity to busy himself offering cream and sugar. Only when they were settled with their cups did he move cautiously on to delicate territory.

"I did not have the chance to see much of your sister and, as you say, she was shocked and bereaved during that time. But one thing puzzled me. Her very first words to me on the night Zabriski was killed were *Stefan would never do anything wrong*. That struck me as odd."

He was happy to see Sofia's gleam of comprehension.

"I told her that was the last thing she should be worrying about. But after all those years of picking up after Stefan, of trying to make him look as good as possible, she just couldn't help herself."

"I suppose so," Oblonski said, careful to match her cadence so the rhythm would not be broken.

"I called her on Saturday hoping to talk about the possibility of her moving, but the story about the terrorists had just been on the radio."

Oblonski stiffened. "The terrorists?" he echoed in spite of himself.

If Sofia had ever shared her sister's dramatic coloring, it had been faded and bleached over the course of years. Her hair had grayed into a rusty dull mass caught back in a bun. Her eyes seemed watery behind strong lenses and her face had sagged with age.

"She was very upset, you understand, crying and breaking off her sentences so that I had a hard time following. But Stefan told her he had made some kind of mistake that was going to become public. He was afraid it would end his career and destroy his reputation. He said he could even be charged with trying to benefit. But he refused to say what the mistake was. That's

247

how Wanda knew it was serious, because he always told her everything."

"Now just a minute." Oblonski was frowning in perplexity. "Frau Jesilko told us that she barely spoke to him before he was murdered."

"Oh, this had to be earlier. To make things worse he then fled out of town, pretending he had to go away on business. Of course she kept trying to justify him. She said he'd been misled by other people, that he'd gotten himself into a mess by allowing himself to be led by the nose. When she was protecting Stefan, Wanda tended to talk about him as if he were ten years old—he got overexcited, his companions led him astray, he meant well. But the period before the funeral had been torture for her. She was waiting for the other shoe to drop."

"All right, but what did the story about the terrorists have to do with that?"

Sofia's voice had now become that of an older sister looking back on a lifetime of coexistence.

"She claimed that was the other shoe. It sounded insane to me, but you have to realize that Wanda could always get carried away by her own imagination and drive herself into a frenzy. When I said as much she told me I didn't understand how these things work, that the terrorists had to have somebody tell them about the schedules of ships using the canal and the cargoes they carried. Absolutely nobody was in a better position to do that than Stefan. So she thought he had been talked into helping someone stage what was supposed to be a minor accident."

Rapidly considering what he had been told, Oblonski was inclined to dismiss it as the fears of a hysterical, grief-stricken woman. Ringing in his ears were the words of the Finnish delegate and a host of others describing Zabriski's good spirits in Kiel and on the plane back. If he had been innocently tricked, he would have been crushed by the first news of the disaster.

There would have been no accordion festival, no sing-along. Zabriski's reaction had come later, after his return to Gdansk.

"Your sister must have had some evidence," he argued. "Otherwise why would she come up with such a horror story, particularly one so far-fetched?"

"That's what I tried to tell her. Stefan certainly had his blind spots. In fact," Sofia confided, "my husband always said that he didn't have the common sense of a flea. But he was basically an honorable man."

Oblonski was still mounting objections. "Besides, from what I hear, Zabriski wanted as much development in the Baltic as possible. He would scarcely unite himself with environmental terrorists."

"That's what Wanda meant by his being easy to mislead. If he'd been told that a small mishap would force everyone to acknowledge the need to modernize the canal, he would have swallowed it whole. According to Wanda he was in total despair when everybody didn't swing into line—as if he'd caused havoc for no good reason."

Oblonski sighed. None of this made any sense. Maybe it was because he did not know enough about the conflict over the canal's future. Casting around for more solid ground, he made a random pass.

"How did Adam Zabriski enter the conversation? Was he involved in all this?"

"Only because Wanda was so set on keeping Stefan's name clean. She was determined to find out if there was any written evidence at BADA linking him to a plot. If there was, she was sure she could persuade Adam, with his ambitions, to use all his influence to suppress it."

"That certainly explains his desire to write off your sister's death as a suicide. No investigation, no unpleasant discoveries."

Sofia snorted. "Suicide! Do you realize, Colonel, that the reason I'm the one who came to Gdansk is that Wanda's daughter is expecting her baby in a week? Have you ever heard of a woman who thought she had nothing to live for when her first grandchild is about to be born?"

She had hit her mark better than she knew. Only a year ago this same event had convulsed the Oblonski family. The colonel could still remember every ludicrous detail of his wife's excitement; his memory was more forgiving about the details of his own folly.

"I see what you mean," he admitted. "In fact I was not prepared to give any weight to Adam Zabriski's theory."

Instead of triumph Sofia was overcome by sadness.

"And now Wanda will never see Katya's baby," she cried, lifting a handkerchief to her eyes.

Sofia's tale certainly accorded with the Wanda that Oblonski had seen in the BADA infirmary. There, ignoring the bloodied remnants of the tragedy still staining her blouse, she had been consumed by the desire to explain away any blame attached to Zabriski's misdeeds. She had said as much at the party in the Old Town. Apparently vodka had caused her to reorganize her priorities, to decide that whitewashing Zabriski would yield place to avenging his death. But was she in any position to name his murderer? And would Wanda, even in the throes of sorrow, have concealed this knowledge?

Stranger things had happened, Oblonski admitted to himself. And he might be doing Wanda an injustice by ascribing her change of heart to vodka. In the first agonizing onslaught of bereavement many people lose their wits. Certainly someone had seen Wanda's new goal as a threat. Unfortunately she had chosen to define it in front of a jostling, moving crowd in which the wrong person could easily have heard her.

"Let's try going over the period before the party, Frau Niemcewicz," he said.

But two hours later, with every possible cooperation from his witness, he was no further along. He could only dismiss Sofia to the sad duty of providing for Wanda Jesilko's final hours above ground.

THE LAST THING he had expected was to hear that Stefan Zabriski was responsible for sabotaging the Kiel Canal, and the whole idea still seemed outlandish. Except for one undeniable fact. Wanda Jesilko and Adam Zabriski, both intimately acquainted with the victim and both with personal reasons to reject the possibility, had been sufficiently alarmed to consider countermeasures.

But surely there was an equally strong objection. Zabriski had said he could even be charged with trying to benefit, as if such an interpretation was the wildest injustice. If he had deliberately enabled someone to damage the canal, where was the injustice? After a moment's reflection the colonel decided wearily that this reading was not beyond Zabriski. Frightened about his career and humbled by his mistake, he might have conceded error. But under no circumstances would he have seen himself as anything worse than an innocent dupe.

Suddenly a grin of pure evil lit Oblonski's face as he dwelled on the reaction of Madame Nordstrom to this theory. So much for her attempts to achieve worldwide exposure for BADA. How wonderful if it all ended in the disclosure that her own chief of staff had been playing games with eco-terrorists.

"That would teach the Ice Queen," he muttered with open relish.

Then, sternly returning himself to duty, he considered practical difficulties in this scenario. These presumed terrorists would have to know all about Zabriski—his technical knowledge, his views on the Kiel Canal, his personal foibles. They would have to meet with him and hold discussions. Somewhere there had to be a point of contact. And with Eric Andersen in the clear, that was not easy to find.

"Bah!" he exclaimed, breaking his pencil in a spasm of irritation and hurling it across the desk.

He would do better to stick to facts. When the ministry of justice had waved the flag of terrorism at him he had replied with the physical constraints imposed by Zabriski's murder. And now Wanda had been killed in exactly the same kind of closed situation. Coming to a decision he rose and bellowed for Alex.

"I want to see this place where they had the party."

When they arrived they found the landlord prowling his premises, looking for damage.

"Wouldn't you know?" he complained. "I rent my house for one week, and now there's a death associated with it and police all over. I probably won't be able to give it away during the summer season."

Oblonski, who knew what Leonhard Bach had paid for his one week, was unsympathetic.

"You'll make out," he grunted.

Rightly identifying the colonel as an unrewarding audience, the owner turned to business. "So what do you two want?"

"Show us the layout here."

Oblonski had been visualizing a back hall, with movement along its length subject to casual observation by the staff. Instead remodeling had created one large kitchen with an outside door smack in the center. Using it meant tramping past the stoves and preparation tables.

Leaving the owner to his self-appointed task of fabricating an artful bill, the two policemen descended to the street.

"We'll do some walking now," the colonel directed, heading toward the river. Today the Motlawa presented a benign appearance, with little ripples crisply sparkling under the sun. As they proceeded they registered details long familiar to them. On their left, massive warehouses stood shoulder to shoulder. The walkway itself had once been expansive wharves.

"It's broad enough here for twenty people to march abreast," Alex commented. "There's no way a drunken lurch could end in the water."

"Not unless Jesilko stopped by the edge to look at the river. People do that when they're feeling moody," said Oblonski, halting at the first corner. "We won't go further here. I want to see where Madame Nordstrom parked her car."

The side street was residential, lined with houses split into apartments like the one Wanda Jesilko had occupied. Cars parked by the curbs, sounds of radio music, women carrying string bags gave evidence of life abundant. Marking off buildings until the right alley, Oblonski finally swung around to peer towards the river.

Uneasily Alex attacked the unspoken theory.

"Madame Nordstrom wouldn't make all that fuss in the kitchen if she was rushing out to murder someone."

"I was wondering if it had to be premeditated. She might have seen the Jesilko woman and decided to speak with her on the spur of the moment. Then a quarrel and a sudden blow! . . . but no, that is too fanciful."

Abandoning one theory Oblonski produced another. "The only way it makes sense is if it was a prearranged meeting."

"Why would Madame Nordstrom want to kill Jesilko anyway?"

"Why was Zabriski killed?" Oblonski asked more comprehensively.

"He at least stumbled onto something dangerous."

"But what?"

Having arrived at the same old dead end, they silently retraced their steps to the market square. Except for a few pedestrians it was almost deserted. The only tour group in sight was a clutch of schoolchildren being instructed by their teacher in the glories of the Hanseatic League. Many of the street-level shops were shuttered.

"Looks nice now, doesn't it?" Alex said approvingly. "Peaceful and law-abiding."

Car ferries into Gdansk during the summer brought a flood of Scandinavian and German holidaymakers. Each and every one of them inspected the marvels of Old Town and purchased amber, vodka or handicrafts. In their wake came enough pickpockets, shady money changers, and gypsy beggars to keep the police on their toes.

With the wind freshening Oblonski huddled lower into his upturned collar. When he finally spoke it was to pursue Alex's casual remark.

"That's the crime we've been used to, but times are changing. Did you read the story about the bank in Warsaw that got looted by the management?"

"Yes," said his puzzled assistant.

"The new wave," Oblonski said sardonically. "That's what we'll be dealing with from now on."

"We'll learn."

This simple youthful confidence evoked a broad smile.

"Of course. But that's why we can't get a handle on this thing. If Bach is right, Zabriski uncovered some kind of commercial fraud. We're not knowledgeable about that, so maybe we'd better consult someone who is."

"OF COURSE I'D be delighted to do whatever I can," Thatcher said on the phone. Then, glancing across the room at his latest visitor, he was inspired by an imp of mischief. "But would you object to my bringing someone else along? I think you might find him very helpful."

After hanging up, Thatcher smiled blandly over the desk.

"The officer handling the investigation into Zabriski's murder is seeking expert counsel about financial chicanery in shipping. I'm dining with him tonight and it occurred to me that you'd be just the man for the job."

The deadpan expression on Pericles Samaras's face never wavered.

"As a successful practitioner of these arts?" he inquired politely.

Then his gravity crumbled and he broke into laughter. "To think that I should come to this. But you're right. I am just the man and it would be my pleasure."

25. Prevailing Westerlies

ITHIN TEN MINUTES Oblonski and Perry Samaras were getting on like a house afire. Thatcher, who had suffered belated qualms lest the colonel be disconcerted by Perry's rollicking approach to white-collar crime, soon realized that these fears were groundless. Off-duty, Oblonski was not only a genial companion, he was an eager student.

"It's marvelous what we have to look forward to in Poland," he commented when Samaras completed his razzle-dazzle survey of possibilities. "But wouldn't most of this be beyond Stefan Zabriski?"

"Probably," Thatcher answered. "I'm afraid he was a man working within the confines of very limited experience."

"Like me," the colonel said ruefully.

Perry Samaras shook his head.

"No, you're willing to accept change. From what I hear, Zabriski regarded anything novel as subversive."

"Then why did everybody tell me how knowledgeable he was about Baltic shipping and what a wonderful administrator he was?"

"Join the club," Thatcher murmured. "We've all been disillusioned. But remember, the man spent most of his life working under a system that he did understand. In addition, he was an astonishing compendium of isolated facts. Unfortunately knowing that the *Polaska* usually docks at Stettin while the *Germania* regularly services Rotterdam is not so useful, especially if you don't understand the economic factors behind the Polish fishing fleet and a German freight line."

Considerably impeding the waiter, Samaras planted both elbows on the table to lean forward helpfully.

"Here's a case in point, Colonel. The system that Zabriski put into effect for handling losses from the Kiel disaster is, from my point of view, a distinct improvement. It actually does make the processing of bulk claims easier and faster. But, for all I know, he may have dumped some time-honored safeguards against fraud without ever realizing their function."

Oblonski had grown more reflective with every word. "Maybe I've been giving too much weight to Zabriski's abilities. It's not just the delegates who resented his pettiness. Even the BADA staff complained, but I assumed that was because he kept their noses to the grindstone."

Samaras sniffed contemptuously.

"If you always watch the help to make sure they don't take five minutes off, you're not looking in the right direction to prevent major losses."

Oblonski delayed proceedings in order to disembowel the dish with which he had just been served, a massive beef concoction baked inside a loaf of Polish bread. Only after his first puncture produced a satisfying gush of steam did he resume.

"Do you think Zabriski might have been a thief?"

"In order to enrich himself? No." After a moment's consideration Thatcher expanded. "I would not put it beyond him to transfer funds from a program he disliked to one he supported."

Oblonski mulled this over. "You know," he said reflectively, "everybody assumed that Zabriski's last trip around the Baltic was an excuse to get away from headquarters until things cooled down. But what if he was touching base with secret allies on some pet project?"

Thatcher could see what was coming.

"You're thinking of the Kiel Canal?"

"Yes, the Jesilko woman may have been right about the big picture but wrong about the details. The Germans are now ready to forget about eco-terrorists. The writer of one of the notes has been identified and he's out of it. The other one didn't come from any known group and has been branded a fake."

Samaras finished the thought for him. "Even so, the canal could have been sabotaged by other interests."

Oblonski ducked his head in acknowledgment. "Exactly. Some development group could have figured that an accident would get them their new Kiel. And Zabriski was a lot closer to them than to the environmentalists."

"That would explain one thing," Thatcher reasoned. "If Zabriski was part of the plot, his baffled fury at finding the opposition alive and well after a major disaster would be understandable."

The colonel was too deep in his reconstruction of events to pause for an examination of Zabriski's psyche.

"Given the lack of results, the conspirators might have decided on further action, and Zabriski could have gotten rattled enough to blow the whistle. So he had to be killed before he could do anything."

Perry Samaras made another contribution. "Then they decided to get some extra mileage by blaming the whole thing on the ecologists."

"Well, those notes have actually done the trick," Oblonski continued. "The Germans aren't taking any chances. You've heard, of course, that they've decided to expedite work on the canal."

"So I understand," said Thatcher, without betraying how central this decision was to his own plans.

Colonel Oblonski was plucking his lower lip in dissatisfaction.

"It doesn't carry much conviction, does it? If Zabriski was appalled by bloodshed, why was he so invigorated and sunny at the canal?" he demanded. "And none of this ties in with what Leonhard Bach remembers from the night of the murder."

With Everett Gabler's cautions still in mind, Thatcher said, "I would not rely too heavily on the bits and snatches that Bach produced."

"He seemed to be fairly responsible," Oblonski protested, going on to cite the reluctance with which Bach had named Eric Andersen. "But I agree his story doesn't take us anywhere."

"You're facing two barriers. Zabriski himself did not intend to convey precise information. And Bach was trying to interpret what little came his way. There are bound to be errors in the result. Bach obviously made at least one mistake—either about the millions of dollars or about BADA being the source of loss."

At this point Thatcher was allowed to proceed no further. Calculations of this sort were meat and drink to Perry Samaras. After learning the context, he firmly endorsed Gabler's views.

"A young man in our office came up with an ingenious attempt to reconcile the inconsistency," said Thatcher when he could continue, "but that didn't work either. My point, however, is that you probably have to dismiss the details as unreliable and concentrate on the chief thrust of Bach's account—that Zabriski had stumbled onto an illegality connected with BADA and planned to expose it."

"If BADA wasn't the one losing money," Oblonski argued, "there was no reason for Zabriski to be as upset as everyone agreed he was."

"Like hell there wasn't," caroled Samaras. "You say he was hoping that BADA would expand its jurisdiction. If the first time they tried there were major losses—to anyone—you could forget further concessions."

"There would be personal grounds for dismay as well," Thatcher added. "Zabriski was in a struggle with Madame Nordstrom and his strength lay in his reputed administrative skills. He was the one who devised each and every system used by BADA. The emergence of serious flaws would make it difficult for anyone to support him."

Looking at his companions rather as if they were unpromising police recruits, Oblonski muttered, "You're not making this easy, are you? What about the barman's testimony? He overheard Zabriski talking about evidence of a crime at the Kiel Canal."

"Now there's a good example of how little use these snippets are," Samaras pounced. "It all depends on where the emphasis was. Zabriski could have meant he found evidence at the Kiel of a crime centered elsewhere. Alternatively he could have been referring to a crime involving the canal."

While Oblonski and Thatcher followed this reasoning, neither was cheered by Samaras's ingrained habit of broadening every possibility to the point of no return.

"Wanda Jesilko was at Zabriski's side every minute at Kiel and she didn't notice a damned thing," the colonel observed gloomily.

"Not every minute," corrected Thatcher with a lively recollection of the polka performed by Wanda and Casimir Radan. "But if Zabriski's great insight came from the piano accordion, then we're really sunk."

Samaras frowned. "But if she didn't notice anything, then why was she killed?"

"Because she was going through the files," Oblonski said instantly.

Thatcher was not so sure.

"If I were the murderer," he mused, "I would have been more afraid of Madame Nordstrom's examination."

Mellowed by good food, good beer, and good fellowship, the colonel had recovered sufficiently from his last session at BADA to produce a balanced reply.

"Most likely the killer did not know about her activities. Madame Nordstrom is so closemouthed that I learned of them only yesterday."

Pericles Samaras, as head of the Oracle Line, lived in a world where his slightest action was a subject of interest.

"When the chairman of an organization calls for someone's files, a lot of people notice," he objected.

"Undoubtedly, but which people?" Thatcher asked cogently. "Mostly it would be messengers and secretaries. With the system at BADA, nobody in the delegates' lounge would hear about it."

Pondering some internal theory, Oblonski was studying the tablecloth's design as if it held the key to his problems.

"Maybe I should be paying more attention to the bookkeepers," he said at last. "If we are no longer guided by Herr Bach's idea of the dimensions of the loss, we are no longer confined to the upper reaches of BADA."

"But Zabriski was neither a trained accountant nor a computer expert," Thatcher reminded him.

"You keep coming back to that," Oblonski almost groaned.

Thatcher tried to be encouraging and realistic at the same time.

"Don't be disheartened by Perry's imaginative sketch of criminal ingenuity. Most schemes boil down to getting something for nothing, whether it's a confidence man substituting old newspapers for cash or a corporate treasurer making payments to a nonexistent firm."

Samaras was incapable of not taking this ball and running with it.

"Or floating a new issue of stock with financials that conceal a major legal liability." Turning to Thatcher he said, "You remember that case in Paris? And the one in Chicago?"

Now Thatcher was gripped by the joys of nostalgia.

"Or fooling your outside accountants with impeccable paperwork about a warehouse stuffed with inventory—when there's nothing there at all."

The colonel held up a restraining hand.

"Just one moment," he said amiably. "I do not think I will benefit from a review of every malefactor you people in the West have produced. How do you find out these things anyway? And if the paperwork is so good, how in the world do you protect yourselves?"

"Insofar as possible, you don't believe a word you hear or read," Thatcher summarized.

A great light was breaking for Oblonski.

"My god, you're all in police work and you don't know it."

"Very possibly. Everett Gabler is an outstanding exemplar of distrust. When he first came to Gdansk he read about projects BADA had already completed, then insisted on a tour of the sites so that he could see for himself. When Madame Nordstrom justified BADA's location by referring to the historic appeal of Gdansk, he verified her claims by tramping through Old Town. Frankly, I think he went too far there. Why in the world would she make the whole thing up?"

"Real estate speculation," Samaras said promptly.

Thatcher was too taken with his own train of thought to be distracted.

"The more I think about it, the more I'm convinced that sort of thing will be your answer, Colonel. Zabriski saw something that contradicted a written record. After all, he was in charge of BADA's operations; he was the repository of most of its paperwork."

Samaras was the smallest man present and, as is so often the case, was proving the mightiest trencherman. Having emptied his plate down to the last crumb, he had been judiciously studying the contents of a dessert cart on its way across the room. But he now returned his attention to the table.

"And you think that would have been enough?"

"Don't you see? Once his suspicions were roused, his limitations would no longer be a handicap. The man was inexperienced, not unintelligent. He had access to all information; he would know how to check any irregularity he spotted. Swindles usually succeed because they are surrounded by a forest of confusing detail. But in its stark outlines, fraud is simple."

Oblonski promptly incorporated this into his own experience.

"As is most crime. People resort to theft because they want more money, they kill wives and mistresses because they are jealous, they get drunk and disorderly because they're unhappy."

Perry Samaras went even further.

"Life is simple. Most of the so-called hard decisions can be clarified by stripping away elements that are largely irrelevant."

Thatcher was not concerned with philosophy at the moment. Watching Everett Gabler turn into a wholehearted partisan of Madame Nordstrom had made him sensitive to certain undertones. Colonel Oblonski, he realized, could not be numbered among the lady's admirers. Nonetheless he forged ahead.

"I think your best course, Colonel, would be consultation with Annamarie Nordstrom." Choosing his words with care, he continued his advocacy. "She is head of BADA, she is there all the time and she is immersed in its activities. While she might not have the intimate familiarity with Zabriski that Frau Jesilko had, she worked closely with him. She might give you some pointers about what he was likely to notice."

Signaling for another beer, Oblonski formulated his objections.

"Only if she's willing to be helpful, which she hasn't been

so far," he said sourly. "And, always assuming she's not guilty."

"That possibility shouldn't stop you," advised Samaras brightly. "She's proud of what she's accomplished at BADA and people always like to talk about their achievements. Very often, too much."

Thatcher simulated disbelief.

"Even you, Perry? I find that hard to accept."

"When I was a young man I practically had to put a lock on my tongue. In those days some of my activities were not the sort to . . ." he paused, eyeing Oblonski, ". . . to invite inspection."

Tonight the colonel was still learning.

"You mean you were operating illegally?" he asked curiously.

"Certainly not," replied Samaras, in no way offended. "But I was sailing so close to the wind that often I myself had no idea which side I was on. And I still did too much bragging. I'd talk to Madame Nordstrom if I were you."

"All right, all right," Oblonski capitulated. "But I'll bet nothing comes of it."

"Sometimes," said Samaras, *"nothing* can be informative."

This obscure utterance coincided with the arrival of dessert, which prevented Oblonski from pressing for clarification. Given Perry's pervasive cynicism, the diversion struck Thatcher as fortunate. So in the interests of sociability he too desisted. Colonel Oblonski was an apt pupil but only so much can be packed into one lesson. Asking him to explore the murkier corners of the universe according to Pericles Samaras might be premature.

As it was, communication between yacht-owning tycoon and underpaid policeman was going better than Thatcher could have expected and, by the time the party broke up, cordiality reigned.

A pleasant evening, everybody agreed, with only oblique reservations.

". . . and very educational," said Oblonski before he disappeared into the night.

Samaras, scenting disappointment, offered modest encouragement. "Look at it this way, John. We may have aimed him in the right direction."

Thatcher kept his own impressions to himself, examining them in the privacy of his room at the Hevelius. There, as he sat unbuttoning his shirt, he reviewed the evening. As a social event it was a success. As a work session he found it wanting.

True, Colonel Oblonski had received instruction, but it was of dubious practical value. And Perry's *right direction* was a nebulous signpost pointing nowhere. What Oblonski needed was one target, not a sweep of the horizon.

This criticism led Thatcher back to another. That gnomic *nothing* was fuzzy too unless it could be reduced to a blank spot as sharply defined as reality—as clear and comprehensible, Thatcher thought lazily, as Oblonski himself explaining negative conclusions by the German police.

Then he paused when the colonel's voice was replaced by Perry Samaras again, but this time at Janow Podlaski spinning ingenious theories.

"And, my god, good old Everett, running true to form," said Thatcher aloud, startled where memory was leading him. "This could explain everything."

With his motionless hand arrested over the next button, he considered these three random sound bites. They did not build a case, of course, but did they lay a foundation? Undressing slowly, he examined this structure for flaws. When he found no holes to pick, he could only shake his head. Nighttime flights of fancy are rarely shot down on the spot by arm's-length logic. They stand or crumble in the cold hard light of day.

"Well, one hour should be enough to tell," Thatcher reasoned bracingly. Then he drew the blanket over his head against the unpleasant moment when he, like Colonel Oblonski, would have to confront Annamarie Nordstrom.

BUT MADAME NORDSTROM was not available the next morning, nor for two long days thereafter. Instead she was embarked on what her office had been instructed to describe as a routine tour of BADA facilities. How Colonel Oblonski and John Thatcher were responding to this unscheduled absence had become a matter of indifference to her. By the time she reached St. Petersburg only BADA and BADA's future mattered.

"Is there anything else you want to see, Madame Nordstrom?" the harbormaster inquired.

"Nothing," she replied with bleak finality.

f

26. Battle Stations

WHEN ANNAMARIE NORDSTROM returned to BADA she found John Thatcher and Everett Gabler waiting. Looking every year her age, she was for once inhospitable.

"Not now," she muttered, bearing down on her secretary's desk.

But Thatcher's next words froze her in her tracks.

"Exactly what Zabriski said to Peter von Hennig in the delegates' lounge."

Flushing a dull red she forced herself to say, "You must forgive me for being so preoccupied. I did not mean to be discourteous."

"That was not a reproach, merely recognition that you and he covered the same ground. And I should tell you that Gabler and I have been busy on the BADA computer."

Through half-hooded eyes she examined him in silence. Then:

"Stefan's files have been examined a number of times."

"Yes, but by people convinced that there was something there. They would have done better to look for what was missing."

He had finally convinced her.

"You'd better come inside."

AN HOUR LATER Madame Nordstrom's powers of persuasion had spent themselves against a stone wall.

"Just one day," she pleaded. "What difference can that make?"

But Everett Gabler was the embodiment of rectitude.

"Leonhard Bach has committed two murders. There can be no delay."

Abandoning the contest, she said, "Oh, very well. While you call the police, I'll call my lawyers."

John Thatcher had no difficulty convincing Oblonski of Bach's guilt, but when the colonel finally arrived he was irritable, harassed, and ripe for murder himself.

"The ministry of justice wants the lid kept on this for the time being. No publicity! No action!" he fumed. "They want a diplomatic huddle to explore the consequences of any steps. My god, just because the man is a German, they'll let him get away with two killings."

"Oh, I wouldn't worry about that, Colonel," Madame Nordstrom said blandly.

He glared at her. "What can I do? My hands are tied."

"But mine aren't," she retorted. "In about one hour my lawyers will be filing a civil suit against Herr Bach."

"A civil suit?" Oblonski snorted contemptuously. "You're as bad as the ministry. You want him to pay a fine."

Conciliatingly, Thatcher intervened.

"That's not what Madame Nordstrom means. Her suit is a major story. By tomorrow morning it will be on the front page of the financial press around the world. Publicity is now unavoidable."

The colonel carefully examined this statement before the beginnings of a smile emerged.

"How soon before Bach is warned?"

"He probably knows by now," Annamarie replied with undiminished calm. "You know what docks are like. I'm sure that word of what I was doing leaked out."

"You have endangered everything!" Oblonski accused. "Simply in order to achieve your own ends."

But today he was dealing with an Annamarie who had discarded her usual armor of formality. Early in the discussion she had shed her suit jacket and rolled up the sleeves of her silk shirt. Now, tilting back in her chair, she kicked off her shoes and deposited her feet in the lower desk drawer.

"Pooh," she said, deliberately fanning the flames. "I had to gather enough evidence to file suit. And that suit is giving you the only leverage you have with your ministry. Besides, I still don't have enough to persuade the court to attach two of Valhalla's ships. What I really need is another day or so, preferably with Leonhard Bach out of action."

Oblonski was bitter. "You think I couldn't use that? If I could go through his belongings and his papers without causing an international incident, I too could acquire evidence. I did question his hotel before I came here. Herr Bach left suddenly several hours ago but he did not check out."

"That doesn't make any difference. He's long gone," she said fatalistically. "Already on the way to Rostock to gut his office."

But Colonel Oblonski had not been lying as low as the ministry would have liked.

"No. He has not yet taken a plane. So I could still stop him using his passport if the ministry were not so obstructive."

"Why don't you warn them about the publicity, Colonel?" Thatcher advised. "Germany may well prefer to avoid an extradition wrangle."

The first ray of hope was dawning on Oblonski's face when Annamarie interrupted.

"Bach may not need a passport, Colonel. The Valhalla Line has a ship in Swinoujście."

Rising, she padded across the floor in stockinged feet to the large wall map. Thatcher and Gabler joined her to follow the finger she laid on the mouth of the Oder River. Any ship leaving this Polish port would reach German waters very quickly.

"But Swinoujście is a long train trip from Gdansk," Gabler pointed out. "Surely the police could be waiting for him at the other end."

"They can do better than that," Annamarie chortled. "There's only one more train today and it doesn't leave for hours."

His heavy eyebrows knotted in furious thought, the colonel said, "If I don't get him before he boards, I've lost him."

"But—"

Oblonski groaned. "Don't you remember, Madame Chairman? There are many special trains today."

"Oh, my god, I forgot the date."

While she and Oblonski stared at each other in rare sympathy, Thatcher tried to make sense of their exchange.

"Ahem!" he finally said. "There's something unusual happening?"

Both stares swiveled towards him.

"Football, or soccer if you prefer," said Annamarie in tones worthy of World War III.

"Berlin against Gdansk," Oblonski amplified heavily.

Taking pity on ignorant Americans, Madame Nordstrom explained the magnitude of the event.

"It's the semifinals. We've been building up to this all year. There will be thousands of Germans pouring into the station to go back home."

"And thousands of Poles as well."

Annamarie was examining her desk clock. "But surely the extra trains don't start until after the game."

"No," said Oblonski, rising hurriedly, "and that gives me about two hours to persuade the ministry and make my arrangements."

Looking back on a life of police work interrupted by periodic soccer frenzies, he made his parting words into a prayer.

"God willing, Bach will turn up at the station before the crowds let out."

ORDINARILY THE STATION staff would have been consumed by curiosity at the descent of a police colonel, accompanied by a team of uniforms and flanked by two foreign businessmen.

But not today.

There were radios blaring from every nook and cranny, each with its cluster of avid listeners. Not a head raised, not an eye turned. A squad of scuba divers, complete with masks and spearguns, could have minced along in flippers without attracting a single glance.

After deploying his men, Colonel Oblonski cocked an intelligent ear.

"They're already in the second half," he explained. Then, remembering that he was speaking to ignoramuses, he went on. "A game half lasts forty-five minutes."

Alex, at his superior's side, felt that he had omitted the important part. "Gdansk has one goal and Berlin is scoreless."

"Splendid," said Thatcher unconvincingly.

With commendable attention to duty, Oblonski dismissed the match and concentrated on the clock. "The first special to Swinoujście leaves in eighty-five minutes. If Bach is going to make a break for it from here, that'll probably be the one he goes for."

Settling himself by the window of the stationmaster's office,

Thatcher examined the spacious square outside that was the hub of Gdansk's transportation system. Commuter trains and long-distance services left regularly from within the station but, in the center of the square, a broad island contained the tracks and platforms for the elaborate trolley system linking different sections of the city. Further constricting the free space was a long line of charter buses parked at the far side. In the narrow lanes remaining a constant stream of cars and trucks sped by. Underpasses made it possible for pedestrians to reach the station without encountering the busy traffic above.

"Are any of those buses for German fans, Colonel?" Thatcher asked. "Would Bach try to board one of them?"

"I've posted some men there, but I doubt it. None of them run near the coast."

Oblonski's last words were almost drowned by the cheers that erupted around him.

"Another goal?" Thatcher hazarded.

"No, just a miraculous save by the goalkeeper."

"Almost as good," said Thatcher politely.

But a quarter of an hour later it was impossible for even him to ignore the prevailing tension. The score remained unchanged and there were only five minutes left in the match. The unlikely source of this information had just come hobbling back into the office.

"You know," Everett said cheerfully, "they really are amazing athletes. They almost never get a chance to stop because there are no time-outs."

Thatcher stared at him speechlessly.

"No doubt that's why soccer's never become successful on American television. There's no place for commercials."

Hardened as Thatcher was to Gabler's remorseless thirst for information, this scarcely seemed the time for research.

"Where have you been?"

"Didn't you know? They have a TV set in the back. Come along."

In the baggage room the crowd was holding its breath and the same seemed to be true in the stadium itself. Earlier the announcer's voice had been heard over a background of cheers, yells of alarm, appreciative applause. Now there was silence, punctuated every now and then by a mass sigh of relief. At the two-minute mark the packed gallery began chanting a countdown.

Then came a sudden interruption!

The announcer's voice soared in excitement, rising above a ragged cheer.

"All tied up," Oblonski muttered. "Now they'll have to go into overtime."

But he was wrong. With only fifteen seconds to go, the ball suddenly squirted out of a scrimmage, received a vicious cross kick, and sailed past the exhausted Polish goalkeeper.

The Gdansk fans were still reeling when the closing whistle sounded. For a moment there was stillness. Then a vast savage roar swelled into the air.

"The riot police had better be at their stations. That happened too fast," Oblonski said sadly.

Thatcher thought he understood. The Polish fans had not sat through an afternoon despairing of their team's performance. They had not even suffered the suspenseful ups and downs of a hard-fought bout. Instead they had gained an early lead and seen that lead defended through two long periods, only to have victory diabolically wrenched from their grasp.

And sports enthusiasts all over the world are the same. That sullen roar could be easily translated.

"We've been robbed!"

"Fortunately," Oblonski continued, "Major Wroclav is an experienced man. He'll clear that stadium fast before any violence can erupt."

* * *

THE COLONEL'S PREDICTION was largely accurate but Major Wroclav, arriving a short time later, was not ready to call it a day. After a hasty consultation, he sped off to inspect the station, leaving Oblonski to explain.

"In a local match, after the game is over, the crowd disperses in different directions. Today they're all coming to the same place."

In view of the fact that Major Wroclav had been the leading edge of a wave of riot police, Black Marias, and ambulances, Thatcher knew where that place was.

Fascinated, he returned to the stationmaster's office to watch the preparations. All doors fronting on the square were closed and bolted. Across the street barricades were being manhandled across the entrance to the underground passage. Major Wroclav was taking no chances that violence would leak into the station and disrupt train service. On the same principle, he had detailed a cordon of police to encircle the center island where the streetcars continued to come and go.

"But what is the point of keeping the trains operating if nobody can get in or out of the station?" Gabler demanded severely.

Oblonski shrugged. "This has happened before. Everyone knows the drill and the radio is telling them in case they've forgotten. To take a train, people must circle around the square and enter from the rear. That door is easy to control and arriving passengers will be shuttled out that way too."

The sounds of advancing disturbance were already beginning to make themselves heard.

The colonel was philosophical.

"From my point of view it's all to the good. Now there's only one door for my men to keep under observation." Suddenly he leaned over Thatcher's shoulder for a better view. "Ah, there they are."

276

The triumphant Germans were returning to the railroad station in parade formation, chanting lustily and raising clenched fists in a sign of victory. A hundred yards from their goal, they halted briefly to allow two heavily burdened young men to struggle to the front. There they raised two long poles with a banner stretching between. Too excited for prudence, they had daubed their message on the spot and were flaunting it before all of Gdansk. The legend was simplicity itself: WE WON!

"An open invitation to mayhem," Oblonski grumbled.

Certainly the mob of Poles streaming on either side of the Germans interpreted it that way. There were instant catcalls and jeers. There were insults hurled in both directions. Finally the inevitable happened. A flying wedge from the crowd attacked the offensive banner and the parade formation broke in order to mount a defense. It was impossible to tell who struck the first blow.

But what difference did that make? Within seconds the square had become the scene of an enormous melee, with bodies launching themselves into combat, noses blossoming into fountains of blood, and substitutes rushing forward to save the threatened banner.

The police for the most part simply watched the fray.

"Aren't they going to do anything?" asked Gabler.

"When several thousand young men want to punch someone, there's no point in letting them practice on the police," Oblonski said wearily. "Wroclav will have his men concentrate on rescuing innocent bystanders and protecting vital services. Then, when these hooligans have exhausted themselves, the troops will move in."

Thatcher was unable to tear himself away from the window. One vignette after another emerged from the pandemonium, to be briefly glimpsed, swallowed up, then replaced.

A white-haired woman was emitting one eldritch screech after another as she flailed her market bag at everybody in her vicinity. When two policemen appeared to lead her to safety she transferred her attentions to them, belaboring them mercilessly.

Then there was a decorous young woman with perfect makeup and carefully groomed hair who did not wait for assistance. Assuming an expression of unparalleled ferocity, she pointed two long talons in a menacing V and daintily picked her way to the sidewalk.

But Thatcher's favorite was the dignified elderly man who descended, examined the disorder, then reboarded the trolley where he could be seen unfurling a paper and plunging into the day's news.

Everett Gabler, however, was falling prey to the stirrings of a Puritan conscience.

"It scarcely seems proper," he announced, "to stand here and witness this carnage as if it were a spectator sport."

"Now, Everett. These people are not early Christians forced into the lion's den. Every roughneck down there has chosen this method of passing the time. The fault does not lie with us."

But Gabler was no longer listening. He had stiffened, peering excitedly through his glasses.

"Colonel! There's Leonhard Bach! He's on the far side of the square, by the underpass."

Rushing forward, Oblonski double-checked. Leonhard Bach, briefcase in hand, had halted by the barricade. His normally cherubic countenance was etched with strain as he surveyed the disturbance.

"The train leaves in three minutes," said Oblonski in a voice creamy with satisfaction. "He'll miss it if he goes all the way around."

Leonhard Bach had apparently reached the same conclusion. Lowering his head, he hunched his shoulders and charged off the sidewalk into the eye of the storm.

For some moments Thatcher followed the stocky figure, bob-

278

bing and weaving and sidestepping. But Alex watched Bach's progress more knowledgeably.

"He's played soccer in his time," he decided before judiciously adding, "probably as a winger."

Then a shout of jubilation distracted them. The attack on the banner had finally overcome the defense. One of the wooden poles was wobbling seriously, its supporters vanishing under a wave of bodies. Germans tried to fight their way forward, Poles moved to block them, the banner dipped to one side, rose again, dipped to the other side. With the second support wavering, the issue was no longer in doubt.

Combatants from both sides swarmed upward, the whole superstructure swayed under their weight, and the banner crumpled downward, its ample folds engulfing the struggling figures beneath.

It was the moment that Major Wroclav had been waiting for. His whistle sounded a shrill signal and the riot police moved forward.

27. A Painted Ship

L EONHARD BACH WAS hit on the head, then trampled," Oblonski explained. "He's in the hospital and he won't be out for another week."

"Isn't it wonderful?" Annamarie said exuberantly. "We managed to attach two of his ships while he was still under sedation."

John Thatcher examined his dinner party with indulgence. His duties as host were minimal in view of the general air of fiesta already well established. Tomorrow morning the Kiel Canal, with banners flying and trumpets sounding, would officially reopen. And BADA's Homeric assistance in this endeavor was so widely recognized that Finanzbank had already reverted to its original plans for the bond issue. As icing on the cake Everett Gabler, having assured himself that BADA would not lose a penny by Bach's shenanigans, had approved a substantial loan.

Madame Nordstrom was on top of the world.

"And it's all due to you, Colonel," she said handsomely. "You produced just the right evidence."

"It turned out well from my point of view too," he acknowledged.

Oblonski was now a hero in the eyes of his ministry. With Valhalla plunging into bankruptcy and its owner identified as a killer, Bonn was only too grateful to leave its embarrassing wunderkind in the hands of another government. Tonight the colonel had shed his uniform and, looking remarkably distinguished in civilian attire, was prepared to be expansive.

"They not only unearthed all the documents for the fraud in Bach's office, they even found the typewriter used for the second terrorist note. He was doing his best to spread suspicion in every direction," he said.

But probably the happiest person present was Everett Gabler. A free man at last, he had dispensed with cast and canes that morning.

"I regard those final moments at the railroad station as providential," he announced solemnly. "It seemed as if Bach might escape in all the confusion, but there he was under the banner at the bottom of the heap. I have rarely been so pleased as when they carted him off on a stretcher."

"Oh, unkind, Everett," Thatcher chided.

"Nonsense. It is a matter of simple justice. If Bach had not murdered Zabriski there would have been no funeral. If there had been no funeral, I would not have been injured. The man was directly responsible for my pain and inconvenience."

But it was neither pain nor inconvenience that Everett found so hard to forgive. It was, Thatcher knew, the sheer mortification of dependence. Everett would probably never forget requiring assistance to the men's room on the trip from Warsaw to Gdansk. Fortunately there were other things he remembered as well.

"An ordeal rendered far more endurable thanks to the help I received from the Gomulkas," he ended graciously.

The Gomulkas, blushing and modest, were moving in their own cloud of elation. Tomorrow would see the beginning of Bill's new and lucrative career as a computer consultant.

Only Peter von Hennig evinced mild discontent. "It's unfair that I missed all the action at the end," he grumbled. "I still don't understand how you concluded that Leonhard Bach was the murderer."

"I'm more amazed that it took us so long," Thatcher confessed. "The clarification process started when Perry Samaras was explaining to Colonel Oblonski the fundamentals of fraud. In order to be encouraging I said that fraud is usually simple."

"But you spoke only in the most general terms," Oblonski objected.

"That should have been enough. Particularly when we pointed out that Bach's recollection of his talk with Stefan Zabriski was not entirely reliable. There was no way millions could be missing from BADA's coffers."

Madame Nordstrom made no attempt to suppress a snort. "Don't I wish!"

Ignoring her dreams of glory, Thatcher continued. "We ought to have taken the next step directly. What if we rejected everything that Leonhard Bach said? Suddenly the whole scene took on a new character. Zabriski returned from his trip so preoccupied he acted abnormally. He was rude to Peter—"

"The man was always a menace," von Hennig interjected.

"Now Peter, try to be objective. Zabriski had many failings. His judgement may have been poor, his estimate of his own talents overinflated, but his manners were punctiliously civil. Yet that night he was gratuitously offensive, not only to you but to Eric Andersen as well. He was consumed by one overriding goal—to seize Leonhard Bach and sweep him off to a private session. If Zabriski had been found murdered without any intervening red herring, Bach would have been the obvious suspect. That would have been the simple explanation and, in fact, the correct one."

Frowning over this new interpretation, Oblonski nodded slowly. "You're absolutely right."

"Bach was quite shrewd about people. He realized that the police would be very skeptical of any story he produced after the body was discovered. So, *before* murdering Zabriski, he returned to the delegates' lounge with a disjointed tale that spread suspicion far and wide."

"But surely that was taking an immense gamble," protested von Hennig. "What if Zabriski had changed his mind and blurted out his news to someone before going home?"

"Where was the risk? If Zabriski did that, all was lost anyway. But there was still a major problem. Snatches of Zabriski's remarks had been overheard and Bach had to tailor his version to fit them. I'll bet he racked his brains trying to remember every word."

Colonel Oblonski had reviewed all those statements so often he was letter-perfect.

"That's why Bach didn't mention Eric Andersen at first," he added eagerly. "I never bought that business of his being so scrupulous. He'd just forgotten that Wanda Jesilko was present."

"Of course he made some mistakes," Thatcher agreed. "He must have been badly rattled when, without warning, Zabriski confronted him. Probably there was only one thing Bach could cling to. Zabriski had not accused him until they were alone. Even so, Bach wanted suspicions that led someplace else. That's why he suggested embezzlement within BADA and unspecified doings at the Kiel Canal."

"He had to throw in the canal," the colonel observed. "The barman overheard that."

"Psychologically Bach was right on target. By the time Zabriski's body was found everybody was already thinking the way he wanted them to."

"I certainly was," Annamarie said ruefully. "I was convinced there was a major scandal inside BADA. Stefan's behavior was so unusual I couldn't think of anything else that would distress him to that extent."

Thatcher shook his head. "After those rebuffs he received in Kiel, Zabriski virtually fell into Bach's arms. Then he discovered that the man he had publicly adopted was stealing from BADA. On top of that the fraud was possible only because of faulty staff procedures. He must have seen his career tumbling into ruin."

With a vivid memory of Stefan Zabriski snarling threats at her, Annamarie Nordstrom sighed. "That would do it, all right."

Von Hennig was simmering with frustration. He had barely been able to extract one word from anybody in Gdansk since Leonhard Bach's arrest. His phone had been ringing nonstop from Germany with laments about the lawsuit by BADA, the condition of the Valhalla line, the rumors of impending bankruptcy. Peter could be forgiven for considering airy theories about Stefan Zabriski's inner conflicts as mere digressions.

"I'm a good deal more interested in this scam by Bach," he complained to Thatcher. "Nobody in Bonn seems to know the details."

"One of the oldest frauds in the book, Peter. Nonexistent assets."

"Just how nonexistent?"

Thatcher grinned sympathetically. A good many creditors in Germany wanted an answer to that question.

"When Bach applied for a BADA loan to fund the acquisition of two more ships he presented documentation proving that he already owned five. In fact, he had three. The other two were nonexistent but Bach knew they would put him ahead of the other applicants."

Every doubt Peter von Hennig had ever experienced about BADA's chief of staff was now confirmed.

"And Zabriski fell for that?"

"Indeed he did. I expect he had never heard of Billy Sol Estes."

"So that's how you pronounce it!" Colonel Oblonski broke in. "I couldn't begin to imagine."

The Gomulkas were still lost.

"And who is Billy what-do-you-call-him?" asked Carol.

Before any of the experts could reply, Oblonski spilled over. "Mobile collateral! Salad oil!"

Thatcher beamed approvingly. On leaving Gdansk Pericles Samaras had presented the police department with a parting gift—a book describing the classic frauds of the West. Colonel Oblonski had already read every word. The next sharpie in Poland who thought he had invented a new scheme to fleece the innocent was in for a rude surprise.

"Salad oil?" Bill Gomulka echoed in bewilderment. "What in god's name are you talking about?"

"You are too young to remember," Gabler said with the pity he reserved for those who had missed great moments of history. "But Estes made quite a sensation. He was the largest wholesaler of salad oil in Texas and a prominent public figure there. The collateral he offered for loans consisted of tank cars of salad oil. Only after his empire collapsed did it emerge that, by moving the tank cars around, he had shown the same ones again and again."

Carol still saw a problem. "If he was so successful, why did he have to resort to something like that?"

"Because Estes was not a good businessman," said Gabler. "He couldn't continue operations without an infusion of additional capital and that was the only way to get it."

Events at Kiel were proceeding so swiftly that Peter von Hennig and John Thatcher were flying to Frankfurt in the morning. While Thatcher's thoughts turned to the Finanzbank meeting, Peter's circled more and more about his reunion with a large, gray stallion. Nevertheless he was paying attention.

"Many men who can start a business are incapable of handling expansion."

"Leonhard Bach certainly couldn't," Thatcher said. "The first time Valhalla posted losses Bach thought enlarging his fleet was the only way to survive. After all, he had served his apprenticeship in the same stifling bureaucracy as Stefan Zabriski and knew what documentation would satisfy the official mind. So he could produce beautiful forged paper and, with suitable camouflage, move around the ships he did have for visual inspection."

Once again Peter von Hennig was reminded of Janow Podlaski. "My god, we should have paid more attention to Perry. You remember he boasted he could put an imaginary freighter in the canal and get an insurance company to pay him for it. He was probably thinking of a shell game too."

"And poor Stefan wasn't," added Annamarie sadly. "He probably never even thought of looking at the ships themselves."

There was a hiss of indrawn breath from Everett Gabler.

"Gross incompetence," he said at his most unyielding.

"Only on some levels," Thatcher corrected. "Because Zabriski was not skilled in our areas of expertise, it was too easy to dismiss his other attainments. I remember saying to the colonel that Zabriski's collection of facts about individual ships was useless. But I was very wrong. That's what finally alerted him to what Bach had done."

Annamarie was all attention. "Now that I'd like to hear about. I suppose it had something to do with his review of shipping when he got back from Kiel. That sent him racing around the Baltic, didn't it?"

"Actually it started in Kiel the night of our party at the Maritim."

Bill Gomulka was beginning to take an intelligent interest in the social habits of big business. "Another party? I didn't realize it was nonstop. Carol, we'll have to get more clothes."

Recalling the doldrums of that evening before Stefan Zabriski snatched up his accordion, Thatcher hastened to rectify a misimpression. "*Party* was a misnomer. Never mind about that. After the musical performance," he said pressing forward, "Zabriski condoled Bach on Valhalla's loss from the canal disaster. Bach didn't know what he was talking about until Zabriski reminded him of the supposed movements by one of his phantom ships called the *Gudrun*. Bach then tried to sugarcoat his forgetfulness and succeeded for the moment. But Zabriski later realized how odd that moment was. For that matter, I should have as well."

Peter von Hennig felt there were limits to the omniscience to be expected from bankers. "Why?"

"Partly because of you. The Maritim was stuffed with people discussing their losses. Then you came in from your night out complaining the evening had been a dead bore because your companions reviewed the dislocations of every one of their vessels. For heaven's sake, back in Janow Podlaski Perry had all the details of the insurance claim he was bringing to Gdansk. If people with worldwide operations knew where they stood, it was inconceivable that a small fleet did not know chapter and verse about its losses. And by the time Zabriski was back at BADA, information was pouring into his computer about the plight of every freighter stuck inside the Baltic or prevented from accessing it. When he found absolutely no reference to the *Gudrun*, his suspicions were roused. He probably conned his memory of past schedules and became alarmed when he could recall nothing about two of Bach's vessels. Then he took off on his trip and Madame Nordstrom is the one who can tell you about that."

Obligingly she took up the tale. "Everywhere I went it was the same story. Stefan had reviewed all movements in major harbors by Valhalla. Apparently I wasn't as quick as you were. It took me until St. Petersburg to catch on. The *Gudrun* and the *Brunhilde* simply didn't exist. Stefan must have been devastated."

"Particularly as he expected to be charged with complicity," Thatcher commented.

"Now why in the world would he think that?" she protested.

Bill Gomulka had not wasted his long hours in the BADA

cafeteria awaiting Gabler's pleasure. "Probably because he was always making accusations like that himself. If this had happened to anybody else, Zabriski would have claimed he was a silent partner in Valhalla."

"Oh dear, you're absolutely right." But Madame Nordstrom was still extending tolerance to her late chief of staff. "If only Stefan had had the sense to protect himself. He shouldn't have tried to handle things on his own."

"A strange criticism," Oblonski said severely, "from a woman who ran around by herself doing the same thing."

Her serenity unimpaired, she said sweetly, "But scarcely in the same way. Every night I sent a tape back home to Stockholm. In the unfortunate event of my demise there would have been proof abundant of my activities."

Once again she had the last word and once again the colonel did not like it. "It is unbelievable to me," he muttered, "that Zabriski thought a confrontation with Bach was the ideal procedure."

"Zabriski must have longed for an alternative explanation," Thatcher reasoned. "Bach probably said there was a minor mistake and that he could prove it the next day—anything to prevent immediate action."

"And Stefan would have wanted to believe that so much," Annamarie lamented.

"Then, with time in hand, Bach planted his rumors in the lounge before lying in wait by Zabriski's car. After you left us that evening, Madame Nordstrom, Bach started to speculate in a way that almost forced Peter to snub him. No doubt he wanted an excuse to leave that seemed inspired by someone else. As I said, he was clever about people."

Von Hennig did not like to think that he had been manipulated by Bach, even in so inconsequential a matter.

"Cold-blooded bastard," he grated.

A somber nodding of heads attested general agreement.

"At least he was facing a genuine threat with his first murder," Carol said indignantly. "But with poor Wanda Jesilko, he didn't even wait for that."

Annamarie was stony-faced. "It took me a day to realize that she was going to retrace Stefan's steps. Bach was faster off the mark than I was and he was taking no chances."

"He took plenty of chances. The man was a fool," Oblonski said angrily. "Without a motive for him, I had to place Herr Bach to one side. But after Frau Jesilko's death there was no doubt who led the pack when it came to opportunity."

Thatcher could almost hear the jovial voice of his host at the party. "Bach arrived just as Wanda was unveiling her travel plans."

Everett was more property-minded. "Furthermore Bach rented the house and was familiar with the geography."

"It was more than that," Oblonski insisted. "Whenever I questioned the staff, their replies were filled with complaints about Bach. He was always bursting into the kitchen, he was always dashing out to hurry the deliverymen. Nobody would have noticed his absence outside for five or ten minutes."

"You know," Thatcher said thoughtfully to Annamarie, "you have plenty to complain about in Bach's dealings with BADA. But you must have paid him back when you asked to leave by the rear door. The last thing he wanted was attention drawn to that exit."

Colonel Oblonski reinforced this impression. "That's why he never mentioned your departure to me," he told her. "It wasn't until you described it that he pretended to remember. And no wonder he was nervous. By my calculations you approached him just after he returned from murdering Frau Jesilko."

"He must have been appalled," she decided with open satisfaction.

"But motive was the real problem with Frau Jesilko," the colonel continued, "because I could never understand what she was up to—with you, with the younger Zabriski, even with Eric Andersen."

"That is because you misread Wanda from the start."

Oblonski raised arctic eyebrows. "Indeed?"

"Although Wanda was fond of Stefan she did not have a high opinion of his common sense. She saw herself as someone who had to protect him from the consequences of his own folly," Annamarie expounded. "When he was murdered I'm sure she felt she had failed him. But she was convinced that Stefan had gotten himself into trouble with his canal enthusiasm. Wanda was on the wrong track entirely and I wonder how Leonhard Bach will feel about that."

"I wouldn't count on a wave of remorse," Oblonski advised. "If I didn't understand the Jesilko woman, you don't understand types like Bach. He's convinced that he had no other choice. It was hard luck that Zabriski became suspicious, it was too bad that Wanda Jesilko couldn't leave well enough alone."

Carol was taken aback by this analysis. "I guess I don't know much about people," she confessed. "Mr. Bach seemed like such a nice man when I talked to him at his party. I would have sworn that he was a cheerful, uncomplicated optimist."

Out of his newfound knowledge, Colonel Oblonski said gravely, "Just such a one was Billy Sol Estes."

Thatcher thought Carol deserved a fuller explanation.

"Basically there are two kinds of people who commit fraud. There is the professional with his intricate system and then there's the casual optimist, like the clerk who needs a hundred dollars for a sure thing at Belmont. He's always confident he can replace the money after he's won his bet. Bach and Estes didn't think they were stealing—they were simply arranging financial accommodation. It is a form of irresponsibility, and the colonel is saying that Bach goes one step further. He doesn't feel accountable for any action, including beating a man's brains in with a tire iron."

Shuddering delicately Carol said, "I'll take the professional any day then."

"There's another distinction between him and the cheerful amateur. The money he steals sticks with him. The lowly clerk simply enriches his bookie."

"And what about the big-time company men?" asked Bill Gomulka.

"Estes was so determined to succeed that he undersold his competition. That's why he didn't make sufficient profit. The same was probably true of Bach. The real beneficiaries were the customers who got salad oil and freight shipping at bargain rates."

Gabler could not resist pointing a moral. "And so, young man, build your business prudently with adequate attention to your price structure. Do not expect easy, painless solutions."

Carol broke into gales of laughter. "But I'm the cheerful optimist in this family, Mr. Gabler. Bill always spots ten thousand difficulties at every turn. He even saw problems with the suggestion that Gerhardt Enteman made."

German software kings were right up Everett's alley. Within minutes he and the Gomulkas were deep in the subject.

At the other end of the table trouble was brewing.

"You're lucky you didn't manage to become another corpse," Colonel Oblonski was saying to Annamarie.

"I had the sense not to make my plans public."

"You mean you displayed your customary reticence about taking the police into your confidence."

"And how glad I am that I didn't," she flashed back. "With my methods BADA was able to file its lawsuit and you, I might add, were spared the ministerial haggling that would have allowed Leonhard Bach to escape."

Before these hostilities could escalate Peter von Hennig weighed in with a more tactful rendition of Madame Nordstrom's defiance.

Momentarily ignored by his guests, Thatcher had time to examine this variegated trio. They could have been figures in a morality play. To the right sat the policeman, dark symbol of the rigidities of the East. On the left was the banker, epitome of the freewheeling West. In the middle sat Scandinavia, embodying the conviction that extremes were unnecessary. Then, more realistically, Thatcher decided this was the theater of the past. The one thing certain about the continent exploding under his feet was that the new Europe would in no way resemble the old.

Madame Nordstrom, noticing her abandoned host, sent him a friendly smile. Raising his glass to her, Thatcher assembled his stray thoughts.

"To all of you," he said in obscure toast.